Marriage, Monsters-in-Law, and Murder

THE ELLIE AVERY MYSTERIES*
by Sara Rosett

MOVING IS MURDER

STAYING HOME IS A KILLER

GETTING AWAY IS DEADLY

MAGNOLIAS, MOONLIGHT, AND MURDER

MINT JULEPS, MAYHEM, AND MURDER

MIMOSAS, MISCHIEF, AND MURDER

MISTLETOE, MERRIMENT, AND MURDER

MILKSHAKES, MERMAIDS, AND MURDER

*Available from Kensington Publishing Corp.

Marriage,
Monsters-in-Law,
and Murder

Sara Rosett

KENSINGTON BOOKS
http://www.kensingtonbooks.com

KENSINGTON BOOKS are published by

Kensington Publishing Corp.
119 West 40th Street
New York, NY 10018

All Kensington titles, imprints and distributed lines are available at special quantity discounts for bulk purchases for sales promotion, premiums, fund-raising, educational or institutional use. Special book excerpts or customized printings can also be created to fit specific needs. For details, write or phone the office of the Kensington Special Sales Manager. Attn.: Special Sales Department. Kensington Publishing Corp., 119 West 40th Street, New York, NY 10018. Phone: 1-800-221-2647.

Library of Congress Card Catalogue Number: 2016933893

Kensington and the K logo Reg. U.S. Pat. & TM Off.

ISBN-13: 978-1-61773-147-1
ISBN-10: 1-61773-147-1
First Kensington Hardcover Edition: July 2016

eISBN-13: 978-1-61773-149-5
eISBN-10: 1-61773-149-8
First Kensington Electronic Edition: July 2016

10 9 8 7 6 5 4 3 2 1

Printed in the United States of America

To Jan, my own sweet mother-in-law, who is nothing like the mothers-in-law in this book. Thanks for being so supportive of me and my writing.

Chapter One

January

"Ellie, I need your help. Someone's going to get killed—I don't know who, but someone is gonna die," Summer said. "It may be me."

"That's a pretty extreme statement for a bride to make about her wedding," I said. When I first met Summer, my husband's younger sister, she had been a tad flighty and impulsive. She was also seventeen. Recently, she had settled down. Now twenty-six, she worked for a Florida state congressman and was engaged to Brian Abernathy, a contract lawyer.

"Okay, so I'm exaggerating a little bit, but only a little. They hate each other, they really do." The worry in Summer's voice came in loud and clear despite the hint of static on the hands-free device broadcasting her call from my minivan's dashboard.

I eased up on the brake and inched forward in the carpool line. "Who?"

"My mother-in-laws. Or is it mothers-in-law? I can't believe I have *two* of them. I'm beginning to appreciate the term monster-in-law."

"I thought you'd met them before."

"Yes." Summer's gusty sigh carried over the phone line. "But separately. Brian's mom, Yvonne, lives about an hour away on the Gulf so we've seen her a lot. His stepmom, Patricia, and dad live in Savannah. We all met for dinner last night, and it was a nightmare. That's why I need you. You're an organizer. You can help me figure out seating arrangements and, well, basically how to keep them apart. It could be a new niche for you, you know," she said in a wheedling tone.

"Keeping angry relatives apart?"

"No, wedding organizing."

"I don't know, Summer. I hate to say no to one of my favorite relatives, but I'm not a wedding planner."

"You wouldn't have to do any actual planning," she said quickly. "That's done. All the decisions have been made—invitations, food, bridesmaid dresses, hotel reservations, even the reception. Now it's just about checking and double-checking to make sure everything is delivered and set up. Detail stuff. You know I stink at that."

It was true. Summer took after her brother. Mitch always had the big picture in view. Unlike my husband, I was a detail person. I loved lists, and I especially loved lists with checkmarks. Finishing a to-do list really did make me happy. I'm weird that way.

"Anyway," Summer continued, "it could be a service you offer to brides, to give them peace of mind."

"Maybe an à la carte service," I murmured. I was always looking for innovative ways to grow my organizing business. Now that I wasn't the only organizer in North Dawkins, Georgia, I was more motivated than ever to explore new possibilities. I'd done many different types of organizing. Why not add organizing a wedding to the list?

Helping Summer would be a good test run to see if the idea was feasible. "Okay, I'll help you out with the follow-up details and mother-in-law wrangling. You just need to keep them apart, you said?"

"Oh, thank you, Ellie. You have no idea how much better I feel. Yes, they're like two chemical compounds that are stable when they're separate, but put them together, and—*boom*!—they explode."

"So we're talking logistics." How hard could it be to keep two women apart during the rehearsal dinner and the wedding?

Summer said, "As far apart as possible. Dinner last night started okay, if a little awkward. There were lots of undercurrents and pointed looks, but things were tolerable until Yvonne—that's Brian's mom—mentioned her dress. She wants to wear red."

Surely I hadn't heard that right. "Did you say red?"

Summer's tone was exasperated. "Yes. Red. Her signature color, apparently. She always wears it."

"Well, I've heard that red is a bridal gown color in China," I said.

"But we're not in China, and she's not Chinese."

"Or the bride," I added. This might be harder than I thought.

"Exactly."

Summer sighed. "I suppose I should have expected something like that. She's a little kooky. She teaches high school drama and spends her free time at the local community theater. She loves Shakespeare and is always dropping quotes into the conversation. Anyway, Brian's stepmom, Patricia, went ballistic. You would have thought Yvonne said she was going to show up naked. It went downhill from there."

"So what happened?"

"No actual punches were thrown, but it was close. Brian

and his dad calmed everyone down. I told Yvonne that any pastel color would be fine."

"Do you know what your stepmother-in-law—Patricia, was it?—is wearing?"

"A blue Diane von Furstenberg wrap dress."

"Sounds appropriate," I said, eyeing the clock on the van's dashboard. One minute until the school bell rang.

"Of course. Everything Patricia does is perfect. Perfectly calculated." There was an abrupt silence, then Summer said, "Forget I ever said that. I can't believe I'm running on and on. I know you're busy, so I'll let you go."

"Summer, you can't stop there. If I'm going to help you, you have to let me know what I'm dealing with."

After a pause she said, "You're right. Okay, Yvonne is exotic and quirky. Patricia is rigidly controlled, and she's got one goal, to get into the cream of Savannah society. She spends all her time volunteering for causes and going to society galas."

"They have money?" I asked. Summer and I talked on the phone and e-mailed quite a bit, and the subject of Brian's family being well-off never came up. "I thought his family was . . . I don't know . . . comfortably middle-class."

"I did too. Until we drove up to Savannah for this dinner. Their house is a mansion. I'm not exaggerating. Thirteen bedrooms, fifteen baths, a pool with a separate pool house—and not a little dinky changing room with a shower. This pool house is bigger than your house, Ellie. They have three cars—a Jag and two Mercedes. Okay, I'm stopping because I'm beginning to sound like Patricia. She catalogued everything for us, house, cars, boat, and jewelry, even the place settings."

"I suppose when your bedrooms are in the double digits, you're doing pretty well," I said. "And Brian never mentioned this?"

The school bell rang, and kids flooded out the doors, a

fast-moving tide of colorfully clad bodies surging to their appointed waiting zones on the sidewalk. The carpool pickup line worked like a well-oiled machine. Teachers and aides monitored the tsunami of students, communicating through walkie-talkies to summon the correct child to the pickup point at the front of the school when parents' cars pulled up.

"No, and when I asked him about it, he was surprised. Said he hadn't thought it was important." She blew out a sigh. "And he's right. It doesn't matter that his dad and stepmom are loaded. I love him for himself, not for his family or his family's money."

I'd met Brian once. "I didn't pick up on it either—the coming-from-money thing. He seems like a regular guy."

"Oh, he is. He didn't grow up with money. He told me all about it on our drive back to Tallahassee last night. His dad invented and patented a part that improves the water efficiency of sprinkler heads. If you see an underground sprinkler system, it has one of his parts on it. Up until about five years ago, before the invention caught on, Gus managed the electrical department in one of those big-box home improvement stores."

"And now he's attending society galas. Interesting."

"Only under duress. Gus doesn't really want to do anything besides improve his golf swing. He could care less about moving in the best circles. It's ironic that it was his golf buddy's cancellation that got us into the resort."

"Oh, is this about the honeymoon? Do you know where you're going?" The cars ahead of me moved, and I stopped even with the front doors of the school. The principal spoke into her walkie-talkie as she opened the minivan's door and waved hello to me.

"No, for the wedding," Summer said. "We were able to get into the resort on Camden."

My wrinkled forehead filled the rearview mirror. "A resort? I thought you were getting married on the beach."

"Well, we were. But how could we pass up Camden? It's beautiful and secluded. And it means a lot to Brian. His dad took him there several summers after the divorce. It was kind of their summer retreat."

"Wait. Camden as in *Camden Island*?"

"Yes. Can you believe it? To be able to get married at a historic Southern mansion on one of Georgia's most exclusive barrier islands—how lucky are we?"

"But you wanted a small ceremony, just family and close friends." I spotted Nathan, chugging along, his backpack bouncing with every step. Arms extended, he held a shoebox, which contained his show-and-tell item, an elaborate Lego spaceship. Livvy trailed along behind him and the aide, trying to read one book as she walked, while carrying several more in the crook of her arm.

"Originally, that was the plan," Summer said. Was there a note of wistfulness in her tone? If there was, it was gone the next moment as she added, "But the resort has everything, a spa, great restaurants, tours of the ruins of the original plantation house, lots of sports and activities. I guarantee that no one will be bored during the four days."

"Four days?" I asked faintly.

Nathan climbed in. "Hi, Mom. Justin brought a frog for show-and-tell."

Livvy dropped into her seat. "Hi," she mumbled, and turned a page.

"Is that Livvy and Nathan?" Summer's voice came from the hands-free device. "Hi there!"

Nathan bounced in his seat. Livvy looked up from her book. "Aunt Summer, is that you?"

Summer confirmed it was indeed her.

"A whole sentence," I informed Summer. "You should

be impressed. Livvy actually stopped reading to talk to you." The kids buckled in, and I put the van in gear.

"I'm honored," Summer said. The kids had stayed with her for a few days during our last vacation. She knew how deeply Livvy could get into her books.

"So what's this about four days?" I asked.

"A long weekend over spring break. Guess what, guys?" Summer said, addressing the kids.

"What?" they chorused in their squeaky voices.

"Not only do you get to be my flower girl and my ring bearer, you get to spend four whole days on an *island*. You ride a ferry to get there, and it's really cool. There's a ruin, giant climbing trees covered with Spanish moss, and you can go swimming at the beach or ride a horse. It won't be during turtle season so we can have a bonfire on the beach one night. There's a huge pool and bike trails and even paintball."

"I think they're a little young for paintball," I said over the excited chatter from the backseat.

"Ellie, I feel so much better after talking to you. With you helping me, I know it will all work out."

"Glad I can help," I said, wondering what I'd gotten myself into. The organizing bit for the wedding wouldn't be a problem. I could do follow-up and confirmations, but dealing with the hostile mother and stepmother? I'd do my best, but I'd found that organizing people was a lot harder than organizing closets and schedules. "Send me the details on the wedding stuff," I said before we hung up.

And that's how I agreed to organize a four-day wedding for 250 people at Camden Island Resort.

Chapter Two

March

"Where's the beach?" Nathan asked. "Mom, Aunt Summer said there was a beach." The Hot Wheels cars, action figures, books, and even the handheld electronic game console lay forgotten, strewn around the back of the van as Nathan strained against his seatbelt for a better view of Camden Island.

"The beaches are on the other side," I explained as the car ferry drew closer to the island.

We'd spent the majority of the short ferry ride from the mainland of Georgia to Camden Island out of the car with the kids draped over the ferry's railing as they licked ice cream cones. We were on spring break and the kids felt it was only right to begin our vacation with ice cream. Mitch agreed wholeheartedly and ordered a double scoop of dark chocolate. While he was normally an extremely healthy eater, ice cream was the one place Mitch indulged. Chocolate in any form is usually an automatic yes for me, but I had thought of the pale pink linen sheath dress I had packed for the wedding and requested a kid-size scoop of peach sherbet.

We were all in a vacation sort of mood. The kids were out of school for a week. Mitch had leave from the squadron for five days, and I had cleared my organizing schedule, except for Summer. Besides enjoying the wedding, following up on Summer's wedding tasks and keeping an eye on the mothers in the wedding party were the only things on my agenda.

I closed the thick white binder I'd spread out across the dashboard and tucked it into my large tote. "Did you get your list made?" Mitch asked.

"Yes. Today is all about getting the final head count to the catering staff, finalizing the seating chart, and reconfirming with the florist, the photographer, the minister, and the deejay."

Mitch shook his head. "I still can't believe Summer roped you into planning her wedding."

"It really hasn't been that bad." Summer had been true to her word. All the big decisions had been made. "So far, all I have had to do is make phone calls and send reminder e-mails. It's been easy."

"I have a feeling the hard part is about to start," Mitch said.

"The mother-in-law wrangling? Yeah, I am a little worried about that. Although, Summer says Brian has talked to both his mom and stepmom and they've agreed to a truce," I said doubtfully.

"You're afraid it won't hold?"

"Well, for a couple of hours, I'm sure they could do it, but four days . . ."

"Whatever happens, I'll have your back."

"I know," I said, smiling at him.

"How much longer?" Nathan asked from the backseat.

"I thought we had to get back in the car because we were almost there."

"We are," I answered as the ferry neared the island. "We're almost to the dock. Did you know we're on the first ferry of the day?" I asked to distract him. Until I became a parent, I'd forgotten the innate competitive nature of kids. Anything that could be claimed as first, oldest, or best was very important to the grade-school set. That news perked Nathan up, and I knew he was filing it away so he could inform various cousins of his arrival on the *first* ferry.

The car ferries usually ran three days during the week and daily on the weekends, but since it was spring break there were more runs scheduled. We'd caught the earliest one along with a few other people, who I assumed worked at the resort because of their bored expressions and lack of beach equipment visible through the windows of their cars.

Mitch winked at me as the ferry bumped against the dock. "If you'd been paying attention, Nathan, you'd know that this side of the island is mostly marsh."

I'd tried to read from the guidebook and tell the kids about the island on the drive over, but they hadn't seemed too interested in the history of Camden Island.

"I was paying attention," Nathan said. "It doesn't look like a bean to me."

Okay, maybe he had been listening. I glanced at Mitch and tried to keep the smile out of my voice as I said, "*Shaped* like a bean, honey. That means that the barrier islands are long and narrow. One side of Camden Island, the side next to the mainland, curves inland, but the side next to the ocean is more rounded. If you saw it from above it would look like a bean."

"Like a *giant* bean." Nathan wiggled in his seat. "And the forests are in the middle of the bean," he all but shouted.

Livvy's head, which had been bent over her book, popped up. "Would you be quiet? I can't read."

The cars ahead of us inched forward, down the ramp to the island. "Here we go," Mitch said, releasing the brake. "Hang on." His dramatic tone silenced the brewing fight in the backseat.

Mitch eased over a bump onto the ramp then punched the gas, and we sailed down to the asphalt road. A weathered sign with faded red letters on a white background welcomed us to Camden Island. The dock area consisted of a stand selling ferry tickets and a building with two gas pumps and a small convenience store with a sign proclaiming burgers, sandwiches, and ice cream could be found inside. The area had a no-frills vibe of a national park during the off-season.

"Nathan, how many roads are there on Camden Island?" Mitch asked.

"One!"

"Very good. You were paying attention," Mitch said.

"We can only drive to the hotel. No cars allowed anywhere else," Nathan said. Ninety percent of Camden Island was a conservation area and no additional development was allowed.

"How will we get around? Are we going to have to ride the horses?" Livvy asked suspiciously.

"Golf carts!" Nathan shouted. "You'd know that, if you hadn't been reading your book."

"Nathan, inside voice," I said.

Livvy made a face at him, then turned her shoulder and propped her book up on the window, but I could see she wasn't reading.

The road left the clearing by the dock and entered the forest abruptly. The sharp-edged fanned leaves of low-growing palmettos crowded the road while live oaks, their twisting branches draped with Spanish moss, rose on either side. Branches thicker than telephone poles arched over the road. Spanish moss hung motionless in curtains from the thick limbs.

We drove a few more minutes, the flat road ambling through the trees. The sun splashed down on us occasionally through gaps in the canopy, then the shade swallowed us again. The asphalt ended at a gate set into a stone wall. Gateposts connected with a curved iron arch marked the switch to a crushed shell road. The gates stood open, grass and vines entwined through them, indicating that it had been a long time since they had been closed.

The wild growth ended at the gate. Inside the stone wall, a grassy lawn spread, broken only by the widely spaced massive live oaks. In the distance, a single spot of white blazed against the green background. As the road curved closer we could make out the lines of a white gazebo positioned between two fountains.

"Is that where Aunt Summer will get married?" Livvy asked, breaking the silence, and I realized that the kids had been quiet for the last few minutes as we drove through the forest. It was probably the sheer uniqueness of the scenery that had kept the kids' attention. We had stands of pine trees in North Dawkins, but those copses were nothing like the lush vegetation here.

"I think so. I don't see any other gazebos, so that must be it," I said.

We crunched around a bend in the road and the resort came into full view. I'd seen plenty of pictures of it as I planned and prepped and double-checked wedding details, but the photos didn't compare with a firsthand look.

Built in the late 1800s by a wealthy sugar baron as a winter escape, it was a blend of Italianate and Queen Anne architecture. A mix of stone, stucco, and shingle, the two-story white central building glowed blindingly in the sun. The dominant feature was a square bell tower with tall arched window cutouts that rose above the main roofline in the center of the building. Orange roof tiles glowed warmly in the sunlight, giving it a Mediterranean flair.

Mitch parked at the foot of a wide stone staircase that led to a covered veranda, which ran across the right-hand side of the building in front of a row of large bay windows. A turret with curved windows rose on the left-hand side of the shallow stairs. Two stories of balconied windows marched along the wings stretching out on either side of the main house.

"Wow." Livvy closed her book. "That doesn't look like a cottage."

I'd read them the part of the guidebook that described how the wealthy industrialists from the North discovered the Georgia barrier islands and built "cottages." Most of these retreats were located on nearby Jekyll Island, and their owners were members of the Jekyll Island Club, the roster of which included names like Morgan, Vanderbilt, and Pulitzer. But even among millionaires there are some quirky folks. Archibald Q. Trumont liked his privacy and built his "cottage" on Camden Island, after purchasing the entire island, of course. "These were very wealthy people," I said. "These houses were small in comparison to their other houses."

Mitch unbuckled his seatbelt. "Let's go check in."

"Yeah, I want to see inside the cottage-mansion," Nathan said.

I stepped out of the van and stretched, enjoying the pleasantly clear air that only held a faint trace of humidity. I'd been worried that the muggy Georgia summer would arrive early and we'd all be sweltering during the outdoor wedding. The aroma of freshly mowed grass mingled with the scent of flowers. I thought I caught a whiff of jasmine and perhaps gardenia.

A slim figure in white flew down the stairs, arms wide,

her red hair streaming behind her. "You're here! Group hug." Summer crushed Livvy and Nathan to her. They submitted for a moment then wiggled away. Mitch gave Summer a one-armed hug as he said, "Hey, Sis. How you holding up?"

"Great. So excited you're here."

The kids were impatient to see the resort, and Mitch let himself be dragged to the stairs. As the kids peppered him with questions about the pool and the beach, he called over his shoulder to me, "I know you two have a lot to talk about. We'll check out the room and come back for the luggage."

Brian, his brown hair with red highlights glinting in the sunlight, followed Summer down the stairs at a slower pace. He and Mitch paused to shake hands.

Summer squeezed me close, then tucked her sleek long bob behind her ears. "So good to see you."

"You too. How are you?" I leaned back to look at her. Her naturally pale skin was flushed with a happy glow, and she was smiling widely.

"Great. I'm so glad it's finally here. This waiting is killing me. It's worse than waiting for Christmas when I was a kid."

Brian joined us. Looping his arm around Summer's shoulders, he pulled her close. "I told her we should have eloped." He wasn't movie-star handsome—no square-cut jaw or elusive charisma gene that drew all eyes to him when he came on the scene—but he was good-looking in a more conventional sense with his dark hair, a tall, broad-shouldered build, and soft brown eyes. He was dependable and reliable and thought Summer was the best thing that had ever happened to him, which made him a keeper in my book.

She grinned and rolled her eyes. To me, she said, "He just wants to go on the honeymoon."

"You bet I do."

Summer's cheeks flushed. "Yeah, well, too late now. The napkins have been printed with our names. Patricia would kill me if we skipped out now."

"Yeah, she wouldn't be happy with all the bigwigs she's invited," Brian said, but the idea of an angry stepmother didn't seem to bother him. "The elopement option is still on the table," he said firmly.

"A few days and then we'll be on our own," Summer countered as she sent me a glance. "He says that, but there's no cutting and running now."

"We wouldn't be cutting and running. It would be a strategic retreat," Brian said.

"I doubt your stepmom would see it that way," Summer said.

The crunch of tires on the shell drive sounded, and we turned to see a MINI Cooper emblazoned with a Union Jack making its way leisurely up the drive. "That's my aunt Nanette. She must have come over on the ferry from Jekyll Island," Summer informed Brian. "She's an Anglophile."

"Never would have guessed." Brian said, deadpan. The car eased to a stop beside the minivan. The door opened, and Nanette emerged. "And that's Queen," Summer said as a gray Afghan hound leapt out lightly.

I'd heard about a study that found dogs tend to look like their owners, and I'd been ready to scoff, but then I had thought of Aunt Nanette and Queen. With their feathered gray hair and pointed noses, there was an uncanny resemblance between owner and pet.

Mitch and the kids descended the stairs, and the next few minutes were a confusion of greetings. Nanette gave Livvy a quick hug and asked what she was reading. Nanette was almost as big a bookworm as Livvy.

"*The Secret Garden*." Livvy pulled her book out from under her arm and held it out.

"Excellent choice for a weekend at a Victorian estate." Despite her rather reserved manner, Nanette had developed a rapport with Livvy and Nathan. She fanned through the pages. "And you have the edition with the classic illustrations. This is one of my favorite books, you know. You'll have to tell me later about what you think of Robin." Nanette was a favorite with the kids, and I thought it was because she didn't talk down to them, but treated them exactly like she treated everyone else. She turned to Nathan and formally shook his hand. "And what about you, young man? It's not all video games for you, is it?"

"No. I can read," Nathan informed her. He'd been reading basic, one-syllable words last year in kindergarten, but now that he was in first grade he was reading chapter books on his own. "I brought *Nate the Great* books with me."

"Glad to hear it," Nanette said.

Queen was sitting prettily as Livvy ran her hands down the dog's back while Nathan rubbed one ear. "Mom, we could have brought Rex," Livvy said, referring to our dog.

"Rex is having a wonderful time at the doggie kennel, playing with his friends." And I was glad he was there. I loved Rex, but I had enough things to juggle on this trip without adding a dog to the mix.

"Come on, kids, let's get these suitcases upstairs," Mitch called.

"I'll be there in a minute." I watched Nathan tug his heavy roller bag through the shell drive. "I think his suitcase is half filled with toy cars and action figures, and Livvy's is mostly books," I said to Summer and Nanette.

"Smart kids to bring their own entertainment, not that they'll run out of things here," Nanette said, then turned to Summer. "Now, I have a message for you. Your mom and dad couldn't leave town this morning. Caroline has a finicky client who—wouldn't you know it—picked today to turn in a contract on a house. There's a bidding war and her assistant's son broke his leg, so she can't leave until she gets it squared away, but she'll be here as soon as possible. Might be tomorrow, depending on how the negotiations go."

"Well, if that's the only thing that goes wrong this weekend, I can handle that."

Aunt Nanette patted Summer on the arm, an extreme show of affection, coming from her, then went to check in.

A car horn tooted and a vintage red Corvette with the top down whipped around the curve and slowed to a stop next to the MINI Cooper, spraying bits of the shell drive. "And that's my mother," Brian said before moving to open the car door for her. The woman's brassy red hair swung around her shoulders as she climbed out of the car. She wore a red tank top and a pair of white capri pants with little red hearts embroidered across the fabric. She'd accessorized with a gauzy red and white scarf, white-framed sunglasses, and three-inch red heels.

"Darling!" She gave Brian a quick death-grip hug, then moved to Summer. "Sweetie!" She grasped Summer's hands and drew her arms wide. "Shall I compare thee to a summer's day? Thou art more lovely and more temperate."

"Er—thanks, Yvonne," Summer said.

Nanette stepped forward, extended her hand, and said firmly, "I'm Nanette." I suspect it was to prevent Yvonne from calling her something like *Honey*. Summer introduced me as well.

"Charmed," Yvonne said, then turned back to Brian, dismissing Nanette, Summer, and me. Yvonne looped her arm through Brian's elbow. "Let's get my luggage. Now, tell me . . ." Her voice faded as they walked across the crushed shell drive toward the cars.

I raised my eyebrows. "Shakespeare?"

"She's always doing that. Just roll with it—it's easier." Summer's forehead creased in a frown as she watched Yvonne and Brian.

"Everything okay?" I asked as Brian hefted several Louis Vuitton suitcases out of the trunk of Yvonne's car.

"She's always doing that, pulling him away to go chat on their own. And lately she's been hinting that Brian and I should put off the wedding. I wish—" Summer broke off as a stocky blond woman strode down the stairs. "Oh, boy. Brian's stepmom, Patricia. Here we go."

The two women met on the staircase, paused, nodded to each other, and then continued on their way. Summer let out a *whoosh* of breath. "Okay, we might actually make it through this weekend."

"So Brian's stepmom and dad didn't come over on the ferry today?"

Summer nodded to the silver Mercedes parked at the front of the line. "No, they've been here since last night. Helping," Summer said in a tight voice.

Patricia crunched across the shell drive, her pale blue linen jacket and wide-leg trousers flapping around her. She raised the cell phone she held in her hand and waved it like a flag. "Great news," she said in nasal tones. "I just heard from Judge Ratliff and his wife, Colleen. They can make it. And so can the Mayburns."

"I don't know if we can do that." Summer looked at me. "Do we have any open seats left?"

I'd slung my tote on my shoulder when we got out of the car, and now I reached for the white binder.

"What are you talking about?" Patricia said, "*Of course* we can find room for the judge. And the Mayburns are top-notch. You don't want to turn them away and get off on the wrong foot with *them*. So influential, you know."

I paused with the binder in my hand. "I know you had a few last minute add-ons yesterday and that filled the extra table we'd left open."

"Well, add another table." Patricia tossed her champagne-colored bangs and eyed me critically. "And you are?"

Summer threw me an apologetic look. "Patricia, this is my sister-in-law, Ellie. She's the reason everything is running so smoothly."

Patricia thawed slightly and turned up the corners of her lips. "So nice to meet you. Do you have the seating charts in there?" She reached for the binder. "I've been waiting on those."

I shifted the binder to my other arm, away from her. "Yes, but Summer hasn't had a chance to look at them. We were just about to go over them."

"Yes, let me sort this out," Summer said, "and I'll drop off a copy for you once we have seats for the Ratliffs and the Mayburns."

"I'll help," Patricia said in a voice edged with steel.

Summer's gaze focused on something beyond my shoulder. "That would be lovely. Let's sit there in the shade and work it out." She moved across the lawn to a white wicker table and a trio of chairs under the spreading branches of a massive live oak.

Patricia hesitated, then said, "On second thought, you take care of that. I have to make sure that caterer got my message about the beef."

"Nice to meet you," I called to her departing back.

Patricia turned, waved like the Queen of England, a perfect little half swivel of her forearm. "Don't shove the judge and Colleen somewhere in the back. They need to be near the head table," she called before resuming her trek to the resort.

Summer moved in the direction of the table, her sandals

sinking into the thick grass as she walked from the drive to the lawn. "I knew she wouldn't stay. She hates being outside."

The wicker creaked as I dropped into one of the seats. "No wonder you're such a success in politics."

"She's tougher than some politicians I've come across, that's for sure. Okay, quick, let's sort out the seating, but no one who RSVP'd weeks ago is getting bumped to a back table."

We huddled over the binder, shifting names and table placements until we'd worked out a new arrangement. Then, Summer made a call to the resort's catering department, who agreed they could squeeze in another table at the midpoint of the room.

"But that will leave four open seats at the new table. Do you want to move someone else over?" I asked.

"I have no doubt that the table will be full before tonight," Summer said as she sent a text.

A golf cart decorated with white tulle, gold ribbons, and a BRIDE AND GROOM sign attached to the canopy bumped off the shell path onto the grass and headed our way. Brian wheeled the cart to a stop and removed a picnic basket from the seat.

"Peach ice tea or lemonade, compliments of the catering staff." Brian removed three glasses, an ice bucket, and two carafes from the basket along with a container of nuts and dried fruits.

"There." Summer put the phone down on the wicker table. "Done." She reached for a glass. "This is nice, although I might need something stronger than ice tea."

"A Long Island ice tea?" Brian said. "I saw you talking to Patricia."

"Two more late RSVPs. It's taken care of," Summer said.

Brian handed me a glass. I took a long gulp as Summer and Brian clinked their glasses and recited together, "Three more days."

I took a sip of the lemonade. "Oh, this is good. Such a rich, tangy taste, but it's not too sour."

"Yes, it is. It tastes exactly like Aunt Gloria's lemonade." Brian ran his thumb over the glass through the thin layer of condensation that had already formed, his face suddenly sad.

Summer reached out and squeezed his hand. "I wish she could be here too."

Brian nodded. "She was looking forward to it."

Summer looked toward me and explained. "Brian's aunt Gloria passed away last month."

"Oh, I'm sorry to hear that," I said.

Brian shifted his gaze toward Camden House. "She really wanted to be here to see this place. I talked about it so much when I was a kid, though, she probably didn't need to see it in person. I used to come here camping with my dad when I was a kid for a few weeks in June, then we'd go to Aunt Gloria's house for Fourth of July. I'm sure I talked her ear off."

"I bet she loved it," Summer said. "She wanted to see this place because you love it, but there's a more important reason—to see you get married. She was so proud to have two nephews go into law." Summer leaned toward Brian and lowered her voice to a mock-whisper. "I think you were her favorite, though."

A small smile appeared on Brian's mouth. "Don't say that around Graham. That's what he thinks, too. But if I was her favorite, it was only because I didn't cause nearly as much trouble as Graham did. I wasn't the one who nearly set her lawn on fire playing with her magnifying glass."

"That sounds like Graham," Summer said, wryly. As an aside, she said to me, "I haven't met him, but I've heard plenty about him."

"Oh it was exactly like him, and he tried to pin the blame on me." Brian looked toward me. "Don't look so worried. Graham has calmed down."

Summer said, "Or as Aunt Gloria put it, 'he's reformed quite nicely.'"

"So he's a lawyer, too?" I asked.

"Yes, in Macon." Summer said. "He works in a firm there."

Brian still must have been thinking about his childhood because he took another sip of his lemonade, then said, "Graham would go to Valdosta for Fourth of July, too. Aunt Gloria had a little rancher on the outskirts of town. We'd sleep in a tent on the lawn. When I think about it now"—he shook his head and laughed—"it must have been blazing hot. July in Georgia, and we wanted to sleep outside. We were crazy, but I don't remember the heat. There was a pond for fishing, and we'd do that, too. Never really caught anything. And there was always her home-made lemonade." Brian lifted his glass and took a sip.

The growl of a powerful car engine carried through the trees. "The next ferry from the mainland must be in." Summer set down her glass and rose to greet the new arrivals. A black Ferrari roared up the drive. The car shot by our group. Brian half stood, a frown crinkling his face. "That's not . . ."

Brake lights flared and the sleek car swung backward in an arc, slipping into a slot at the front of the line by the Mercedes.

"Oh, good. It's Graham," Summer said. To me, she added, "You can meet the infamous Graham right now, Brian's cousin and best man." She turned back to Brian. "When did he get that car?"

Brian shrugged. "No idea. Last I knew he was driving a Camry." There was something about his voice that made me look closer at Brian. He sounded distracted. He was squinting, not at Graham, but at the woman getting out on the passenger side of the car.

"Oh, he brought someone for his plus one," Summer said. "I didn't know he was dating anyone."

Summer walked across the lawn to meet the couple. Brian followed more slowly, his gaze fixed on the leggy, tanned woman walking in Graham's wake. The woman and Graham were quite a pair. Even from a distance, I could see that she was beautiful. Everything about her was long and slender, from her graceful neck to her long, tanned limbs, which glowed against the fabric of her pale pink halter top and white Bermuda shorts.

With a head of shining blond hair, deep blue eyes, and a squared-off jawline, Graham wasn't a slouch in the attractiveness department either. He hadn't dressed as carefully as the woman had. His faded denim shirt, wrinkled khaki shorts, and boat shoes didn't exactly go with the Ferrari, but I supposed when you drove a car like that you didn't worry too much about your clothes, especially if you were a guy. Despite the wrinkles, I recognized the shirt as an expensive designer brand. It was just like one I'd given to Mitch for Christmas last year. Together, Graham and his date looked like Hollywood A-listers. I half expected a couple of paparazzi photographers to pop out of the surrounding greenery.

I dropped the binder into my tote and trailed along behind Summer and Brian, figuring it would be bad manners to sit in the shade while everyone else was meeting and greeting.

I intended to say hello and continue on to the resort to find Mitch and the kids, but I ran into Brian's back when he stopped abruptly at the edge of the drive. I apologized, but he didn't hear me. He was focused on the face of the woman as she pushed her big sunglasses up into her mahogany hair, revealing dark brown eyes fringed with long lashes.

She looked . . . embarrassed, I realized, as she hung back a step behind Graham as he slapped Brian on the back. Because of my collision with Brian, I heard Graham say in an undertone, "Sorry, man. I'll explain later," as I shifted around the immobile Brian.

Brian seemed to shake himself, reminding me of our dog, Rex, when he woke from a nap. "Summer," Brian said slowly as if he was having a hard time finding the right words, "you've talked to Graham on the phone."

"Yes. Finally, we meet." Summer gave him a quick hug.

"And this is Julia." Brian's voice had a strained quality to it, and I looked at him, but his face was blank.

Summer hesitated for a second. "Julia?" Her voice held a question as she shot a glance at Brian.

"Julia Banning." The leggy brunette stepped forward and extended her hand. "So happy for you both. Thanks for having me." Her words came out in a rush and carried some extra significance that I couldn't identify.

Summer made a choking noise, then cleared her throat. "Of course."

Graham ran his fingers through his blond hair, pushing it off his face as he grabbed Julia's hand and backed away. "We better get our rooms. See you in a few." Julia waved, then they crossed the shell drive to retrieve their suitcases from the car.

As soon as Graham and Julia climbed the stairs and disappeared into the cool dimness of the resort's front door, Summer spun to Brian. "Julia? *Julia Banning*? I can't believe it. It's not enough that we have to deal with the family feud between your mom and stepmom, now we've got your psycho ex-girlfriend, too?"

Brian held up his hands. "Hey, I didn't invite her. Obviously, Graham asked her as his date." His face darkened. "But he should know better."

Not eager to witness a lovers' spat, I eased to the side, trying to make myself invisible, but it didn't matter. They were so focused on each other that they didn't take any notice of me.

"He should know better, but it doesn't matter." Summer rubbed her forehead and turned away. "We can't ask her to leave."

"You're right, it doesn't matter. I didn't ask her to marry me." Brian put his hands on Summer's shoulders and turned her around. "I asked you. I don't care that she's here. . . ." Their voices faded as I tiptoed away.

I almost made my escape, but the sound of a wedding bell ringtone cut through the air, then Summer called out, "Ellie, wait. The florist wants to go over the final numbers for the corsages."

I turned back. After Brian gave Summer a kiss that didn't leave any doubt about where his affections lay, he left to catch the ferry to the mainland so he could pick up some guests at the local airport. Summer and I huddled at the wicker table again, the phone on speaker between us as we went over the flower order.

When we were done, Summer ended the call and fell back against the chair.

"So, ex-girlfriend, uh?" I asked.

"Yeah. I've never met her, but I've heard about her." Summer was seated facing the resort. She stared straight ahead, squinting at the central bell tower, then looked sideways at me. "Julia went a little crazy when Brian broke up with her a few years ago. She kept going to his office, camping out in the lobby for hours, refusing to leave, and scrawling weird notes written in lipstick on the mirror in the women's restroom. There were a couple of instances of

vandalism—Brian's car was keyed and the building his office was in had a couple of windows broken. Another time,
paint was splashed on the front door. There was never any
proof that she did it, but that's what everyone thinks."

"Wow, and she looked so innocuous."

"And beautiful."

"You have nothing to worry about," I said. "Brian loves
you. Like he said, he's marrying you, not her."

Summer's mouth quirked down. "I know, but it's not
what you want a few days before your wedding, the groom's
old flame showing up." She ran her fingers up into her
hair and gathered it into a ponytail. "I'm beginning to understand the bridezilla phenomenon—all the focus and expectations and the pressure. Maybe we *should* have eloped."

I opened my mouth to reply, but there was a *pop*, then a
whooshing sound. I looked around as it repeated, but
didn't see anything. Summer gasped, and I turned back to
her. Three bloody spots bloomed on her chest, crimson
against the white of her dress.

Tips for an Organized Wedding

To keep track of all the small details for the big day,
make a wedding binder or notebook. You can create as
many sections as you need, but here are some basic ones to
get you started:

- Budget
- Time Line
- Invitations
- Guest List
- Wedding Location
- Reception Location

- Flowers
- Catering
- Attire
- Transportation
- Lodging
- Music/Entertainment
- Officiant
- Legal
- Photography/Video
- Honeymoon

Dividers with storage pockets will come in handy as a place to store samples as well as receipts. Or you can add zippered plastic pouches between sections.

In addition to your hard-copy materials, you'll also want to keep track of all the electronic communications you'll receive. A dedicated e-mail account or a folder within your existing e-mail account can help you keep all the details at your fingertips.

Chapter Three

Summer collapsed forward, slipping off her chair and landing on her knees in the grass. I was so stunned, my mind couldn't seem to take in what I was seeing. Another *pop* and whooshing sound cut through the air, snapping me out of my frozen state. I jerked down below the table beside Summer.

I gripped her hand. "Summer—"

"I'm okay," she said in a dazed voice. Red smears covered the skirt of her sundress now.

This cannot be happening. "Hang on. No, don't move. I'll call for help." Cautiously, I peeped up over the table, snatched my phone, and hunkered down again.

I punched buttons. "No service. I'll go for help. I'll hurry—"

"Wait." She rose up a few inches.

"No, stay down. In fact, you should lie down."

"Ellie." She squeezed my hand. "I'm okay. I'm not hurt. Well, not much." She rocked forward again. "Oh, that stings."

She was delirious. "Not hurt? Of course, you're hurt. You've been shot. . . ." I said, but my voice trailed off as I realized the red stains weren't spreading. In fact, they were only splotches on the fabric. Garish and scary-looking, but only splotches.

Still hunched over, her breathing rough, Summer touched one spot gingerly. "It's paint."

I breathed out and glanced around, my heart still skittering around in my chest. It was quiet. No more pops or whooshing sounds.

Two red stains marred the carpet of the green lawn a few yards behind us. "Paintball. That has to be what happened. But how—?" I scanned the grounds. No one was in sight, except for an older couple bumping up the shell path in a golf cart. The resort was quiet. The windows marched across the facade, reflecting the sun, and the staircase and the veranda were empty.

A shrill scream cut through the air. Summer and I flinched and hunkered down again. It was the woman in the golf cart. She pointed at Summer, her hand shaking as she continued to scream.

"She's okay," I called, but the woman couldn't hear me over the piercing wail of her own scream, which brought the resort staff and enough commotion and people that I felt reasonably safe abandoning our little white table that we'd used as a barrier.

I thought we were going to have to call for medical help for the manager, Mr. Markham, when he saw Summer.

"Don't worry. It's not as bad as it looks," I said to him. "That's not blood. They were red paintball pellets."

He was a small man with puffy gray hair, a beaky nose, and coal black eyes. "But the paintball range is quite a distance from here. There's no way . . ."

I touched the chair. "She was sitting here, facing the resort."

"But then that means—" He glanced at the resort. "That would mean . . ."

"That they came from the resort."

*   *   *

I knocked on the door to Summer's room a few hours later. She pulled it open, her cell phone tucked into her shoulder. She'd changed into a loose, turquoise V-neck tee and a pair of jean shorts. "I'm fine, Mom. I promise," Summer said into the phone, then waved me in and closed the door. "Yes, I have an ice pack." She picked one up from the marble-topped dresser and pressed it to her sternum. "No, I don't think we can ask her to leave . . . well, no one actually saw her do it, for one thing."

I shifted the fabric-covered box I held from one hand to the other and mouthed, *Do you want me to come back later?*

Summer shook her head. "Mom, I've got to go. . . . No, I'm fine. Really. I promise. . . . Yes, I'd tell you if I wanted you to come right now. Brian's here and Mitch, too. You know how he gets when he's in his protective-older-brother mode. . . . No, you and Dad wouldn't make the last ferry anyway. Don't worry. Just get that contract squared away, and I'll see you tomorrow."

Summer ended the call and dropped down onto the bright yellow duvet, propping her back against the white iron headboard with glass accents. The bed was covered with boxes, rolls of ribbon, stacks of paper, and her laptop computer. "I should have known someone would call Mom. Between her, Brian, and Mitch, I feel like I'm trying to rein in an army ready to do battle on my behalf."

I smiled. "The Avery family never does anything halfway. I guess you should be glad you have so many people to defend you."

"I am, but at times it gets a tad overwhelming. Especially when you're the youngest."

"But you're really okay?"

"Yeah. Just a few welts. They won't go away before the wedding, but no one will be able to see them anyway. All the hits were squarely in my midsection." She waved her hand at her chest and stomach, then put down the ice pack and reached for a stack of small boxes and gold ribbon. "The last of the favors." She tied a piece of precut ribbon around one of the boxes and put it in a basket on the bed.

"I brought the box with everything for the reception." I put it on the dresser. "But you can check it later. I'll help you with that." I moved over to the bed, sat down cross-legged, and went to work helping her tie the ribbons. I shook a box. "What are they?" I asked because she didn't seem to want to talk about the paintball incident.

"A small jar of peach jam and postcards of the island."

"That's nice. I like it."

We worked in silence for a while, then without looking up Summer said, "Brian talked to Graham. Julia went immediately to her room as soon as they checked in and stayed there. She says she was lying down because she had a headache."

"Where's her room?"

"A few doors down, on this side." Summer made a miniscule adjustment to the bow so that each side was exactly the same size.

"So, facing the lawn." We were on the second story of the resort. Our rooms, one for me and Mitch and one for the kids, were adjoining and were located on the opposite side of the hall, almost directly across from Summer's room. We had a lovely view of the sumptuous back terrace and gardens. Summer's room was in the turret portion of the resort and had curved walls set with windows that overlooked the resort's front sweeping shell drive and the wide lawn.

"I suppose Brian was too polite to insist on searching Julia's room or luggage?"

Summer tossed the box into the basket. "That would be going beyond the bounds of Southern hospitality, wouldn't it? You can't accuse your guests of shooting paintball pellets at you, can you? It just isn't done."

I met her gaze. "Well, Julia did have a really big suitcase." After I met them, Graham and Julia had returned to the sports car and retrieved their luggage before going to check in. I'd noticed Graham struggling with Julia's large suitcase. "It was so big he could barely get it out of the car."

Summer jumped up from the bed and paced to one of the windows overlooking the lawn. "I'm sure Brian and Mitch will keep a close eye on her from now on." She stared out for a moment, then said, "I can't believe someone would do that. It means that she brought it with her—the paint gun and the pellets. It's crazy."

"What does Graham say?"

Summer went to the dresser and selected a chocolate from a gold box. "He's in denial. Says that it had to have been a mistake, probably some kid from the paintball area sneaking around where he shouldn't have been who's too freaked out to own up to it." Summer bit into the chocolate and made a face. "Coconut, ugh." She tossed it in the trash bin, then picked another from the box. "Brian says he can tell Graham really likes her. Brian is afraid that if he asks Julia to leave it will make everything worse. He *is* Brian's best man. We can't really ban his date from the wedding. So even though Brian doesn't want to do it, he's going to let it ride." She came back to the bed and held the box out. "Want one? There's two left."

I was tempted. I hadn't brought my typical stash of chocolate Kisses that I always carried with me, and the chocolate aroma made my mouth water. I shook my head, cursing the pink sheath dress. "I have to pass, if I want to wear the dress I brought for the wedding."

"You're right." Summer shoved the lid on the box and tossed it in the trash.

"I wouldn't go that far," I said, straining across the bed and retrieving the box. "There's always the day after the wedding."

"Keep it." Summer squared her shoulders, her gaze on her wedding gown, which was hanging in splendid isolation in the room's closet. The folding doors were pushed back, allowing the swell of the skirt to bell out. Summer had chosen a gorgeous strapless gown with a crisscross bodice in a soft ivory color. The skirt was a filmy A-line style without a train. She gave a brisk nod. "I'm not going to worry about crazy Julia. You're right. Mitch and Brian will keep an eye on her. This weekend is about Brian and me and our families celebrating together. That's what is most important and what I'm going to focus on. Where are the kids?"

"Livvy and Nathan convinced Aunt Nanette that they had to go to the pool. She offered to take them."

"She's so tough on the outside, but inside she's a big softy," Summer said.

"I know! I never would have imagined it, but she is," I agreed.

"But never let on that you know it," Summer said.

"Never."

Summer clasped her hands together and scanned the room. "Okay," she said briskly. "I've got the guest book and the fancy pen to go with the other things for the reception." Summer nodded at the box I'd brought with me. "I'll add those to the box later. That's taken care of. What else do we need?" She checked the time on her watch. "We have to get ready for the bachelorette party."

"What's the plan for the party?" I asked.

Summer shrugged. "No idea, except I told Meg it had to be tasteful. I thought Mom would be there."

Chapter Four

Summer's mom, Caroline, a true Southern lady, would have been perfectly comfortable at the party. Summer's maid of honor and former college roommate, Meg, had planned a perfect, classy bachelorette party, which consisted of a cooking demonstration with dinner included.

"Not a stripper in sight," Yvonne commented sadly as she took her seat next to me at one of the tall tables positioned around the resort's kitchen. A demonstration table with a large, angled mirror sat in the middle of the room. A mix of cookware, utensils, and ingredients covered the table. Delicious aromas of baking bread and savory meat already filled the kitchen. "Of course, I shouldn't be surprised," Yvonne continued, "her maid of honor doesn't exactly look like she'd know how to party, even if she wanted to."

Meg, a sturdily built yet soft-spoken woman with raven-black hair, did radiate competent calmness as she shuffled everyone into their seats and consulted with the chef.

Patricia was passing in front of our table and overheard Yvonne's comment. Patricia paused mid stride. "Meg made an excellent choice. Strippers would be tacky."

Yvonne muttered, "Thou art as loathsome as a toad," to Patricia's back.

Patricia's steps checked. "What did you say?"

"She hopes no one got stuck on the road," I said quickly. "You know, coming in from the ferry," I said. *Lame*, I thought, but it was the best I could do on the spur of the moment. Patricia frowned, and I hurried on, scanning the room for a diversion. "I think Meg needs some help getting everyone's attention."

"Of course she does." Patricia's voice held a note of exasperation. Patricia crossed the room to the demonstration table, her linen skirt snapping like the sail of a ship under full steam. Meg had been saying, "Everyone—please—can I have your attention?" But her voice didn't carry across the room, and only a few people noticed.

Patricia struck a mixing bowl with a spoon, producing a gong-like tone, and the noise level dropped. Meg cleared her throat. I could tell she wasn't comfortable speaking in front of a group. She spoke quickly, rushing along through her story, but it was a funny anecdote about her and Summer's first attempt at a dinner party, which ended in disaster. By the end of the story, I could tell she felt more comfortable. She said, "Unfortunately, neither of us has improved as a cook, so that is why Jean-Pierre is here."

She turned the floor over to him. While Meg couldn't wait to get out of the spotlight, Jean-Pierre thrived on it. He was a hit, flirting with everyone with his French accent, which I thought had to be contrived. I'm no expert, but he sounded more Pepé Le Pew than Gérard Depardieu, but, then again, maybe I'd seen too many cartoons lately. I might just have cartoons on the brain. As Jean-Pierre chopped and seasoned and smiled at us, I wondered what Mitch was doing.

"The boys" were ensconced in the Camden Room, a dark-paneled room, which usually held a conference table for meetings, but tonight green felt tables had been set up for the bachelor party. Mitch and I had recruited one of the older cousins to watch Livvy and Nathan. The baby-sitter and the kids were in our hotel room watching as many kid movies as they could fit in while we were gone. It felt slightly odd for Mitch and me to be out and away from the kids, but on our own separately. If we had a sitter—a fairly rare and unusual occurrence—we usually hoarded that time as couple time for a date, but tonight we'd gone our separate ways.

Summer and her bridesmaids finished mixing the ingredients for the chocolate soufflé dessert and slipped it in the oven. Summer raised her fisted hands as if she'd won a boxing match. She wore a white T-shirt with the word BRIDE spelled out in sparkly letters and looked as if the paintball incident hadn't even happened. The wedding photographer, a lean man who kept pushing a swath of his black hair off his forehead, circled the room, slipping in and out of groups, taking candid photos.

My gaze strayed to the far side of the kitchen where Aunt Nanette and Julia were seated. The bachelorette party invitation had been a blanket invite to all the women who arrived at the resort the first evening, so Summer couldn't uninvite Julia. We paired Julia with Aunt Nanette. I was pretty confident that Aunt Nanette would keep everything in check where Julia was concerned.

Summer had also insisted that we not mention the paintball incident. Only Summer, Brian, Mitch, the resort manager, Summer's mom, and I knew about it, which sounded like a lot of people, but that was only a handful of people compared to the number of guests who would be arriving soon. Summer wanted to keep the news limited to as small a group as possible, and I agreed. The fewer people who knew, the better.

Of course, the golfing couple knew as well, but they were only on the island for the day and didn't know anyone in the wedding party. The resort manager was more than happy to keep it quiet. Summer said she didn't want to have to answer questions about it, which I completely understood. The last thing you want before your wedding is to be asked how the paintball welts are healing.

Jean-Pierre demonstrated how to make a beef bourguignon. Fortunately for us, he'd prepared it earlier in the day and was only showing us the steps. When he finished, we were served a plate of the delicious beef and vegetable dish along with a tossed salad and fresh rolls. By then, he was removing the soufflé dessert from the oven and the heady smell of chocolate wafted across the kitchen. They had baked the soufflé in individual ramekins. Jean-Pierre placed one on a plate. "It is all about the appearance, no? This looks good, but . . ." He dusted the top with powdered sugar, then positioned two raspberries on the side. "This looks even better, yes?" A murmur of agreement rippled through the room.

As I took a bite of the dessert, a flash blinded me. *Great, just what I wanted, a photo of me with my mouth gaping open.* I blinked away the spots on my vision. I'm sure I was scowling at the photographer as he sauntered closer to our table. I swallowed and dabbed my napkin to my mouth. "You've got to delete that last one."

"Oh, no. Don't worry. It is flattering." A name tag clipped to his white oxford shirt read NED. "Very flattering."

"I doubt that, Ned. I'd appreciate it if you'd delete it."

I'd used my no-nonsense tone of voice that I employed on the playground when Livvy or Nathan misbehaved and I wanted them to stop whatever they were doing, which was usually something like climbing up the slide the wrong way. Ned shrugged, but pushed some buttons on the camera. "Very well. It's gone," he said in a tone that indicated he thought I'd made a big mistake.

"Thank you."

He looked up and held my gaze. "But there are very few things as sexy as eating." His gaze dipped to my lips, then leisurely drifted lower to the neckline of my top.

Where did Summer find this guy? Did she know he was hitting on the wedding party? I was about to tell him I was too old for him—he looked to be somewhere in his mid-twenties—but before I could say anything else, Yvonne leaned toward him. "I couldn't agree more."

Ned turned to her, and it was as if I'd never existed. Within seconds, they were involved in a deep conversation about art, which he reluctantly pulled himself away from when Patricia called out that she wanted formal photos of the bride and bridesmaids.

Yvonne downed the last of her champagne. "Well, things are looking more interesting now."

I really didn't have a good reply to that, so I kept quiet. We got through the rest of the dinner with only one other Shakespeare quote and a couple of entertaining stories about her time in the theater.

After the photos were taken, Meg announced that a behind-the-scenes look at the resort would round out the evening and introduced a guide who would lead us through the mansion on a tour from the perspective of the servants. "Oh, what a wonderful idea," Patricia said.

Yvonne picked up her glass and motioned a server over. "Good grief. I do not understand this enthrallment with the servant class."

"I think it's an offshoot of our fascination with the opulence of another era," I said.

"Oh, fascination with opulence, I understand," she said as she fingered a gold hoop earring. "It's the fixation on the domestics that puzzles me. Don't people realize the servants lived restricted lives of drudgery?" She downed her champagne in one swallow and slid off the barstool. "I'm hitting the bar instead. Care to join me?"

"No, I better stay here," I said, thinking that with Patricia safely on the tour and Yvonne in the bar, I could relax for the rest of the night.

"Your loss. Enjoy those poky little rooms and depressing back stairs."

I watched her stroll away and noticed that Ned took note of her departure as well. The rest of us followed our female tour guide, a redheaded woman with ivory skin dotted with freckles, who announced, "My name is Emma, and I'll be your guide for the behind-the-scenes tour. You'll see parts of Camden House that are normally off-limits. I grew up on the island and I didn't see these areas of the house until last year when this tour was added." She led us down a hall to the butler's pantry where she informed us that Camden House did have a kitchen. "Surprisingly, a kitchen wasn't a standard in these holiday island homes," Emma said. "Many of the grand cottages on Jekyll Island don't have kitchens at all. The builders of the cottages wanted to encourage socializing at the island clubhouse, so they eliminated kitchens from the building plans," she continued as we moved into Camden House's original kitchen, a relatively cramped space, considering the size of the rest of the house.

"This is only a little bigger than the kitchen in my apartment," Summer said. "Can you imagine preparing elaborate meals or food for huge dinner parties? I've got to take a picture." Summer patted the pockets on her jeans, then turned back the way we came. "I must have left my phone on the table."

"I'll get it," I said.

"Are you sure? You'll miss part of the tour," Summer said. On the side of the room, Emma was pointing out ledgers displayed on a rickety wooden table, explaining the entries for household purchases.

"I can miss a minute or two of the tour," I said. "You're the bride. Enjoy the perks. I'll catch up."

I hurried back down the hallway and reentered the resort's kitchen. The scents of beef bourguignon and the rich chocolate dessert lingered, but were mixed with the smell of cleaning supplies. The tables had been cleared, and the servers were moving around the room, washing dishes and mopping the floor. I spotted Summer's phone on a table and tiptoed in that direction, careful to avoid the wet areas of the floor. As I moved to the table, I heard Patricia's unmistakably nasal voice. "That's not possible."

I turned, searching for the source of the sound. Maybe Yvonne hadn't gone to the bar after all. It would be just my luck for Patricia and Yvonne to cross paths when I thought they were safely separated. But then I spotted Patricia standing next to the door that opened to the parking lot, talking to a man. He was halfway out the door and had turned back to speak to her. I couldn't see his face, but I recognized Ned's white oxford shirt and dress pants.

"No, I won't do it again." Patricia's voice was firm. There was a palpable tension between them that made me pause. With all the activity in the kitchen, neither one of them noticed me.

"Are you sure about that?" Ned asked. "You wouldn't want"—a clatter of dishes cut through his words—"to find out."

I swiped Summer's phone from the table and moved back toward the hall as quietly as I could. Whatever they were talking about, it wasn't any of my business. As long as Patricia wasn't speaking to Yvonne in that tense, almost angry tone, then I was out of there.

I rejoined the group at the top floor of the mansion where I handed off Summer's phone, then peeked into a typical servant's room. Yvonne was right. It was a sad little room with only the barest of necessities. Two single iron bed frames with thin mattresses were positioned against the walls. Between them sat a beat-up pine dresser. A small mirror along with a washbasin, pitcher, and two chamber pots were the only other furnishings of the room. After a glimpse at a few more rooms as well as a tour of the servants' dining room, Emma led us to the lobby. "That completes our behind-the-scenes tour. Any other questions I can answer for you?"

Summer motioned to a roped-off doorway near the grand staircase with a CLOSED sign dangling from the red velvet barrier. "I don't suppose we could get a look at the bell tower?"

"I'm afraid not," Emma said, moving toward the closed door. "It's under renovation because it's not safe at the moment." A sign propped on an easel showed several black-and-white photos of the bell tower alongside an artist's drawing of what the reconstructed bell tower would look like when it reopened in the summer. "The rotted floorboards are being replaced and safety rails are being installed. Once those changes are complete, it will reopen. The bell is original. It was brought over from Amsterdam and is made of solid bronze. It's been taken down to be cleaned, but will be replaced when the renovation is finished."

"I bet the view is spectacular," Summer said.

Emma said, "Oh, it is. You can see everything—the whole island and even the mainland on clear days."

"Are you sure we can't take a quick look?" Summer asked. "We'd be very careful."

Emma grimaced. "I'm sorry. I wish I could show it to

you. It's strictly off-limits. No one is allowed up there but the workers, and they have to have harnesses."

Summer looked at Emma out of the corner of her eye. "Then how do you know how good the view is?"

"Oh, I went up when I was a little girl. Years ago, before the floor in the bell tower deteriorated, anyone could go up. You didn't even have to be a hotel guest. All you had to do was climb the seventy-two steps."

"I'm out," muttered one of the bridesmaids. "I get enough of that at the gym on the StairMaster."

"Well, I'm not," Summer said. "The chances of any of us getting back here this summer are pretty slim. Are you sure we can't take a look? Just a quick peek? This *is* the behind-the-scenes tour, isn't it? What's more behind-the-scenes than a closed bell tower?"

"Well, I suppose it wouldn't hurt to give you a glimpse of the staircase. It's not very exciting, though."

Emma opened the door, and I asked, "It's under renovation, but the door to the tower isn't locked?" I was thinking of Livvy and Nathan. Their curiosity was boundless. I'd seen the sign and roped-off door, but I'd assumed the door was locked. I could imagine one of the kids sneaking over and trying the doorknob just for kicks. If the door opened, they'd be around that barrier and up the stairs in a moment.

"It's a fire exit for the upper floors," Emma explained. "It can't be locked here, but the upper area, the part that connects to the actual bell tower, is closed off. Only the construction people can get in there."

"Oh, that's good," I said, glad that I didn't have to keep an eye on the kids every second while we were in the hotel or try to warn them away from the door, which would be like pointing out forbidden fruit. And every mom knows that forbidden fruit is the only fruit kids want.

We craned our necks to get a look at the circular metal staircase that wound up and out of sight. Emma was right. It was a bit of a letdown. "This staircase runs alongside the grand staircase and has access to all the floors," Emma said. "That's why it can be used as a fire exit. The servants used it as another set of back stairs because they couldn't be seen on the grand staircase. Well, that's it. Now you've really seen everything." Emma firmly closed the door and stood in front of it. "I hope you enjoyed the tour and have a wonderful wedding."

Summer thanked Emma for the tour, and I joined her. "Very interesting," I said to Emma before she left our group. As she moved away, I turned to Summer. "Great party. Really unusual bachelorette party, but lots of fun."

"I know. Meg is wonderful." Summer scratched her sleeve as she lowered her voice. "Thanks for heading off that argument between Patricia and Yvonne at the beginning of the night."

"No problem. Yvonne was fun to talk to. She told me some funny stories about the local theater company she belongs to."

"Did you hear about her next play?" Summer said with a wicked grin. "*Taming of the Shrew.*"

"Tempting, but no comment."

"I admire your self-control." Summer rubbed her hand along her collarbone, moving the fabric of her V-neck shirt a few inches as one of the bridesmaids, Regina, joined our group.

"Some of us are thinking of hitting the bar. Do you—" Regina pointed at Summer's neck. "Oh my God. You've got a rash."

"What?"

"It's all red and bumpy." Regina's voice rose.

Summer rushed to a mirror hanging on one of the lobby's

walls and pulled at the edge of the neckline of her T-shirt, exposing blotchy, raised skin. "I felt itchy, but I thought it was just a bug bite or something." She twisted her arm and pulled up her sleeve, revealing more inflamed skin.

"It's on your arms, too," Regina said in a voice usually reserved for delivering news of famine and death. "Oh, this is horrible. The wedding is only two days from now. And your wedding gown is *strapless.*"

I pulled her away from Summer, who already looked devastated, and caught Meg's eye. She moved toward us as I said, "It's not too bad. Some anti-itch lotion will fix you up."

Meg ran a critical eye over the red patches. "Probably best not to rub it," she said.

Regina squinted. "I think it's getting redder by the moment."

"Regina, you go ahead to the bar and order Summer a drink," I said, "We'll get some cream on this and join you later."

Meg gave Regina a shove in the direction of the bar as she said, "Order me a glass of white wine, would you? I'll be right there."

After Regina was out of earshot, Meg looked critically at Summer's skin. "That looks like poison ivy. I got into some last summer. Benadryl and calamine lotion is what you want."

"Come on, Summer," I said, "let's see if the resort has some sort of medical person on call."

Camden House had a nurse practitioner on duty. She arrived at Summer's door within a few minutes of my call. "Hello. I'm Rebekah. You've got a skin irritation that you'd like me to look at?"

"Not me. I'm just here for moral support." I stepped

back so that Rebekah could come in. As she stepped by me, Ned strode down the hall, his camera bag slung over his shoulder. He saw me, gave me a quick nod, then pulled out a key card and entered a room two doors down the hall from my room.

Rebekah took one look at Summer's neck, diagnosed poison ivy, and sent Summer to shower, instructing her to wash in tepid water to remove any of the plant oil that was still on her skin.

Summer emerged from the shower wrapped in one of the resort's generous bath towels. "Ellie, could you find my robe? It's in my suitcase somewhere. Where could I have gotten into poison ivy? I haven't been in the woods or the gardens even."

I looked up from her suitcase. "We were on the grass today." I hated to bring up the paintball incident, but it might be a possibility. I didn't say anything else since Rebekah was in the room, but Summer picked up on my meaning immediately.

"But that was just my knees and they're fine. And my hands and forearms aren't itchy."

They were indeed clear of any inflammation, unlike Summer's upper arms, shoulders, and chest. With the towel still wrapped around her, she turned around to look at her shoulders in the mirror. "How could I get it here, but not on my lower arms?"

"Perhaps a vine," Rebekah murmured, looking closer at the rash. She had a squat figure and coarse dark hair cut short. She pushed her purple-framed glasses up, then slipped on a pair of gloves and disappeared into the bathroom. I found Summer's robe, and she slipped it on. Rebekah came out of the bathroom holding Summer's T-shirt, which was turned inside out. "There does seem to be some residue on the fabric. . . ."

"On the *inside* of the T-shirt?" I asked, already not liking where this conversation was going.

"Yes. It's slight, but it is there."

Summer dropped down onto a flowered chair. "How could . . . ? That shirt—it was in a package."

"Where? Where did you put the package?" I asked.

"In the trash. There, under the desk. The T-shirt was in the gift basket that the hotel delivered." She gestured toward a basket on the bed. Decorated with a white bow, it contained several candles, a magazine on honeymoon destinations, and a bottle of lily of the valley–scented lotion. "The shirt was so cute, I decided to wear it right away," Summer said.

Rebekah handed me a pair of gloves, which I donned, then she gave me the T-shirt. "Hold this." Rebekah turned to Summer and opened a small zippered bag she'd brought with her. She began to dispense medicine and instructions for dealing with the rash.

I poked through the trash with my free hand and found a cardboard sleeve printed with the words BRIDE TO BE T-SHIRT. The back had two grooves that fit together. No sticker or tape held it in place. Anyone could easily open the wrapping, then later refasten it around the shirt.

Rebekah sent Summer back to the bathroom to apply a lotion. As soon as the door shut, Rebekah took the shirt from me, went to the desk, clicked on the lamp, and spread the shirt on Summer's discarded bath towel. As she bent over the shirt, I stripped off one glove and dialed the front desk, requesting information about the gift basket that had been delivered to the room. Rebekah examined the shirt without touching it as I waited on hold.

Rebekah stood and used the back of her hand to adjust her glasses as they slipped lower on her nose. "There *is* something on the interior of this shirt. I don't know for certain that it is urushiol."

I tilted the phone away from my chin. "Urushiol?"

"It's the oil produced by the poison ivy plant. It is the oil that is the irritant."

"So you think the rash is from whatever it was you called it, the oil, on the shirt?" I asked.

"No, I don't know that for sure. This could be from some other oil or lotion that Summer applied herself. Or Summer could be reacting to something she came into contact with previously. Sometimes it takes weeks for the rash to show up after someone has come into contact with poison ivy, or urushiol, to be more specific, but considering the pattern of the rash now . . ."

Summer opened the door, again swathed in the robe, her skin shiny with the ointment. "I can hear you, you know. I didn't put on any lotion today. I forgot to pack my lotion and meant to pick up some in the resort's gift shop today, but haven't done it yet."

"What about the small bottle of lotion, the resort supplies? Did you use that?" Rebekah asked.

"No. I didn't like the smell of it," Summer said. "Too rosy. And I haven't been hiking in the woods or even working in the yard—I don't have a yard, actually, so I think it's got to be from the shirt. If someone wanted to get poison ivy on the shirt, how would they do that? Rub it against the plant?"

"I suppose it could be done that way," Rebekah said. "But every part of the plant contains the oil that causes the allergic reaction. Anything from the plant has it—the leaves, stems, even the roots. And it does stay active, even on dead plants, for years."

"Ma'am, sorry to keep you waiting," said a voice in my ear.

I repositioned the phone. I had almost forgotten I was on hold. "I'm still here."

"We didn't deliver anything to room two-twelve today."

"Nothing?"

"Yes, ma'am."

I looked at Summer. "This basket came today?"

"Yes. Right before you came to my room this afternoon," Summer said.

I spoke into the phone again. "Can I talk to the person who was on duty earlier today? There was a delivery today and we need to find out exactly who sent it."

"That's a different shift, but I can assure you that we record all deliveries. Nothing is allowed to go to a guest without us noting it, and there is nothing on the list for that room."

I hung up and looked at Summer. "It wasn't sent through the hotel."

"Well, we all know who sent it." Summer glowered at the basket as she reached up to scratch her ribcage. Rebekah made a warning sound, and Summer fisted her hand.

"Don't scratch. I know it's hard," Rebekah said. "I'll bring you back a prescription from the dispensary. Best-case scenario is that it will clear up quickly."

"How quickly?"

Rebekah shrugged. "A day or two."

"And worst case?"

"Could be up to a week to ten days."

Summer flexed her hands open and closed. "I want to throw that basket out the window."

Rebekah looked from me to Summer questioningly. "Perhaps I should contact resort management?"

Summer blew out a breath and lowered her tense shoulders. "No. We're going to keep this as quiet as possible."

I raised my eyebrows at Summer.

"Damage control," she said. "I won't give her the satisfaction of knowing she's gotten to me." Summer shoved her hands into the pockets on her robe and circled the bed, her gaze fixed on the basket. "I had a minor skin irritation. That's all." She looked toward Rebekah, who had finished calling in the prescription.

"Hey, you don't have to worry about me," Rebekah said. "Patient records are confidential."

"Good." Summer gave a sharp nod. "And I know you can keep a secret, Ellie."

"Of course." I gestured to the basket with my hand that was still gloved. "How about I get rid of that?"

"Please. I think I'll try a cold compress." Summer headed back to the bathroom.

I shoved the basket into the trash can under the room's desk, pulled up the plastic liner, and knotted it together at the top so the maid could just grab the plastic in the morning when she came to clean the room. It seemed the irritant had been on the T-shirt, but I wasn't taking any chances. I didn't want Summer or anyone else handling the basket . . . just in case.

Tips for an Organized Wedding

Mothers of the bride and groom can create emergency kits for all those unexpected incidents that pop up. A few items that might be helpful to include are: a mini sewing kit, bandages, breath mints, fabric tape, pen or pencils, crackers or energy bars, a lighter, safety pins, bobby pins, pain medication, a magnifying glass, batteries, a compact mirror, a lint roller, and plenty of tissues.

Chapter Five

"Close your eyes," I said to Nathan before slathering sunscreen across his upturned face. He stood motionless, arms extended as I layered on a thick coat of sunscreen across his neck and arms. "There. You're done." We were on the terrace outside the front doors of the resort. The morning was still a bit cool and the scent of jasmine floated up from the flower border that enclosed the terrace.

I turned to Livvy to repeat the process, but she handed the bottle of sunscreen back to me. "I did mine myself."

"Let me see." I examined her face, which did indeed have the glossy sheen of freshly applied sunscreen. "You even got the back of your neck. Good job." I covered her arms with sunscreen, then shook the bottle of bug spray. "Arms out."

Livvy wrinkled her nose as I coated her in the fine mist. "That smells terrible."

"Yes, but it's better than coming back covered in bug bites." I repeated the process on Nathan. "Okay. I think you're ready." Sometimes getting ready to spend time outdoors was almost as exhausting as the outdoor activity.

I kissed both kids on the top of their heads and waved them off on their expedition. The resort had a kids' program of activities. Today's agenda included exploration of the island's tide pools as well as a talk about sea turtles at the nature preserve's outdoor classroom. Livvy hadn't been too excited about the outing. It cut into her reading time, but I'd convinced her to go and let her pack three books in her string backpack in case she got bored.

"Have a good time!" I called as they scampered down the steps to join the group of kids being herded into place by several adults wearing the resort's outdoor uniform of a navy polo shirt and khaki cargo shorts.

Livvy turned and ran back to the bottom step. "If I had a cell phone you'd be able to call me during the day and check on us."

"Yes, but the leaders have walkie-talkies and our cell phone numbers. Good try, but you're nine. You really don't need a cell phone yet."

Livvy blew out a long sigh, then spun on her heel and ran back to the group.

Mitch appeared at my shoulder. "Lobbying for a cell phone again?"

"Yes."

"Why does she want a cell phone, anyway?"

"Lots of her friends at school have them. And by that, I mean exactly two girls in her class at school have them." I shook my head and watched the group of kids depart in a heaving, shifting throng that reminded me of a rugby scrum.

Mitch broke off a piece of blueberry muffin and offered it to me. The breakfast buffet had been so sumptuous that Mitch grabbed another muffin on our way out the door.

"No thanks. I'm stuffed. I don't know how I'm going to be able to eat again at the picnic in a few hours." While the kids were seeing the edges of the island, the adults of the wedding party were scheduled for a golf cart tour of the interior of the island that included a picnic lunch at the ruins of the original plantation house. I transferred the sunscreen and bug spray to the crook of my arm and consulted my watch. "We've got a while before we have to meet everyone here. What should we do?"

Mitch dusted the crumbs from the muffin off his fingers. "You don't have a mother-in-law to keep an eye on or a wedding emergency to handle?"

"No. Yvonne said she planned to sleep in this morning, Patricia is dealing with her e-mail until the tour, and everything is running smoothly, wedding-wise."

"In that case, we should probably retire to our room . . . and rest."

"I don't know," I said in mock seriousness. "We don't get a chance to explore a world-famous resort very often. We could go to the pool or the beach."

"We don't get to be alone in our hotel room at a world-famous resort very often either."

"Good point. And I haven't had time to check out the minibar."

"Well, we *have* to do that."

"Summer seems to be recovered," Mitch said, his gaze on his sister, who was perched on a white wicker chair at the center of what had once been a wide sweep of lawn in front of the ruins of the old plantation house.

"She does look good, doesn't she?" I said. Summer wore a loose white linen camp shirt over a pair of navy shorts along with boat shoes. Her hair was caught back in a ponytail, and she was laughing at something Brian had whispered in her ear.

"I checked in with her this morning after breakfast, and she said the rash had faded quite a bit already, so the medicine is helping."

I'd kept a close eye on her today. She did seem relaxed and happy, but I'd noticed her sending occasional assessing glances at Julia. I couldn't blame Summer for keeping an eye on Brian's ex-girlfriend, but Julia didn't seem to be interested in Summer. If Summer happened to catch Julia's eye, Julia smiled, almost sheepishly it seemed to me, then looked quickly away—usually focusing her attention back on Graham, where it had been firmly fixed all day. Graham and Julia had shared a golf cart during the tour of the island, and she'd been snuggled close to him the entire time.

Now, Julia and Graham were relaxing in chairs planted close together on the opposite side of the table from Summer and Brian. Graham had his arm slung along Julia's shoulders, and she was leaning toward Graham, who was telling a story in a very animated way. I caught a few of his words and realized he was in the middle of a story about his and Brian's law school days. Whatever the story was, it had all of them grinning, even Summer.

Beyond our little group stood the ruins of the old plantation house. I remembered from my reading about the island that it had caught fire sometime around the turn of the century and had never been rebuilt. The roof was completely gone, leaving only the shell of the outer walls jutting up to the sky. Vines and greenery crisscrossed the stone and brick walls, the slow creep of the vegetation as it claimed the ruin. The highest point was a massive central brick chimney, which still soared straight up three stories into the cloudless sky.

The staff from the resort had arrived before us, and when our caravan line of golf carts had chugged up the asphalt path that hugged the lawn of the ruin, we'd found a fancy picnic lunch of cold ham, potato salad, and warm rolls along with strawberries and champagne, all served with fine china, silver, and crystal. They had also brought in wicker chairs and tables. For people who felt like roughing it, they spread quilts on the ground over tarps to keep anyone from getting a damp behind.

I scanned the group quickly, noting that the mothers-in-law were still separated. Yvonne was easy to spot in her red-and-white-checked halter sundress as she sprawled on one of the low stone walls that had once formed a terrace along the house. The slimy photographer, Ned, had one leg propped up on the wall and his arm rested on his knee as he leaned over her, his unused camera dangling from his neck. Although, to be fair, it did seem he'd put in a fair amount of time photographing the wedding party. He'd been with us the whole time as we toured the island and had snapped candid shots of everyone during the morning. We'd begun with a circuit of the golf course, then looped around to the far side of the island with its abrupt change from land to sea. After lunch, our route back to the resort would take us along the strip of beaches on the opposite side of the island.

Ned had obviously been telling a story, waving his hands around, and when he finished both he and Yvonne laughed. I put my plate down, glad I didn't have to worry about him snapping a shot of me with my mouth full again. "Another luscious meal. Too many great meals are on the agenda." I handed my half-empty plate to Mitch and he raised his eyebrows.

"You don't want the rest?"

"Of course I want the rest, but I want to fit into my pink dress more."

"If you're sure . . ." Mitch scooped up the last of the fluffy roll.

"Don't worry, I plan to eat well at the reception."

"Or, you could eat all this and we could walk back to the resort," Mitch said between bites.

"Maybe. It depends on how hot it gets." We were deep in the shade of a grove of huge live oaks, but it was warm, even considering it was only March and not yet midafternoon. "Besides, I call driver for the golf cart on the way back. I like zipping around in the cart."

I glanced beyond a cracked circular fountain to check on Patricia as I spoke. She and her husband, Gus, were seated at another table but the sun had shifted since we began eating and now they were partially in the direct sunlight. Gus worked his hand along the collar of his button-down oxford shirt. His loud voice carried over the low murmur of the conversations going on at the other tables. "I want a beer."

Patricia caught his arm as he began to stand, extending her other hand with the crystal goblet of champagne away from her body so that none of it sloshed out when she halted his progress and yanked him back toward his seat. "They don't have beer," she said in her nasal tones.

"Of course they have beer. Place like this *has* to have beer."

"I assure you they don't. I approved the menu myself."

"You mean to tell me that I'm paying through the nose for this weekend, and there's no beer?"

Patricia sighed. "There will be beer at the bonfire on the beach tonight and at the reception, but not here. This is a classic garden party."

"What?" Gus asked. "It's a party. You have beer at parties."

"It is a themed party, and the theme is classic garden party, so no beer," Patricia said.

I looked over at Mitch. "Let's not ever let our marriage get to that point," I said in a low voice.

Mitch raised his glass. "Agreed."

Our glasses clinked together as Gus stood, deftly avoiding his wife's hand. "I'm going to ask about that beer," he announced. Patricia rolled her eyes.

Ned left Yvonne and worked his way across the lawn, snapping a few photos as he moved through the group until he was near Patricia, then he slipped into Gus's empty seat and leaned close to Patricia.

"That's an odd pairing," Mitch said, watching Ned and Patricia.

Patricia kept her voice low, but it was clear from her expression that she wasn't happy. And they'd argued after the bachelorette party, too, I remembered. "You'd think he'd stick with Yvonne. She seems more his type," I said, and looked over at Yvonne. It appeared she agreed with me. Yvonne watched Ned, a pout on her face. Her glance cut away from Ned. She fixed her attention on Summer and Brian's group for a moment, then lifted her arm and called, "Brian, darling, come here a moment."

There was something about the preemptory way she called for Brian and the way he hopped up immediately that made me feel a little worried for Summer. Summer had been in the middle of a sentence, and whatever she'd been saying, she had the rapt attention of everyone at her table until Yvonne called out. Summer's eyes flashed as Brian stood. He shrugged and moved away.

"Looks like the fireworks may not be between the monsters-in-law," Mitch said.

"Shh. Don't say that, but yeah, there could be trouble in paradise," I said, a low-level worry growing. Ned stood and walked away from Patricia. She didn't look happy, but come to think of it, unhappy seemed to be her default expression.

Gus returned from the food tables holding a beer dripping with condensation. "Told you they'd have beer." Patricia's face shifted into a deeper frown of disapproval.

Gus's path crossed with Ned's as Ned moved toward the golf carts, which were lined up along the narrow asphalt path that curved steeply up to the house, which had been built on a rise of ground. Ned waved to get Summer's attention and pointed to his camera. "I have to get a new battery from the resort," he called. "It won't take long."

I felt a wave of drowsiness come over me and fought off a yawn. "Come on." I uncrossed my legs and struggled to my feet. "Let's explore this ruin before I fall asleep."

Mitch, settled deep into the wicker chair, his back against several cushions, squinted at me. "You sure about that? A walk?"

"Yes. Look, everyone's going."

Mitch struggled upright. "Just because everyone's doing it doesn't mean you have to," he said with a grin as he echoed some of my many conversations I'd had with Livvy and Nathan.

"Yes, but we're being sociable, so we're doing it."

Mitch groaned. "There's a reason guys hate weddings."

I grabbed his hand and towed him up two sets of shallow stone stairs to a terrace sprouting grass and vines between the flagstones. "And we just promised not to end up like the Bickersons down there," I said quietly, glancing at Patricia and Gus as they made their way to the stairs, Patricia steaming along with Gus trailing behind her, still sipping from his beer. "I won't drag you all over the whole ruin," I said. "I promise."

I turned to the view and spread out my hands. "You have to admit it's a wonderful view. I bet they were able to get a glimpse of the sea from the upper stories. Look, you can just see a golf cart moving through the forest there." The raised elevation of the house let us look out over the terraces across the lawn to the thick mass of green forest that enclosed the grounds. The bit of white, the golf cart, disappeared into the deep shadow of the forest.

"How did the photographer get that far away so quickly?" Patricia asked as she arrived beside me.

"That's someone else," I said. "He hasn't left yet. He's just now getting into one of the carts." I gestured toward the side of the grounds where the golf carts were parked in a line along the single path.

Gus used his beer bottle as a pointer and motioned to the speck of white disappearing through the trees. "Probably someone from the golf course, hunting for one of their golf balls. The ninth fairway runs along there, beyond the belt of forest."

"It's hard to believe there's a golf course not far away. It feels so isolated here," I said, looking at the thick forest that enclosed the grounds of the ruin. "It's like someone scooped out a bit of the wilderness and replaced it with civilization. Well," I amended, "it was civilized at one point, but the wilderness is reclaiming it."

Yvonne came to stand beside us, her arm firmly hooked through Brian's. "'Where every something, being blent together, turns to a wild of nothing.'"

Summer trailed along behind them, her hands shoved firmly in the pockets of her shorts. I sent her a sympathetic look.

Yvonne bounced up on her toes and pointed. "Look, there goes Ned." The golf cart, which looked like one of Nathan's toys, bumped over the grass to get around the other carts, then rejoined the asphalt road that dipped and curved sharply down the hill. I squinted. Something fluttery was caught on the front edge of the cart's roof.

The movement of the square golf cart roof, white against the surrounding green, drew everyone's attention, and we all let out a collective gasp when it rounded a tight left-hand turn in the road and flipped onto its side.

Chapter Six

We all stood motionless for a second, waiting for Ned to climb out of the cart, but there was no movement. Mitch was the first to react.

He jumped down from the terrace where we stood and sprinted across the lawn toward the cart. Brian was right behind him. The rest of us ran across the sloping descent of the lawn behind them. At the point where the lawn ended, I scrambled down the edge of a little embankment that separated the lawn from the path where the accident had occurred.

Ned lay on his side, his legs tangled in the wreck of the cart. A smear of blood on the asphalt near his head made my stomach plunge. Mitch was on the far side of the cart, kneeling beside Ned.

Brian gripped the crumbled roof of the golf cart. "We can lift it off him," Brian said. "I've got this side."

Gus, who must have ditched the beer bottle during the sprint to the golf cart, moved into place on the other side. "We'll move on your call, Mitch."

Mitch shook his head and pressed his hands to his knees as he stood slowly. "Better leave it. He's dead."

We were all stunned into silence for a few seconds, then there was a confused burst of words as someone said he was probably just unconscious and another person asked if anyone had a signal on their phone.

Summer leapt down from the embankment. "But surely we can do something."

The resort waitstaff had followed us across the lawn. One man clad in navy and khaki was speaking into a walkie-talkie, giving our location.

"Can't we do CPR or something until help gets here? Oh—" Summer broke off, clapped her hand over her mouth as she saw the full extent of Ned's injuries, and turned away. Brian left the cart and wrapped his arm around her.

I went to stand with Mitch. He'd moved a few feet back from the cart. "We can't do anything for him," Mitch said.

I nodded and laced my fingers through Mitch's. I shifted so that I wasn't looking at the sprawled body inside the golf cart. I concentrated on breathing steadily, focusing on the group hovering at the edge of the embankment—anything so that I wouldn't look at the golf cart again.

I don't know what drew my attention to Patricia. I had been looking at the group as a whole, a crowd of people perched on the embankment like birds on a wire, but there was something about Patricia that was different.

It was the contrast, I realized. Everyone else had a shell-shocked expression, as if they couldn't believe what had happened. Patricia looked relieved.

We were a somber group as we waited on the lawn in front of the plantation ruin. The wicker furniture still sat in the lengthening shade of the trees and the food was still spread out in a buffet, but the garden party atmosphere was gone. After a short conversation over the walkie-talkie, the resort staff had herded us away from the golf cart, told us not to speak to one another or use our cell phones, and to await instructions at the picnic area.

"I don't know why we're still here," Yvonne huffed as she stalked around the tables in a tight circle, her bright skirt fluttering with each step. "We've been waiting for hours." She glowered across the slope of the lawn to the crowd around the golf cart.

Patricia slapped her hand down on the table and turned toward Yvonne. "For God's sake, a man has died. Show a little respect. You'd think the way you were carrying on with him earlier, you of all people wouldn't be so cold-hearted."

Yvonne's eyes narrowed into slits, reminding me of a cat about to attack a mouse. I quickly stood and said, "I think we're about to be released."

A broad-shouldered man in a dark suit moved quickly across the grass, his long strides covering the distance quickly. His bright yellow tie matched his thin, gold hair. Yvonne marched toward him. "Are you in charge? I'd like to know why we're being held here like prisoners."

He held up a hand and shook his head. "A moment, please. I need to speak to the entire group before I talk to you individually."

He gestured to a chair, pulled it out, and Yvonne reluctantly plopped into it. He addressed the group. "Thank you for waiting so patiently. I apologize for leaving you long in the sun, but in an isolated area like this, we had no other choice. I'm Detective Redding. I'll be working with state authorities and resort officials in an investigation of Mr. Blackson's death. We'll work to resolve this matter as quickly as possible." Behind him, I could see several uniformed officers moving toward the area where the golf cart overturned.

"A detective?" Summer said faintly as she rubbed her hand across her forehead. I exchanged a look with Mitch. Poor Summer—not that I didn't feel bad for Ned Blackson—but to have all these things go wrong at your wedding . . . it was about as far from a fairly-tale wedding as you could get.

"Yes. There are some irregularities with the situation, and we were called in immediately. Now, I'd like to talk to each of you separately." He turned and looked over his shoulder at a noise. Several golf carts motored out of the forest foliage and into view, but instead of coming up the path we'd taken, they stopped at the retaining wall.

"As you can see," Redding said, "we now have transportation back to the resort. Who was first on the scene after the crash occurred?"

Mitch raised a hand. "That would be me. Brian was right behind me."

Redding asked for their full names, jotting them down in a small notebook. "I'd like to talk with you two first. If you'll both go directly across the lawn, avoiding the area where the crash took place, and wait for me at one of the golf carts, I'll meet you there shortly."

Mitch squeezed my hand and whispered, "I'll round up the kids when I'm done and meet you at the resort."

I nodded. "See you there."

"And who spoke to Mr. Blackson today?" Redding asked the group.

Several hands went up. "Names?"

People called out their names, and he wrote them down. Yvonne had been the first one to speak. Redding drew a breath to continue, but Yvonne said quickly, "Patricia, I didn't see your hand go up, and I know I saw Ned chatting with you. It was right before he left in the golf cart, actually."

Patricia's face hardened. "It was only wedding business. It wasn't important."

Redding said, "Nevertheless, I'll need to know what you discussed. Mrs. . . . ?"

"Abernathy," Patricia said tightly.

"Thank you." Redding turned to a uniformed man, a deputy from the sheriff's department, I realized now that he was close enough to see his uniform. Redding tore a piece of paper out of his small notebook. "Send these five people on in the next golf carts, then send the rest of them table by table. Make sure everyone stays away from the scene until forensics is finished. I'll return after speaking to everyone."

Redding turned to leave, but Patricia's peremptory nasal tone rang out. "Detective, are you aware this is a wedding party? We have another event, a beach bonfire in"—she paused to look at her watch—"two hours."

Redding turned back. "Mrs. Abernathy, I understand this is inconvenient for you, but a man is dead. The investigation into his death takes priority—over everything. The bonfire is on hold."

Patricia stood up. "Well, I never—do you know who is coming to this wedding? Very powerful people, that's who. Including several judges and congressmen. They will be very interested to hear how unhelpful you are being, I'm sure."

I swear, it looked as if Redding wanted to roll his eyes, but was able to stop himself. "I assure you, we are doing everything as quickly as possible. I apologize for any difficulty our investigation causes, but the fact remains that a man has died. I'm sorry if the timing is irksome for you, but the investigation will go on."

Redding strode across the grass toward the first golf cart where Mitch and Brian were waiting. Patricia shot a furious look at Gus, but he shrugged. "What the man says is true. They've got to investigate."

The deputy called out several names, including Patricia's, and motioned the group toward the newly arrived golf carts.

Patricia had a set look on her face, a mulish look I'd seen many times on my kids' faces.

I was searching for a way to convince Patricia to go with the officers, when Gus said in a low voice to her, "Better get those interviews rolling. That's the best way to get the festivities back on track."

Patricia blew a long breath out of her nose. "Fine, but I will tell Judge Ratliff about this," she announced before she stalked across the grass to the second waiting golf cart. Somehow I didn't think that news would rattle Detective Redding, even if he had been around to hear it.

Yvonne followed Patricia, but climbed into a different golf cart. I leaned back in my chair, glad that the two mothers-in-law were under police supervision for a little while. Surely, they wouldn't misbehave in front of law enforcement.

I settled in for a long wait. Mitch and I had sat down at the back of the lawn near the live oaks of the forest, and I could tell I would be one of the last people called for a ride back to the resort.

Summer went in one of the next groups, giving me a little wave, her expression grave, before she headed across the grass. I watched the figures of the forensics team move around the golf cart as the caravan of new golf carts came and went, ferrying the wedding party, a few at a time, away from the ruin.

The sun inched lower in the sky, and the shadows of the ruin stretched across the grass until they encompassed the whole picnic seating area. My phone sat on the table in front of me, lighting up every few minutes with texts and missed calls, but the cell phone ban was still in effect, at least for those of us waiting at the ruin, so I left it where it was. The opening lines of the texts popped up on my screen as they came in and showed that the resort manager was working with Summer to reschedule the bonfire to a later time this evening. I could imagine the fit that Patricia had thrown when everything had to be shifted. I was actually glad I wasn't in the vicinity.

I shifted in my wicker chair, trying to see what was going on around the golf cart. I couldn't see much because the golf cart was on the path below the retaining wall, so mostly I saw the tops of people's heads as they walked back and forth. Eventually, a group of people moved several yards away, formed a line, and then moved slowly across the grass.

"Mrs. Avery?"

I looked up to find one of the deputies standing beside me.

"You're the last one. You're in the next cart along with the two resort employees." He pointed to two men in the resort's navy polo shirt and khaki shorts already moving across the lawn.

I picked up my phone and hurried across the grass, catching up with the two men as they climbed in the golf cart. One of them, a sinewy man with a gray mustache, hopped up from his seat on the bench behind the driver of the golf cart and offered it to me, then moved to the seat on the back that faced away from the driver.

"Thank you." I sat down next to the other employee, a plump guy in his twenties. While the deputy who would drive us was conferring with one of the men near the smashed golf cart, the younger man twisted around and spoke to the mustached guy behind him. "They're searching for a lug nut. I heard 'em talking about it. It's missing."

My knowledge of mechanical things is sketchy at best, but even I know that lug nuts are what keep the tires secured.

The guy with the mustache let out a low whistle. "Donny isn't going to be happy about that."

"Or Markham."

The young guy hooked his arm over the seat and leaned closer. "But I don't see how that could be. You know how Donny is. So particular about the morning maintenance check. He wouldn't send a cart out without a lug nut, especially since Markham started that 'never give a guest a reason to be unhappy' thing."

The man with the mustache shrugged. "Maybe it wasn't Donny who missed it. He can't check every cart himself."

"You think it was that new guy—" The younger employee broke off as the deputy approached the cart. The ride through the darkening forest was silent except for the rev of the little motor.

When we arrived at the main building, the two employees courteously stepped back and let me enter first. The deputy who had driven the golf cart escorted us through a side entrance, up a set of stairs, then down a long hall. The resort employees were told to wait in the hall, while I was instructed to go through a set of double doors. I stepped into a large room with paintings of beaches and the resort. Redding sat at one end of a long conference table. He motioned me into a seat near him. "Ellie Avery, is it?"

"Yes, that's me." I sank into the cushy swivel chair.

"I spoke to your husband earlier, so I have your contact information." Redding confirmed the spelling of my name, then said, "Take me through what happened this afternoon."

I summarized how we'd arrived at the ruin, eaten lunch, and then intended to explore the ruin. "That's when Ned left. We were able to see him drive away from the terrace. We all saw the golf cart turn over, but we had no idea how bad the crash was until we reached it."

"Yes, the injury rate associated with golf cart accidents is much higher than most people realize." Redding spoke as he made some notes, then he looked up. "And did you know Mr. Blackson before this weekend?"

"No."

"But you didn't like him."

"Why would you say that?" I asked cautiously.

"Because you sounded repulsed when I asked if you knew him."

I sighed. "Well, I know it's in bad taste to speak ill of the dead, but he hit on me and several other women at the bachelorette party last night. It was . . ." The word that popped into my mind was *icky*, but I replaced it with "inappropriate."

"Hmm. Besides yourself, who else was on the receiving end of his . . . attention, shall we call it?"

I hesitated, and Redding said, "Mrs. Avery, the man is dead. I need to reconstruct what happened yesterday."

I wished I hadn't opened this line of questioning, but there was no going back now. "Yes, of course. He and Yvonne seemed to get on really well." That was as innocuously as I could phrase it, but I had a feeling Redding was reading between the lines.

"And did Mr. Blackson's attentions to Yvonne continue today?"

"He did talk to her at the ruin after we ate. He sat beside her for a while on the terrace at the ruin, but, to be fair, things were winding down then. He had worked the whole morning, taking candid pictures of all of us by then."

"Anyone else?" Redding persisted.

"That he hit on? No, he definitely flirted with Yvonne quite a bit yesterday, but I didn't see him doing that with anyone else. The only other person who I saw him speak to for any length of time was Patricia. He certainly wasn't flirting with her."

"I imagine not."

"Patricia looked upset, quite angry, in fact," I said, thinking of her expression right before he left the ruin.

"Could you hear what they discussed?"

"No." I debated telling about the look on Patricia's face when we realized that Ned wasn't just unconscious, but dead. But it was only an impression, my interpretation of her expression. I could be totally wrong about the way I read her face, but then I remembered the incident in the kitchen after the bachelorette party and decided I had to at least mention that. It wasn't a feeling or impression. It had happened. Angry words had been exchanged. "There was another time, I heard them arguing," I said, and went on to summarize what I'd heard, which wasn't much.

Redding's expression didn't change, but he made a note, then said, "Do you know who hired Ned Blackson?"

"Summer, I imagine."

"You don't know? I understood that you were the wedding planner."

"No, I'm only managing the last-minute details. Summer made all the hiring decisions before I was involved."

"I see. Now, let's go back to the time after you arrived at the ruin for lunch. Did you notice anyone wander off? Anyone go missing for a time?" Redding asked.

"No, I don't think so, but I wasn't keeping track . . . well, only of Patricia and Yvonne."

Redding raised his eyebrows.

"They don't get along, and to help out Summer, I was

making sure that they . . ." I searched for an innocuous way to describe the situation.

"Didn't come to blows?" Redding finished for me.

"You could say that," I said reluctantly.

"Not surprising, really," Redding said. "Get this many people together and there's bound to be someone who doesn't like someone else. Add in the element of the wedding and that only makes things more stressful." Redding got back to his notes. "No one went down to the path area where the golf carts were parked?"

"No, not that I noticed. I think everyone was always around the tables, but I could have missed someone. Even when you're trying to watch someone, it's hard to keep an eye on them all the time, especially when it's two people. I suppose Patricia or Yvonne could have left and I could have missed it."

"Did you see anyone in the forest who wasn't part of the group?"

"There was a golf cart in the forest. We all saw it from the terrace when we went up to explore the ruin."

"Who was driving?"

"It was too far away to tell. I couldn't even see if there was more than one person. It was just a bit of white moving through the trees. Oh, that reminds me. There was something caught on the golf cart roof. I noticed it as Ned drove away. It was white, maybe a piece of fabric or something like that."

Redding nodded. "Decoration. A net type of fabric along with some gold ribbons."

"Tulle and gold ribbons?" The chair creaked as I leaned forward and gripped the edge of the table. "With a sign with the words *bride and groom*?" I asked with a sinking feeling.

"I don't know if there was a sign. Only the fabric and

ribbons were visible at the crash scene. The golf cart won't be moved until the techs are finished with the scene, then we'll know if there was a sign as well." Redding folded his hands, all his attention on me.

"There will be. A sign, I mean." I closed my eyes briefly. "There was only one golf cart decorated with fabric and ribbons, the one for Brian and Summer."

Tips for an Organized Wedding

Create a timeline for the wedding day. List when each person needs to arrive, building in plenty of cushion, in case someone gets caught in traffic or forgets something and has to double back. Also give directions on where everyone should go before the ceremony. A map might be helpful, if everyone in the wedding party isn't familiar with the event location.

Chapter Seven

"And that fact seems to worry you." Redding reached for a tray positioned at the center of the table with a silver pitcher covered in condensation. He poured a glass of water and set it in front of me. "You're very pale. Are you feeling okay?"

I grimaced. "No, I'm worried. Extremely worried." I sipped the icy water. Summer wanted to keep the "incidents" quiet, and I had promised not to talk about them, but I really didn't have a choice. Not now. I had to tell Redding about the paintball and the poison ivy. He needed to know that a mean-spirited prank might have led to the death of the photographer.

I set the glass down carefully. "I overheard some of the resort employees talking about missing lug nuts . . . ?"

Redding sighed and folded the notebook over his pen. "That is confidential information. I would appreciate it if you didn't mention it."

"So the wheel *was* tampered with."

Redding didn't reply. Instead, he folded his arms. "Why don't you tell me what is bothering you instead of trying to figure out where the investigation is going? You know, most people just want to answer my questions and get out of this room as quickly as possible. Why are you asking so many questions?"

"I don't suppose Summer Avery mentioned any problems or difficulties she's had since arriving?"

"Summer Avery. That would be the bride. Your sister-in-law." I nodded, and he shook his head. "No, she was one of the people ready to get out of here. At the time, I thought it was understandable. What bride wants to answer questions from the police a few days before her wedding? But I'm beginning to think I shouldn't have dismissed her so quickly."

"No, it's nothing to do with Summer," I said quickly. "Well, not anything she's done. It's because she's the bride, because she's marrying Brian."

"I'm confused."

"I'm sorry. Let me start with the paintball incident."

Redding's eyebrows flared. "By all means. Let's start there."

I described the paintball incident, the poison ivy, and Julia's stalkerish behavior after Brian broke up with her. Only a few minutes into my narrative, Redding uncrossed his arms and jotted notes. "I didn't mention it earlier because Summer specifically asked me not to. And I'm sure she didn't realize the connection with the golf cart being the cart reserved for them. I know I didn't even look at the golf cart after the accident, except in a passing glance. All my attention went directly to Ned . . . and he looked so awful. Well, it was a shock, and I looked away. I didn't look back or study the scene. Summer probably did the same thing. I'm sure that if she'd realized what had happened she would have mentioned it."

Redding tapped his pen against the table for a moment,

his gaze focused on his notes. "But why keep the paintball and the poison ivy under wraps?"

"Well, I think at first Summer was angry."

"Angry?"

"Not in a vicious way," I said quickly. "She didn't like that someone was messing with her. Anyway, Summer didn't want to give Julia the satisfaction of letting Julia see she'd riled her in any way."

Redding studied his notes for a moment, then looked up. "And you're sure it was Julia?"

"Well, no. Not positive, but who else would it be?"

By the time I'd answered all of Redding's questions, the sun had set and everyone was gathered on the beach around a large bonfire. Despite the death of the photographer earlier, the atmosphere wasn't gloomy, which I supposed was to be expected. As far as I knew, none of the wedding party had been personal friends with Ned, and, except for Yvonne, he hadn't spent much time with anyone else.

I spotted Yvonne sitting by herself up near the dunes. I did what had become an automatic check of the area, looking for Patricia, but didn't see her anywhere. Maybe she'd decided to skip the bonfire. She wasn't fond of being outdoors, and I could imagine that getting sand in her shoes wouldn't appeal to her.

I greeted Mitch's parents on my way across the sand. They were seated on rough wooden benches that were positioned in a semicircle around the fire. The Avery clan had arrived in force and the golden glow from the fire flickered over the adults on the benches and on the kids sitting closer to the fire making s'mores. I ruffled Nathan's hair and squeezed Livvy's shoulder, but they were busy roasting marshmallows with their cousins. Uncle Bud was supervising the kids, and I felt confident leaving that duty to him. With his phoenix arm tattoos and no-nonsense manner, he would make sure the kids didn't get too near the fire. The bridesmaids and groomsmen were scattered around the outer rim of the circle of the fire's light, lounging on the sand closer to the water, which swirled up the beach. The sea stretched out, dark and empty, to the horizon with only the moonlight glinting on the waves. The warmth of the afternoon had vanished with the sunset, and I was glad I'd stopped by our hotel room to pick up a sweater.

I found Mitch at a wooden picnic table between the bonfire and the dunes.

"Hey," he said as I sat down. "I saved you a plate." He pushed over a plate with shrimp, corn on the cob, and potatoes.

"Thank goodness. I didn't think I was hungry, but suddenly I'm starving." I picked up a shrimp. "Where's Summer? I need to talk to her."

"She was here with Brian, but a deputy came and got her. Said they had more questions for her. Brian went with her."

I wrinkled my nose. "That's my fault, I'm afraid."

Mitch wiped his mouth with his napkin. "You didn't tell the detective about Julia, did you?"

I raised my eyebrows. Julia and Graham weren't too far away from us, snuggled together on a single rustic chaise longue. Julia had changed into denim shorts and a loose-weave sweater over a tank top. Graham, again, looked sloppier in a wrinkled white oxford shirt over a pair of shorts similar to a pair that I had bought for Mitch, but had to return because he wouldn't wear them. Mitch had taken one look at the designer plaid shorts and said, "No way. Real men don't wear plaid unless they are in Scotland."

With the glow of the firelight on Graham and Julia, they looked content and happy. How could she sit there, looking so content? If she'd engineered an accident that turned fatal, shouldn't she look at least a little worried?

"I had to." I kept my tone low and tilted my head so that I was turned slightly away from Brian and Julia. "The golf cart that crashed today, it was the one Brian and Summer were using. Someone had loosened a lug nut on it."

Mitch rubbed his forehead for a moment and blew out a sigh. "How do you find out this stuff?"

Between bites of shrimp and corn, I described my ride back with the resort employees. "It's not my fault that they couldn't stay quiet. And all I did was tell Redding that there was something caught on the top of the golf cart—remember, I mentioned it when we watched Ned leave? Redding was the one who told me the golf cart was decorated with ribbons. I didn't even notice it after the crash. One glance at . . . Ned and I couldn't look back."

"No, I didn't notice it either. It was the shock of it. We were all overwhelmed by what had happened." Mitch glanced at Julia then said, "So you think it was another prank?"

"I hate to say it, but yes, I think so. I mean, it fits the pattern. Julia probably wanted to embarrass Summer or, worse, hurt her. Dumping her out of the golf cart would achieve at least one of those goals, maybe both. You have to admit that Summer has handled the paintball and poison ivy really well. If you didn't know what had happened, you'd never suspect someone had tried to put a damper on this event."

A childish shriek came from near the fire and Mitch and I both jerked our attention that way, but it was only one of the cousins holding a wire coat hanger that had been refashioned into a marshmallow toasting tool, but this marshmallow had been toasted a little too long. It was flaming. Uncle Bud took the wire coat hanger and blew the fire out, then proceeded to eat the marshmallow. The girls groaned or murmured, "How gross," while the boys looked on with admiration.

Mitch and I exchanged smiles, then he gazed out across the water and said, "If Julia did plan to cause trouble this weekend, that would mean she would have to have a socket wrench with her today on the tour."

"Well, she apparently packed a paintball gun and poison ivy. I mean, you can't say she wasn't prepared, which makes it worse," I said, wiping my greasy fingers on a paper napkin.

Mitch looked over at the chaise longue. "She doesn't look like a woman obsessed with breaking up her old boyfriend and his fiancée."

"No," I agreed as I watched the cuddling couple. Julia was snuggled onto Graham's shoulder, her dark hair spilling out over the edge of the chair. Graham had tilted his golden head so that it was resting on hers. They looked like one of those commercials for expensive perfume that deluge the airways around Christmas, which always seemed to feature incredibly good-looking people doing outdoor activities like horseback riding, rock diving, and walking on the beach.

"She does look smitten," I said as Julia tilted her head back to get a better look at Graham's face. She gazed at him as if she couldn't get enough of him. "If I didn't know what happened yesterday, and about her history with Brian, I would never think she might have been involved in what happened at the ruins."

"But we do know," Mitch said with a sigh.

"And that's why I had to tell Redding."

"Yes, of course you had to tell him. The golf cart wreck goes way beyond a prank."

"I know." I looked back toward Julia. If she had planned the wreck that killed a man, she didn't look the least bit regretful. "I don't know if it's scarier to think that she did do it and is acting like nothing happened, or that she didn't do it. . . ."

"Then who did?"

Nathan bounded up to the table holding the wire coat hanger that he'd been using to toast marshmallows. "You have to come make a s'more. If you don't come now, all the chocolate will be gone, and the fire is dying down."

"Then we don't have a moment to lose," I said as Mitch and I stood. We joined the kids around the fire. I limited myself to one deliciously melty s'more, then handed off the coat hanger to Nathan. Livvy came and asked if she could go back to the resort with the older kids. "The library has a cabinet full of board games. The guy at the check-in desk said it was okay for us to play with them, but we didn't have time today."

"I don't see why not," Mitch said.

Livvy spun away, her face excited.

"Stay with the group. We'll come get you in an hour," I called as she hurried away, her footsteps kicking up bits of sand. Her high-pitched "Okay, Mom" floated back as she joined the group moving up the path through the dunes back to the resort.

Nathan settled into my lap with his last s'more. I could tell he was tired because of the limpness of his limbs and his stillness. "Nathan, have you looked at the stars?"

He cranked his head up, pressing against my collarbone. "Wow. There's tons of them, like a *hundred billion*. Where did they all come from?"

"They're always there, we just can't see all of them.

There's usually too much light around us from streetlights and lights from stores and cities. That's called ambient light. When you go somewhere without all the lights, somewhere really dark like out here, then you can see more stars."

"Do you see any patterns in the stars?" Mitch asked.

"No."

"Are you sure?" Mitch hunkered down on Nathan's level and pointed out the Big Dipper. They found a few more constellations, then Nathan went quiet and completely still, his breathing smooth and deep.

With Nathan asleep in my lap, I snuggled up against Mitch and enjoyed watching the light from the dying fire flicker over the faces of the younger kids, most of whom were fighting off sleep. It had been a big day of outdoor activities, and I knew both kids would sleep hard tonight. After a while, some of the adults announced they were turning in, and I was just about to suggest to Mitch that we head inside when Summer dropped onto the sand beside me.

"How mad are you?" I asked in a low voice.

"Oh, I was furious at first, but after talking to Detective Redding," she sighed, "I can see that you had to tell him."

Mitch unwrapped his arm from my shoulders. "How about I take Nathan up to bed and round up Livvy."

I shot him a grateful smile and transferred Nathan to his arms. "I'll be up in a few minutes." As he walked away, Nathan snuggled to his chest, I turned back to Summer. In a low voice, I asked, "Redding told you about the lug nut on the golf cart?"

"Yes. Actually, it was all of the lug nuts on one wheel. They'd all been removed."

"All? I heard it was one," I said, surprised.

"No, Redding was very specific. He said they'd all been taken out."

"Then there's no way it was sloppy maintenance or an accident," I said. I knew that was what all the indicators had pointed to, but having it confirmed gave me a sick feeling in the pit of my stomach.

The fire had died down and now we both stared at the red glowing embers. Finally, Summer said, "It means someone intentionally did it, wanted it to happen."

We both looked toward Julia and Graham, who were now walking along the beach, the silhouette of their linked hands barely visible in the darkness.

Summer said, "It's hard to imagine . . ."

"I know. Mitch and I just had this discussion."

I looked back to Summer. "Sorry I wasn't able to give you a heads-up about telling Redding. He mentioned the decorations on the golf cart. I hadn't noticed them at the accident, but when he said that, well, I knew I had to tell him about the other stuff."

"That's okay," Summer said. "I had a feeling it would all come out anyway. I just hoped it would be after the wedding, not before."

"So what did Redding ask you?"

"Most of his questions were about Julia, and I only know hearsay, so I wasn't much help. Brian told him everything that happened when he broke it off with her. Redding wanted to know about Ned, too. But, again, I wasn't much help there either."

"Really? Why did you hire him? Had you worked with him before?"

"No. In fact, I had a photographer I'd worked with for some print ads who was excellent, and I wanted to use him as our photographer for the wedding, but then Patricia called and insisted I hire Ned. She had hired him for something—I forget what—maybe something for Gus? Yes, I think that was it. They needed a good headshot for some public relations thing Patricia had lined up." Summer ran her hand over the sand, creating little ridges. "I wasn't excited about hiring him, but his portfolio was excellent and he had good recommendations. I'd fought Patricia on so many little details by then that I decided to hire Ned. To keep the peace, you know."

"I wonder if he was a friend? Maybe he knew Patricia and Gus socially?" I asked.

Summer's brow crinkled into a frown. "I don't think so."

"They didn't seem chummy," I agreed.

"Is Patricia chummy with anyone?" Summer asked with a trace of a smile. "Anyway, that's all I knew about him."

"I'm sure Redding will dig into his background. On another, much more trivial subject, what do you want to do for a photographer? I know it's a rather crass thing to talk about, but we need to figure out something."

"It's okay. All sorted," she said in a quiet voice. Her voice made me study her face more closely. "The resort manager gave me the contact details of a photographer who has done several weddings here and lives in Brunswick," she went on, her gaze focused on the sand. "I've already talked to her. She is coming over on the first ferry tomorrow."

"That's great. Well done."

Summer shrugged. "Yeah, I guess."

"What?" I asked as I watched Summer struggle not to cry. She pressed a hand to her mouth for a moment, then took it away and said, "It just seems so insignificant. All the details of the wedding. Every little thing that I've been obsessing over—do you know I lost a good night's sleep over whether or not to have a deejay or just recorded music? It's all so trivial . . . when I think about Ned, what his family is going to have to deal with. It makes the debate about what color the tablecloths should be seem . . . well, rather pathetic."

"Of course it's upsetting and when someone dies, it makes everything seem insignificant in the big scope of things," I said as I patted her back as I did for Livvy when she was upset. "But you shouldn't feel guilty for making plans and focusing on your wedding. Someone has to think about seating charts and the color of the napkins and the music," I said. "Believe me, details are important. All those little things don't just fall into place by themselves. You've done an excellent job of planning. You should be proud that things are going as well as they are, considering all the . . . extra things that have come up. I think you're handling it really well."

Summer blinked and sniffed. "I suppose that's true, about the details."

"It is. I've had plenty of experience in that area. Trust me, details matter." Summer nodded, but didn't look any happier, which set off my mom instincts. "Is there something else bothering you?"

"Yes, and this really is selfish. I really do feel bad for Ned's family, but at the same time"—Summer lowered her voice—"I hate it that all these things that have happened have overshadowed the wedding. I mean, Brian's not even here to enjoy the bonfire. He's off answering questions with the police again and this was the one part of the weekend he was really looking forward to. All the other stuff—the rehearsal dinner, the ceremony, all those things—he thinks of as formal . . . duties, I guess, that have to be done. Events to get through. It's only when he's out here, on the beach or in the forest, that he really enjoys himself. The island, the wildlife, the habitats are so important to him."

"Oh, don't get him started on the beaches," said a voice from the beach. Graham and Julia had returned from their stroll on the beach. "Beach habitats are Brian's personal hobbyhorse," Graham said as he stopped beside us, while Julia went over to the chaise and collected her beach bag. "He'll drone on and on about native species and dunes. And sea grass," Graham said with a mock shudder. "Trust me, *never* mention sea grass. He knows every kind and variety and will give you a detailed list. Even if you don't want it."

Summer shook her head at him. "He's not that bad." I was glad to see the shiny film of tears had receded from her eyes. "Besides, it's part of his job."

Julia rejoined Graham. They immediately linked hands as Graham said, "But that's no excuse for boring people. Trust me, sea grass is never that interesting. We're calling it a night."

Julia sent us a tentative smile as she said, "Good night. The bonfire was great."

We watched their meandering progress through the sand dunes for a moment, then I asked, "What did you mean about Brian's job?"

"Oh, Brian does a lot of pro bono work for barrier island conservation groups. Checking the legality of development, helping them draft potential legislation to limit development and prevent habitat erosion, that sort of thing. He is licensed to practice law in Florida and Georgia, you know. He's even on the board of the Camden Island Authority."

"I probably should know what that is, but I have no idea what it is," I confessed.

I was glad to see Summer smile. "Don't feel bad. It's not well known. It's a state agency that oversees the management of Camden Island. The governor appoints board members for four-year terms. It was quite an honor for Brian when he was picked last year. He's the youngest member they've ever had. And he's the only board member who doesn't live in Georgia full-time, but he grew up here and visits often enough that they looked past that detail."

"Wow. I had no idea."

"Yeah. Contrary to what Graham says, Brian doesn't go around boasting about it. I promise you, that if Graham got appointed to anything, he would work it into every conversation. Brian's not like that. He does talk about the island and how important it is to preserve the habitats here, but he doesn't bore people with it."

"No, I've never heard him mention it," I said.

A pair of red flip-flops dropped onto the sand beside Summer, and we both jumped. Neither one of us had realized anyone was that close to us. "What a gorgeous night." Yvonne settled into the lotus position with her back completely straight, making me think that she must do a lot of yoga. She tilted her head up and gazed at the stars. "Amazing what you can see out here, how many 'candles of the night' there are."

Summer looked at me out of the corner of her eye and widened her eyes, conveying, *Here we go again. . . .*

Yvonne had changed out of her sundress into a pair of jean capris and layered an open-weave red sweater over a white tank. She must have been walking along the beach because the cuffs of her capris were wet and her feet were covered in a fine layer of sand, which was getting all over her pants, but she didn't seem to mind. "Such a shame about Ned. That poor young man." Yvonne transferred her gaze from the starry sky to Summer. "I can't believe he's gone. That he could be so vibrant and alive one moment and gone the next." She shivered.

I leaned forward. "I saw you with him, right before he left."

"Yes," she said, and grinned sadly. "He was telling me about another wedding he'd worked where the bride, who was very high-strung and particular, took a Valium. She was so loopy she could barcly walk down the aisle." Her smile vanished and Yvonne blinked rapidly. "It's so sad. It really is."

I waited a moment as she got her emotions under control, then asked, "Do you know what he talked to Patricia about? Did he say what he was going to talk to her about?" The mention of Patricia's name snapped Yvonne out of her despondent state. "No. Something about the wedding, I suppose." She shifted slightly on the sand, turning toward Summer. "It's awful, what's happened, but don't you think—" She broke off as Brian joined us, holding out a Styrofoam cup with steam rising from it.

"Oh, thank you. You're a darling." Yvonne reached for the cup, intercepting it before Brian could hand it to Summer.

Brian and Summer exchanged a look. "Mom, that was for Summer."

"Oh, sorry!" She handed off the cup. "I would love some coffee too. Would you be a dear and get me one too?"

"Of course. Ellie, you want some?"

I declined and Brian set off to the other side of the fire where picnic tables had been set up with drinks.

Yvonne turned back to Summer. "Now, as I was saying, Ned's death is terrible, but don't you think it may be a sign?"

Summer sipped her coffee. "A sign of what exactly?" she asked cautiously.

"An omen."

"*Omen* is a pretty strong word," I cautioned, sensing a gathering tension in Summer.

"Perhaps *omen* isn't the right word. Maybe *portent* is better? In any case, no one should get married after one of the wedding party dies. It's just bad luck."

"Ned Blackson wasn't part of the wedding party," Summer said. "He was the photographer."

"Still. It tinges the whole event with . . . a sad atmosphere." Yvonne put her hand on Summer's arm. "I think you and Brian should delay the wedding. It would be best, for everyone."

Summer had gone very still, and I knew her well enough to realize she was working to keep her emotions under control. "We cannot cancel the wedding."

"Oh, darling, everyone would understand."

"Patricia wouldn't," Summer said in an undertone, but Yvonne hurried on, shifting so she was completely facing Summer.

"Just put it off for a few weeks. Maybe even a month or two. You know, until you're sure."

Brian returned with another cup, but sensed the tense atmosphere and slowed down as he approached. "Hey, everything okay?" he asked, his voice uneasy.

Summer gazed up at Brian for a long moment, her face tight and angry, "No. Everything is *not* okay." She switched her gaze to Yvonne. "Brian and I are sure about getting married—completely sure, but that's what you don't like. You're not worried about the atmosphere. You just don't want us to get married, or more specifically, you don't want Brian to marry me." On one smooth movement, Summer handed off the cup of coffee to me and got to her feet. Her jaw was set and her hands clenched into fists.

The chatter around the fire died away as Summer said, "I'm sick of your insinuations that I'm not good enough for Brian and all your hints that we should call off the wedding. You're trying to sabotage the wedding. Brian and I are getting married. Deal with it." She whirled away and strode out to the beach.

Yvonne uncurled her legs and stood. "Bride nerves," she announced to everyone. "Nothing to worry about."

"Mother," Brian said warningly, his gaze going to Summer's figure as she walked along the waves.

Yvonne gave him a pitying look. "She's a sweet girl, but rather temperamental, don't you think? Are you sure you want to deal with that, day in and day out?"

Brian gazed at her with an expression that I couldn't quite read. It almost looked like fascination. "Summer was right," he said, nodding slightly. "I argued with her, said you'd never be that petty and selfish, but she was right. You *don't* want us to get married." His voice was filled with amazement. "Despite all your outward show, inside you're rooting for us to call everything off." He stepped back and his voice changed. "It's not going to happen," he said firmly. "I'm marrying Summer. Don't make me choose between you and her. I'll choose her. Always." He threw the cup in the trash and set off at a jog along the beach to catch up with Summer.

Chapter Eight

A sudden *thump* jarred me out of a deep sleep. I didn't have to open my eyes to know that Nathan had jumped on the end of our bed.

"Beach! Beach! Beach!" he chatted, matching his mantra to his bouncing, which was shaking the mattress.

I snuggled deeper against Mitch and kept my eyes closed. "I must be dreaming."

Mitch, his voice thick with sleep, said, "I knew I should have locked that door to the adjoining room."

Livvy's earnest tone sounded beside my ear. "Dad promised we could go to the beach this morning, after breakfast."

"You didn't." We had nothing planned until lunch when I was meeting Summer to go over wedding details, and then we had the rehearsal dinner this evening. An early-morning visit to the beach wasn't on my list of things to do.

I felt Mitch's chest move as he sighed. "Afraid so." He shifted and murmured so low that only I could hear, "I thought they'd sleep in after their big day yesterday."

"Silly man." I scrubbed a hand across my face and spoke

through a yawn. "Kids wake up even earlier when they are on vacation than they do at home. It's like a law of nature or something."

I cracked one eyelid open to check the clock on the nightstand. Six twelve. I struggled up on one elbow, ready to decree that the beach would still be there at ten o'clock, when I caught sight of the kids' expectant faces. Nathan seemed to sense that the beach expedition was in danger of being delayed. He'd abruptly dropped onto his knees and stopped bouncing. Livvy stood beside the bed, already dressed in her swimsuit, her body language rivaling those images of saints waiting expectantly at altars.

She deposited the woven beach tote on the bed. "I have our goggles, fins, and beach toys. There's a sign on the bathroom counter that says we can pick up beach towels on the way."

I exchanged a glance with Mitch. "We *are* awake now."

"Yes, I suppose so."

Nathan let out a cheer, bounded up from the bed, and raced around the room, repeating, "We're going to the beach!"

An hour later, after a short stop for breakfast, the four of us were rambling along the trail that led from the resort to the beach. Mitch was loaded down with beach chairs, I had the beach tote, and the kids were each carrying plastic pails and shovels as we moved through the forest. Once we left the wide, manicured lawn around the house, we'd followed the sign pointing down a trail that took us through the forest. We had walked the same trail last night, but it had been so dark that it was impossible to see a few feet beyond the lighted pylons that edged the trail. Now, in the grayish light of dawn, I could see the dense greenery of layer after layer of the forest from the fan palms at ground level to the Spanish moss hanging from the twisty oak branches overhead.

"Sabotage?" Mitch asked in a low voice. "Summer actually used that word?"

The kids were several steps ahead of us, and we were continuing the conversation we'd had the night before. I'd related the blowup between Yvonne and Summer to Mitch.

"Yes. I'm sure she did. That's a very specific word to use, you know," I said.

"You don't think that Yvonne could have . . ." he said, his eyebrows raised.

"I don't know. Until last night, I would have said no, that it would be impossible. But now that I think about it, just in the time I've been around—" I glanced at the kids, who were striding quickly along ahead of us. They didn't seem to be paying any attention to us, but I'd learned that they were like sponges, soaking up everything we said and did, and they often quoted our words back to us verbatim—usually at very inconvenient times, too. Instead of mentioning Yvonne by name, I only said, "She's made several disparaging comments. And, she's constantly pulling Brian away from Summer."

"But to sabotage your own—"

Nathan turned to us. "What's *sabataj*?" he asked, doing his best to pronounce the new word.

I opened my mouth to reply, but Livvy was quicker. "It's when you hurt someone, but do it in a sneaky way," she informed him.

Mitch and I exchanged a glance as we caught up with the kids. "That's my reader," I said as I placed a hand on her shoulder. "You're going to rock your SAT vocabulary portion."

"Sure," Livvy said, but I could see that her forehead had wrinkled into a frown. She had no idea what the SAT was, but she wasn't about to admit it. I was sure she'd ask one of her older cousins later today.

Mitch pointed to a sign posted at a fork in the road. "Only one hundred yards to the beach."

"Oh, look, the ruin is only two hundred yards down the other trail," Livvy said. "Can we go and just take a quick look. Please?"

"I don't know . . . maybe later today," I said, thinking that the smashed golf cart was not an image I wanted my kids to see. "It might not be open right now."

Nathan grinned. "You can't close a ruin, Mom. They don't have any doors."

"It should be okay," Mitch said, checking his watch. "We need to let our breakfast digest a little longer before we swim, anyway. Let's leave our stuff here." He planted the beach chairs against the signpost. The kids dropped their pails and took off down the path toward the ruin.

"Mitch, the golf cart might still be there—"

"It's okay. The police cleared it out this morning."

"How do you know that?" I dropped the beach bag next to the chairs and started up the path beside Mitch.

"While you were with the kids upstairs after breakfast, I went for a walk around the resort," Mitch said. "The golf cart had been loaded onto a flatbed and was being moved off the island."

"Really? So they're done at the ruin?" I asked.

"Yes, all finished. It's open to visitors, and everything has been cleaned up. I also dropped by the maintenance building. One of the groundskeepers came in, and I struck up a conversation with him."

I narrowed my eyes at Mitch. "This is so unlike you. Usually I'm the one nosing around asking questions."

Mitch's face was serious. "Yes, well, this involves my little sister. If someone is determined to hurt her, I want to find out what is going on and who is doing it." Mitch paused, then sighed. "Unfortunately, the guy at the maintenance building said no single person from the resort is assigned to the building all day, and he didn't remember seeing anyone unfamiliar around lately."

I glanced up the trail and saw that the kids were far enough ahead of us that I could speak in a normal voice. "You're thinking about the socket wrench, aren't you?" I asked as we moved deeper into the forest. The foliage became thicker, filtering out more of the weak sunlight.

"Yes," Mitch said. "I suppose whoever messed with the golf cart lug nuts could have brought a socket wrench with them. I said to the guy at the maintenance building that I was thinking of buying a golf cart and got him talking. I found out that most golf cart wheels use the same size bolts and lug nuts, so theoretically, whoever loosened them could have brought a three-fourths-inch socket wrench with them for that purpose, but how would someone know that they'd have the opportunity to mess with the wheels?"

I shrugged. "The details about golf carts being the only form of transportation on Camden Island are online and in all the brochures. It would be easy to find out. Chances are that sometime during the weekend, Summer would take a golf cart somewhere. Maybe Julia just watched and waited for her opportunity. With Summer and Brian having a dedicated 'bride and groom' golf cart, it only made it easier to target her. On the other hand, I can't believe that *someone* wouldn't remember a stunning young brunette or an older but still very attractive redhead, dropping into the maintenance building. That's not on the list of resort amenities, you know."

"No, it's definitely an area of the resort that a person would have to seek out. The building is located out of sight down a forested drive. But all I did was ask a resort employee the way and they pointed it out, so it's not impossible to think someone else did it too. And the place was wide open when I first got there, no one in sight."

"They leave it unattended?"

"Yes, it's far enough off the beaten path that most of the vacationers don't even know it's there."

"And were there tools lying around?"

"Tons of them. I saw three socket sets, and I only got a cursory look around."

The path curved, and the ruin came into view as the forest dropped away and the wide green lawn spread out in front of us. Livvy and Nathan were already halfway across the expanse, making straight for the ruin. Another pair of sightseers were moving around the ruin.

We stayed clear of the path where the accident had happened, but I couldn't help taking a closer look at it as we neared the area. It was empty. There was no trace, not even a speck of blood on the asphalt, that something tragic had happened there yesterday.

When we arrived at the ruin yesterday, we'd come in from the side, and I hadn't looked at the ruin from this angle, from directly in front of it. I could see the steepness of the cart path, and the sharp bend where it turned to hug the retaining wall. We paused a moment, taking in the panorama of the ruin.

"Someone sure picked a heck of a place to remove the lug nuts." Mitch's tone was grim as he studied the path.

"With the short distance between the top of the path and the turn, the cart was sure to flip over," I said with a shake of my head.

"And the steep grade of the path would mean it would probably be traveling at a good clip."

The morning was on the chilly side, but I felt a coldness settle over me that had nothing to do with the weather. I looked away to check on the kids, not wanting to think about how calculating someone had been.

They had reached the ruin itself. "Stay off the walls," I called just as Nathan gripped a stone near his head as if he wanted to climb to the top. I knew what he was thinking—what else could a ruin be for, except to use as a giant jungle gym? Nathan reluctantly released his grip on the wall and moved to follow Livvy through the rest of the house.

"Do you think they're okay in there?" I asked Mitch.

"Yes. The walls that are standing are solid enough, I noticed that yesterday. Nothing is going to come crashing down on them."

As we crossed the slowly rising lawn, I noticed that the increase in elevation partially blocked the cart path from view. By the time we reached the area in front of the terrace where the wicker tables had been placed, I couldn't even see the cart path. Mitch was looking the same direction I was. "Can you see anything?" I asked. "You're taller than me."

"Not a single bit of the asphalt of the upper cart path." Mitch turned to the ruin and climbed the steps to the terrace. "Stay here a moment, would you? I want to check something out."

"Sure," I said.

Mitch waved to the kids, who joined him as he walked through the ruin, then all three of them disappeared through what would have been the back of the house. I watched, scanning the ruin, smiling politely at the other couple, who were taking photos. After a minute or two, Mitch and the kids reappeared from the back of the ruin and made their way toward me.

Nathan jumped off the terrace. "Did you see us, Mom?"

"No, I didn't see anything," I said as I looked at Mitch.

Nathan and Livvy thought it was a great joke that I hadn't seen them and raced off to try to replicate the feat on the other side of the ruin. Mitch said, "We walked all the way around to the cart path. There's enough bushes and trees to screen someone all the way there."

"Which means someone could have slipped away, removed the lug nuts, and rejoined us, without anyone being able to see them, at least not from here."

"Do you remember anyone disappearing for a while?" Mitch asked.

"You sound like Redding. That's what he wanted to know too. But no, but I wasn't watching everyone. I did try to keep an eye on Yvonne and Patricia, but I couldn't say for sure that both of them were always in my sight. I was more concerned that they weren't together than if they were both always with the group."

"Hey there," a voice called from behind us. Mitch and I had been looking in the direction of the hidden cart path where the crash had happened, our backs to the ruin. We both turned and saw Graham trotting down the shallow terrace steps. He wore running clothes that were drenched in sweat. He pulled out his earbuds that were attached to his phone, which was tucked into an armband. "If you're looking for the beach"—he paused to suck in a gulp of air—"you took a wrong turn."

We were all wearing swimwear, so it was obvious we were on our way to the beach. Livvy and I had on swimsuit cover-ups over our suits. And Nathan and Mitch had on bright swim trunks with their T-shirts and flip-flops. The resort was a classy place, and you couldn't just run around in your swimsuit, not that I wanted to run around *anywhere* in my swimsuit.

"The kids wanted to see the ruin so we made a little detour," I said as I checked their location. I could see them motoring around the side of the ruin toward us.

"Is there a running path around here?" Mitch asked, his gaze shifting around Graham to search the forest that ringed the ruin.

"Yeah." Graham turned to point behind him, his words spaced out as he worked to get his breath back. "It goes from the resort through the forest and . . . comes out back there. A three-mile loop . . . It starts by the pool." He pulled a washcloth out of his fanny pack and wiped down his sweaty face and neck. This was quite a different look for him from his usual shabby designer clothes. His face was bright red and his hair was plastered to his forehead. With his sticky clothes clinging to him, I could see that he had the beginning of a potbelly. He didn't look nearly as attractive as he did when his golden hair was swept off his forehead and he was dressed in his expensive clothes.

"Thanks, man. I'll give it a try," Mitch said.

Unlike me, Mitch jogged a lot. I only ran if I absolutely had to. It would take something pretty bad, say a zombie apocalypse, to get me running. My neighborhood walking routine was the perfect exercise for me.

"We won't hold you up," Mitch said, stepping away and calling the kids. Mitch tracked his times and his runs and didn't want to slow Graham down. Graham, on the other hand, looked like he wouldn't have minded lingering.

"Thanks," he said halfheartedly, and set off at the slowest trot I'd ever seen.

I watched him for a moment while we waited for the kids to reach us. "You know, I think I can walk faster than that."

Mitch laughed. "Yeah, well, you're quite a walker. You can really move."

"It's all those years of pushing the stroller. Now that I don't have the stroller I can go twice as fast."

Despite our detour, we were still one of the first groups to arrive at the beach. This morning the water was pearly gray, reflecting the thin layer of clouds that skimmed overhead. Unlike the soft, sugary sand of the Gulf, the beach here was dark brown and densely hard-packed, but the kids didn't seem to mind. Mitch settled the chairs into the sand, and the kids hit the water. Livvy had always been cautious when it came to the water. She didn't splash in as quickly as Nathan did, but I was glad to see she didn't hesitate or cling to me like she had in the past. She took it slow, but she did get in the water.

Gradually, more people arrived and the film of clouds dispersed as the sun rose in the sky. Soon, bright umbrellas and towels dotted the sand and the sunlight became intense, beating down, making me glad I had a pair of sunglasses to slip on.

Mitch and I joined the kids in the water for a while, then the kids transitioned to building sand castles, and Mitch and I returned to our chairs. After about two hours, I closed my book. "I better head back to the room. I need to change and pick up my binder before I meet Summer to go over some wedding stuff."

"Ah, the all-important binder. The notebook of knowledge," Mitch said playfully. "Can't forget that."

"Are you making fun of my binder?"

"No, I would never, ever joke about something as critical as the notebook of knowledge."

"Liar," I said, but I couldn't help but smile at Mitch's mock-serious face. "That binder is what brings order out of chaos. Sanity out of craziness."

Mitch's tone changed. "Too bad we don't have something like that to help sort out Ned's death and everything else that's going on."

"I know," I said with a sigh as I stood and worked my feet into my flip-flops. No matter what we did, the awful things that had happened weren't far from our thoughts. I called out to the kids that it was time to go.

Livvy ran up, scattering sand and water droplets across Mitch and me. "Aww, do we have to?"

Nathan was on her heels. "Can't we stay a little longer?"

I looked at Mitch. "I have to meet Summer for lunch. Wedding stuff."

He tilted his head toward the trail that led back to the resort. "You go ahead." The kids didn't wait to hear more. Excited, they whirled around and made for their sand castle.

"How long will you and the kids stay?" I asked.

Mitch checked his watch. "Probably only another twenty minutes. I'll round everyone up, and we'll get lunch."

"Okay. Don't forget, Livvy wants to go to that kids' tennis lesson this afternoon. See you in a little while." I kissed Mitch, waved to the kids, and headed through the dunes, staying on the path that would take me through the forest and back to the resort.

After a quick shower, I slipped on a loose turquoise shirt, white shorts, and sandals and headed out to meet Summer. As I emerged from my room, I saw Patricia slip out of the room two doors down from mine. Then she moved furtively to the stairway exit.

Why would she be in Ned Blackson's room?

Tips for an Organized Wedding

Outdoor weddings have special concerns.

Comfort:
Have sunscreen, bug spray, high-heel supports, and fans handy for guests and members of the wedding party.

Plan B:
A backup location either indoors or in a covered area is a good thing to have in case of bad weather.

Setting the Scene:
If you don't want the groom to see the bride before the ceremony, screens or indoor waiting areas should be arranged beforehand.

Audio Issues:
Sound is another thing to consider for an outdoor ceremony. Decide if you'll want a microphone for the officiant as well as speakers to amplify music. A setting like a beach may have a lot of wind, which is something that will need to be taken into account when considering sound setup.

Wind:
Wind can also play havoc with hemlines. One solution for the hemline issue is having small weights, like metal washers, sewn into hems.

Chapter Nine

"Why would Patricia be in Ned's room?" I asked Summer.

She took a bite of the calamari appetizer we were sharing and shrugged. "Who knows? I've given up trying to understand anything Patricia does."

I'd met Summer for lunch on the veranda that stretched across the back of the resort and overlooked the pool and golf course. Tables were spaced across the right-hand side of the veranda while the left half had wicker chairs and tables arranged in conversational groupings.

"Besides, maybe it's not his room anymore," Summer continued. "Maybe the management cleared out his stuff."

"No, I asked at the desk on my way down. They said the police have asked them to hold the room until they've finished, so Ned's things are still in there."

Summer tilted her head. "Why are you so interested in this?"

"Because of everything that's happened," I said simply. "I don't want anything else to go wrong." Seeing Patricia had reminded me of the look I saw on Patricia's face after the accident, the look of relief, but I didn't want to mention it to Summer. She already had enough stress, and I didn't want to add to her worry. "I don't know, it is just something odd. With all the other odd things going on . . . well, I just don't want anything else to happen."

"I know." Summer dropped her napkin on the table and pushed her plate away. "I'm not thinking about any of that stuff, not Ned or any of the pranks or even interfering mothers-in-law. The only thing I'm focused on right now is becoming Mrs. Abernathy."

I hadn't brought up the subject earlier, but since Summer had mentioned it, I asked, "So everything is okay between you and Brian?"

"Yes. Better, actually. I've known for months that Yvonne wasn't my biggest fan, but as the wedding got closer, her little campaign to derail us intensified. Brian couldn't see it until last night. Things aren't so good between Yvonne and me, but that's her decision to act that way. I was pleasant when I saw her this morning at breakfast. She gave me the cold shoulder."

"I'm sorry."

"I think she'll come around, eventually." Summer looked out over the pool, squinting against the glare. "At least, I hope so, for Brian's sake. I think she's a little too dependent on him, but he would miss her if she completely refuses to be around him after the wedding."

"You don't think that she'd do anything . . . drastic, do you?"

Summer slowly set down the bottled water she'd been holding and gave me a long look. "You think she might be behind the pranks?"

"After the scene last night, it occurred to me that Julia might not be the only one who wanted you to call off your wedding."

"No," Summer said instantly. "Yvonne wouldn't do those things. Sure, she wanted to break us up, but she's not going to do anything in secret. That's not her way. She has to have attention. No," Summer repeated, shaking her head, "that's not Yvonne's style at all. Those pranks had Julia written all over them."

"But Julia seems so taken with Graham."

Summer's forehead wrinkled. "Yes, I know. I saw the way she looked at him last night. Utter adoration. Maybe it's an act."

"Maybe. But Yvonne is the actress, not Julia."

"You like that theory, don't you?" Summer said.

"The whole situation bothers me. Number one, that someone would try to scare you in the first place. But the golf cart, that wasn't a prank. Someone seriously wanted to hurt you." I gazed out over the emerald lawn to the rectangle of the pale blue pool. "It doesn't fit. Something is off." When Summer didn't answer, I looked back at her. She was sitting with her head tilted forward, her shoulders slumped as she fiddled with the base of her unused fork.

Her despondent air made me feel guilty. I reached for the binder. "Listen to me, doing exactly what you don't want to do, focusing on all the bad stuff that's happened. I'm sorry I brought it up. Let's talk about the ceremony instead."

Summer put down the fork and leaned back in her chair. "Yes, let's switch to a subject where the biggest catastrophe is that Meg forgot her shoes."

"She did?"

Summer waved a hand. "Don't worry. She's already called her roommate, who sent them FedEx. They should arrive this afternoon."

"Well, that's efficient of her."

"Yes, she's a bit like you," Summer said with a grin.

"Okay, then let's get to the to-do list."

"Right. Run them down."

We sorted out the tip envelopes and went over the timeline for the wedding day, double-checking when each person should arrive and where they should go while waiting for the outdoor ceremony to begin. I would contact each person today and make sure they had a copy of the schedule and knew where to go. "Speaking of being outdoors, let's look at the weather." I checked the weather app on my phone. "Looks good for tomorrow, but there may be a storm rolling in later tonight."

"That's fine. The manager said we could use the ballroom for the rehearsal if it rains tonight. The setup for the reception doesn't start in there until the next morning."

"And what about the day of? Just in case there's rain."

"You are a worrier, aren't you?" Summer motioned for our check. "It's not supposed to rain."

"But just in case, is there a backup plan?"

"Of course. There's a small events room that we can use. It would be a squeeze, but we don't have to worry about that because it's not going to rain." Summer signed the ticket to charge the lunch to her room, then slapped the pen down and tilted her head up. "Look at that beautiful clear blue sky. It's going to be gorgeous, exactly like I pictured it."

I couldn't help but smile at her. She looked relaxed and happy and confident, just like a bride should.

Caroline, Summer and Mitch's mom, arrived. "There you are. How are you?"

Summer rolled her eyes. "I'm fine, Mom."

Caroline, exquisitely turned out as always in a pale taupe wrap dress and flat sandals, looked at me with exasperation. "All these strange, awful things happening, and she acts like I shouldn't worry about her."

"I think Ellie's doing enough worrying for the both of us," Summer said as she moved her chair back from the table.

"Yes, being a worrywart is my specialty," I said. "I've got that handled."

"Along with everything else," Caroline said. "I don't know what we would have done without you, Ellie."

"Oh, it was nothing but running checklists, another specialty of mine. Anyway, don't you two have a spa appointment?" I flipped to another page of the binder. "Yes, you do. Facials and nails at one. You better get going."

Summer stood. "We'll see you there. Don't get so wrapped up in this wedding stuff that you forget your own spa appointment."

"Wouldn't miss it for the world," I said, waving them off.

I finished the last of my ice tea and sent a text to Mitch to see where he was, then I closed the binder and was about to stand, but I heard a familiar nasal female voice. Our table was near the balustrade, and the veranda was raised several feet off the ground, so I had a good view of the top of Patricia's head as she stopped on the crushed shell path that wound around the resort's main building and continued on to the pool.

"I'm sorry, Reggie, but I don't see the point," Patricia said to a bald man in golf clothes who stood beside her. He stopped to readjust the strap of the bag of golf clubs he carried, and Patricia paused as well.

"But don't you want to see it through?" he asked as he heaved the bag higher on his shoulder. "It's a sad but very true fact that many artists' work doesn't resonate until after their death. Ned's work was good. And, the news about his death will draw some publicity. I'm sure—"

Patricia shook her head, cutting him off. "I won't continue my sponsorship of the show." Her nasal tones carried a firmness that I recognized. Even in my short acquaintance with her, I could tell she wasn't going to change her mind.

"But the catalogues have been printed and the mailers are about to go out," the man said, undeterred by her tone. "You can't back out now."

"You're welcome to look for other supporters, but I'm out. Now, if you'll excuse me, I have an appointment."

The bald man watched her walk away, then muttered a curse as he trudged on under his heavy load.

Frowning, I flipped to the GUESTS tab in the binder. Reggie was an unusual name. Hadn't someone with that name been invited to the wedding? I ran my finger down the list of names until I found a Reginald and Holly King. Their invitation had been mailed to a Savannah address. I typed his name and the word *Savannah* into the browser on my phone. The results popped up, and I clicked on the third one down, King Galleries. I scrolled down the page, then I sat back in the chair. Reggie owned King Galleries, and he had a photography show scheduled to run next month featuring an "exciting new talent, Ned Blackson." Patricia and Gus Abernathy were listed as sponsors of the show.

"Why would Patricia sponsor a show for Ned Blackson and then back out?" I asked, my gaze following a short rally as a tennis ball flew back and forth over the net from Livvy to the tennis instructor.

Mitch sipped his smoothie through the oversize straw then said, "Maybe they're having financial difficulties?"

"Could be," I conceded, switching my view to another court where Nathan waited in line for his turn to practice his serve. He'd decided he wanted a tennis lesson too. "But they are paying for a portion of the wedding."

"Really?"

"Yeah, Summer told me a while back. I thought I told you. I didn't?" Mitch shook his head, so I continued, "Remember how Summer said she wanted a small beach wedding?"

"Ah—no."

"Right. Wedding plans. You tend to tune those out, I remember."

"Which you actually loved. You got to plan our wedding exactly the way you wanted it without me interfering."

"True. That's why we're a match made in heaven," I said with a smile. "But back to Summer. She really had her heart set on a casual beach wedding. Small, just a few friends and family, but then Camden had an opening, and Patricia wanted Brian and Summer to get married here. Summer said no, it would be too expensive, and then Patricia offered to split the cost with your mom and dad. So doesn't it seem odd that Patricia and Gus can afford to help underwrite this extravagant wedding, but she wants to pull her support from an art show?"

Mitch offered me a drink of his smoothie. I took it and tried the mango-strawberry drink as Mitch said, "Who knows? Maybe this wedding has bankrupted them, and they're cutting costs where they can. Remind me to set up a savings account for Livvy's wedding when we get home. If we start now, we may be okay. That's one wedding that I will want to know about all the details."

I handed the smoothie back. "Ned and Patricia," I murmured, thinking of the snippet of an argument I'd overheard on the night of the bachelorette party. I told Mitch about it, and he said, "But Ned and Patricia could have been discussing something related to the wedding."

"Yes, I suppose so. Maybe some cost overrun that she didn't want Gus to know about, but it seemed like a pretty intense discussion if they were talking about . . . I don't know . . . a larger photo package than they'd originally planned for."

"Excuse me, Mrs. Avery?" I turned to find Mr. Markham, the resort manager, hovering at my shoulder. The poor man had had a trying few days. His puffy gray hair was nearly standing on end and his coal black eyes had a frantic look about them. He was probably counting the hours until this wedding was over, and we were all off the resort property.

"Yes?"

"There is a matter that I would like your assistance with."

"Of course," I said, expecting it to be some detail related to the wedding. Mr. Markham and I had had several chats about everything from the positioning of tables for the reception to whether or not the guests would need special transportation to the mainland after the wedding.

Mr. Markham opened his mouth, paused, then shook his head. "I do not know who else to consult. A man has arrived, a friend of Mr. Blackson's, and he insists on speaking to someone about the death of his friend. He didn't know what had happened, in fact. I broke the news to him, but now he wants to talk to someone who was there. Mr. Redding is not on the property. I've notified him, but he won't return until this evening, and I'd rather not disturb the bride or groom. The bride is in the spa, and the groom is on the golf course."

"Of course not, but I don't see what I can do."

"Well, you are the wedding planner. You met Mr. Blackson. I think his friend wants to speak with someone who was there . . . when the incident occurred . . . to confirm what I have told him. He seems to be having a hard time taking it in."

"I guess I can talk to him," I said, glancing at Mitch.

"I'll come with you," Mitch said. "The tennis lesson has another forty-five minutes to go."

We followed Mr. Markham into the resort and through a winding hallway. He paused in front of a heavy wooden door with his hand on the doorknob. "This is my office. Please take as long as you like."

"Does he know about the investigation?"

"Yes, I told him the police will want to speak to him, but I didn't tell him any of the details."

He opened the door and ushered us inside the large room with a view of the front of the resort. "This is Craig Abbott," Mr. Markham said. "Mr. Abbott, this is Mr. and Mrs. Avery. They were there when the incident occurred."

Mr. Markham asked if we'd like something to drink. "I can have a tray sent up with refreshments or some food."

Mitch and I declined, and Craig Abbott looked as if he'd barely heard Mr. Markham. I'd thought Ned was probably in his mid-twenties and Craig looked to be about the same age, but where Ned had been lean and had rather a dark, debonair look, Craig was shorter, stockier, and had light brown hair cut very short. His arms were disproportionately muscled, and I wondered how many hours he spent in the gym to get his bulky look.

The office had a desk backed by bookcases on one side of the room. A round conference table with rolling chairs sat on the other side of the room. Craig had been seated at the table but stood when we came in.

Mitch held out his hand. "Sorry about your friend. I'm Mitch."

"And I'm Ellie," I said, extending my hand as well. Mitch pulled out a chair for me.

Craig dropped back into the chair, his gaze scanning both of our faces. "So it's true? Ned really is dead?"

"Yes, I'm afraid so," I said as Mitch and I sat down across from him. "We were both there when it happened."

Craig leaned forward, one hand pressed to the table. "What exactly happened?"

"A golf cart he was driving overturned," I said, looking toward Mitch.

"I was the first to get there," Mitch said, his voice somber. "Ned had been thrown out of the cart and he had hit his head on the path. I think he died instantly."

I wondered if that was too much information, told too baldly, but Craig just shook his head and stared at the table. "That's what the manager guy said," he murmured quietly. "Golf cart wreck. I couldn't believe it." He raised his head and looked at us. "Who dies in a golf cart?"

"I'd never heard of it either, but, apparently, they can be quite dangerous," I said as gently as I could.

Craig continued as if I hadn't spoken. "He was showing off, wasn't he?"

"Umm . . . no, I don't think so," I said.

"He always likes to show off—be the best, the fastest, the quickest." He focused his attention fully on me. "Where did it happen?"

"At the ruin. Are you familiar with the island?"

He shook his head.

"There's a ruin of an older home inland from here. He was there photographing the wedding party. He said he needed to return to the resort for a battery. That's when it happened."

Craig sat back in his chair and ran his hand over his mouth.

The silence stretched. "Were you good friends?" I asked.

"Yeah. I've known him since high school. We played football together."

"Do you live in the area?" I asked, wondering if Ned had gotten in touch with Craig and told him he would be at Camden Island.

"Me? No, I live in Savannah too," he said.

I exchanged a puzzled glance with Mitch, which Craig noticed. He rubbed his hand over his mouth again. "You're wondering why I'm here." He glanced at a duffel bag positioned by the door that I hadn't noticed when we came in. A garment bag, which had been folded in half, had been placed on top of the duffel. The garment bag had a clear circle placed on one side, and I could see it contained a dark suit coat.

Craig sighed. "I might as well come clean. The manager says I'll have to talk to the police because his death is under investigation." Craig shook his head and muttered, "Man, *under investigation*. If I'd been smart, I guess I would have turned around and headed out the minute the desk clerk went to get the manager, but I was so stunned. I just couldn't believe it."

"Were you here to help Ned with the photography?" Craig was dressed casually in a collared polo shirt and denim shorts, the ribbing around the bottom of the sleeves cutting into his bulky arms, but he'd obviously prepared to dress more formally. I knew his name wasn't on the guest list. With the last name of Abbott, he'd have topped every list I had from invitations to seating arrangements, even ahead of our last name of Avery.

Craig shook his head. "No, not this time. There were a few times, when Ned had a really big event, that he asked me to help him. I didn't do much, actually, just holding reflective panels a few times and handing him new batteries, stuff like that. But this time, I wasn't here to help. He called to tell me to drop in. These wedding gigs are great. Good food, and what's one extra person? There's usually someone who doesn't show up. Ned always called when there was a good gig, not too far away."

I glanced at Mitch again, and I could see that he was thinking the same thing I was. *Here is a real-life wedding crasher.*

"But didn't people notice that you didn't know anyone?" I asked.

"Nah. I tell the friends of the bride that I know the groom, and friends of the groom that I know the bride. The secret is to ask them first who they're there for, the bride or the groom, then I say the opposite. Besides, no one really listens at these things anyway," he said, then his tone changed, losing its lightheartedness. "It seemed like a good joke, at the time." He focused his gaze on the table and said quietly, "And to have it happen right when he got the break for the show." His words weren't directed at us.

He was talking to himself, but I leaned forward and asked, "The photography show at King Galleries?"

Craig looked up. "Yes, you'd heard about it?"

"Only recently," I hedged. "How did the show come about?" I asked.

"I'm not sure. Ned had been trying to break into the art scene. He wanted to get out of doing strictly wedding stuff, but it paid the bills, really well, actually. He had done event photography for years, but hadn't had much luck with anything else. It's like everything else in life, I suppose. It's all about who you know, because he met some woman who was loaded and liked his stuff. He said she was his ticket into the art world. She could help him get a show."

"Hmm, I see," I said, but I didn't. I didn't see how it fit together at all.

Chapter Ten

"I know that look," Mitch said as we crossed the reception area on our way back to the tennis court.

"What look?"

"That contemplative, slightly worried look. He said something that's bothered you."

"Yes," I admitted slowly. "It was that bit about the woman who liked Ned's work. Ned must have been talking about Patricia. She and Gus are loaded, and she sponsored the show at King Gallery."

"Yes, I think that's right—it was probably Patricia."

"Okay, but if she wanted to support Ned's artistic work, why would she pull her sponsorship of the show only literally the day after he died? I don't think Gus and Patricia are having financial difficulties. If they were, they'd be trying to cut corners with the wedding, and I haven't seen any evidence of that. In fact, Patricia keeps expanding the guest list. No, I'm beginning to wonder if Patricia didn't want to sponsor the show for Ned from the very beginning."

We had left the resort and were walking across the lawn

112 *Sara Rosett*

to the tennis court. I glanced up, automatically checking the weather. A thin layer of clouds lay on the horizon to the west.

"So you're saying that Ned convinced her to help him somehow, and now that he's dead, she's not afraid to drop her support from the show?"

"I think that's exactly it. She's not afraid anymore. Remember that argument I overheard between Patricia and Ned in the kitchen? I can't remember their exact words, but I know Patricia said she'd done something once that she wouldn't do again. She could have been referring to the art show. And then Ned said she wouldn't want someone 'to find out.' I do remember that. Those were his exact words. I don't know who he mentioned—I didn't hear a name—but he had something, some kind of hold over her."

"You think Ned was blackmailing her," Mitch said, his face troubled.

"Well, it fits. And it would explain the look on her face after we realized he was dead, too."

"What look?"

I slowed my steps as we neared the tennis courts. I could hear the *ping* of tennis balls hitting rackets and the shuffle of feet skidding on the rough courts. "It was right after the wreck. I was down on the level of the path with you. I looked up. Almost everyone was lined up on the retaining wall above me. Everyone looked horrified, except Patricia. I think it was because her face looked so different from everyone else's—that's the only reason I noticed. She looked . . . well, the only word I could think of to describe it would be relieved."

"Ellie," Mitch said in a warning tone.

"I know," I said quickly. "I know it was just a look, and I could have interpreted it wrong. That's why I didn't mention it to the detective." I blew out a sigh. "I'll have to tell him now."

"Yes, I suppose so," Mitch said reluctantly.

"I'm not looking forward to that conversation." I slowed my steps. "Maybe I shouldn't say anything at all. I mean, you're right. It's all speculation based on a few words I happened to hear. I could be totally wrong. And Redding will find out about Ned's cancelled show and how Patricia was sponsoring it."

"You have to tell Redding," Mitch said suddenly, and I turned toward him. He'd stopped walking completely.

"I don't know—"

"Ellie, you've got to," Mitch said. A group of people moved by us, and Mitch waited until they were out of earshot before he continued. "Do you remember who Ned spoke to right before he left the picnic?" His voice was so intense that I stared at him.

"Yes, he was with Yvonne on the edge of the terrace and then he spoke to Patricia right before he left. I don't get it. What are you thinking?"

"What if Patricia told him to take Summer and Brian's cart? What if she knew the cart would overturn before he got down that hill?"

I stared at him a moment, then closed my eyes briefly as I put the pieces together the way Mitch had. "I don't know," I said, forcing myself to rearrange my thoughts. "Then that would mean we've been looking at this the wrong way the whole time—that Summer wasn't the intended victim. But what about the paintball and the poison ivy?"

"We assumed the three things were related," Mitch said. "But you said yourself that the golf cart accident is in a completely different league than the pranks. Maybe two different people planned the events—one person planned the pranks and another person planned the golf cart accident."

I rubbed my head and turned to walk a few paces away into the shade of one of the live oaks. The rhythmic *thunk* of tennis balls connecting with rackets filled the air. "I suppose that there could be two people instead of one, but then that would mean that Patricia loosened the lug nuts on the golf cart. I can't quite picture that. Do you think she knows what size socket she'd need? Do you think she even knows what a socket wrench is?"

Mitch leaned one hand against the tree as he answered. "You can find out almost anything on the Internet. Besides, it's not like removing lug nuts requires advanced technical knowledge. It's basically turning a wrench. Anyone who had enough strength could do that. And Patricia isn't exactly frail."

"No. She's quite tough. No, it's not that part that tripped me up. It's the thought of her getting her hands dirty—that seems totally out of character."

"When people are pushed, they do unusual things," Mitch said.

"But then there's also the element of the golf cart with the bride and groom sign," I said. "Why would she loosen the lug nuts on that cart instead of the one Ned was riding in?"

"Because all the other carts were identical," Mitch said. "She wouldn't be able to guarantee that Ned would leave the ruin in the same cart he arrived in. None of the rest of us had a specific cart we used. Remember when we stopped at the other side of the island and looked around before we reached the ruin?"

"You're right," I said with a small nod. "We all got out and looked around, then piled back into the carts, but I don't think anyone paid any attention to which cart they were in before. In fact, I bet you and I were in a different one than we started in because we parked at the back of the group, but we were one of the first to start off again so we took a cart near the front when we left to drive to the ruin."

"Exactly," Mitch said. "So by sending him to the golf cart reserved for the bride and groom, she would know exactly which one he'd take."

"And it was the closest one to the ruin. It would be plausible that she'd suggest he take it," I added.

"But how could she know that he'd need to go back to the resort early? How could she know his camera battery would die?" I asked.

"Well, if she figured out a way to sneak off and remove the lug nuts, I'm sure she could replace his camera batteries with ones that were almost out," Mitch said.

I rubbed my fingers over my forehead. I didn't want to agree with him. It was a tenuous theory, but it was possible, I supposed. "That's a lot of ifs. I'm *really* not looking forward to talking to Redding now," I said. "Oh, Mitch, if we're right, this will ruin the wedding. Summer will be so upset."

Mitch ran his hand along his jaw. "This box is open. Once it's open, you can't put anything back. Don't worry about Summer. She's pretty good at rolling with the punches."

"Mitch, we're talking about a woman's wedding day. You don't mess with a woman on that day. Revealing her stepmother-in-law is a murderer is about the worst thing that could happen."

"No, the worst thing that could happen would be revealing that her new *husband* is a murderer, and I don't think there's any danger of that. Summer's devoted to Brian, and he feels the same way about her. Once all the dust settles, that's the most important thing."

I shook my head at him. "Mitch, we've been married fifteen years, and you still don't understand women at all."

He grinned back at me. "Nope, not women in general. You, I've got a pretty good bead on you . . . at least most of the time. For instance, I know you won't be able to think about anything else until this mess with Ned is sorted out. You go find out if Redding is back yet, and I'll get the kids."

"Okay, so you're not *totally* clueless when it comes to women."

I headed back toward the elegant and imposing facade of the resort, dreading the conversation with Redding, but I also felt a bit relieved. If Ned really had been the intended victim, then that meant Summer only had to worry about pranks, not threats on her life. Of course that left out the possible family complications, if Patricia really had messed with the lug nuts, but I couldn't focus on that right now. And, having seen Julia and Graham leaving breakfast with their arms wrapped around each other's waists today, it seemed that Julia had turned her attention away from Summer. We had gone a whole day without another prank.

I trotted up the shallow steps to the resort and asked at the front desk if Detective Redding had returned. The clerk told me he had arrived back a few minutes ago. "I believe he is on his way to the upstairs conference room. If you'd like to contact him, you may use one of the house phones," he said, pointing to a phone on an end table near a rattan chair. "The conference room is extension twenty-two."

"Thank you." I sank into the chair and dialed. The phone rang, but no one answered. *He must not be in the conference room yet.* I decided I'd walk up and try to catch him there, but the wide grand staircase that doubled back on itself was roped off. A man in white coveralls was balanced on a ladder, which was set up on the landing. He moved his paintbrush over the trim, touching it up. A sign in front of the rope at the bottom of the stairs pointed me around the corner to the elevator.

Because our room was on the second floor and the kids

had boundless energy, we always herded them up the stairs, so I'd never ridden in the elevator. I turned the corner to enter the elevator alcove and found a logjam of people and suitcases. It was after two in the afternoon on Friday, check-in time for the resort. There was one elevator, the kind with an old-fashioned arrow above the doors pointing to which floor the elevator was on. The arrow was pegged out at the right and moving in very slow increments as the elevator descended.

I joined the long line to wait my turn, but then remembered the servants' staircase near the dining room that we had used during the behind-the-scenes tour. It wasn't off-limits to guests; most people just didn't take it because it was out of the way. I left the alcove and moved through the dining area toward the kitchen. The dining room wasn't busy, and the few waiters who were moving among the tables didn't pay any attention to me. I slipped into the little nook between the kitchen and the dining room, and moved to the door that had once separated the servants' "below stairs" world from the "upstairs" world of the wealthy owners. I pushed the heavy wooden door, but it only opened a few inches. I pushed harder, thinking that it must be the age of the door causing it to stick, but it only gave another inch or so. I looked down and realized something was lying on the floor, blocking its path. It was dim in the little alcove and it took me a minute to distinguish that it was an arm. It was a person.

I edged the door back a little bit more, wide enough that I could get my head and shoulders through the opening. "Are you okay?"

She didn't move or respond. All that I was able to take in was that it was a woman before the rapid thud of feet sounded above me, and Graham pounded down the bare wooden stairs.

I was already halfway in the door, so I slipped through the opening, carefully stepping over the woman. She had been on her side, her face turned away from me toward the floor. The door swung closed behind me as I scanned the motionless figure.

"Is she—" Graham hunched over the figure and gently pushed her shoulder, causing her to roll onto her back. It was Julia.

Some of her long, brunette hair covered her face, caught in her lipstick and in a gash on her forehead, which was bleeding at a steady rate, trickling through her hair and dropping into a growing puddle on the floor. Graham brushed the strands of hair out of her face with trembling fingers as he repeated her name.

Julia didn't look good. Her skin was an ashy color and she didn't respond at all to Graham's voice. "I'll get help." My voice came out high-pitched, sounding odd even to me. I stepped over Julia's legs and edged back through the door. I flew out of the little alcove and spotted a nearby table laid with china and linen. I yanked up several of the napkins, causing silverware to fly through the air and crystal glasses to rock.

A waiter coming from the kitchen said, "Hey, you can't—"

I dodged around his outstretched arm. "There's been an accident. Call an ambulance—or no, call Rebekah."

He looked blank, so I said, "The resort's nurse practitioner. Get her, and then call an ambulance."

I opened the door slowly so I wouldn't bump into Julia or Graham, who still hovered over her. I'd only been gone seconds, but her face looked much paler and the pool of blood was larger. Her eyes were closed, and if it hadn't been for the blood and her grayish complexion, she would have looked like something out of a fairy tale, the princess put into a deep sleep.

"Here." I handed the napkins to Graham, and he pressed them to her forehead.

"What happened?" I asked.

"I don't know. We were talking as we came down-stairs—the elevator is taking forever—and then she made a little noise and went flying. She must have tripped."

I looked down her long legs to her feet. She had on thick ankle-strap wedge platform sandals with at least three-inch heels. The navy and white print on the sandals went with her denim shorts and loose poet-style blouse. The strap of a camera, a large professional-looking one with a retractable lens, had been around her neck, but the fall down the stairs had tossed it around. When Graham rolled her over, the camera, with its cracked lens, caught on her shoulder.

I leaned forward and eased it to the side so that the strap wasn't pulling on her neck. I wasn't sure what else to do. She was obviously breathing, I could see that, but she was unresponsive to Graham's words and his gentle shakes of the shoulder. "They're calling for help. Someone should be here soon."

"Help me move her." He shifted around to her shoul-ders, still holding the napkin to her head as he moved. He motioned for me to stand at her feet. "I'll get her shoul-ders. You take her legs. We can carry her to the front, so we'll be in the lobby when the ambulance gets here." Gra-ham worked one hand under her shoulder.

"I don't think we should move her," I said, looking at the way Julia's head lolled to one side as Graham worked to get one hand under her shoulder. The loose, rag-doll limpness of her limbs set off warning bells. "No, we should leave her here."

"The ambulance will come to the front of the resort. If we're there it will save time." Below the bright fringe of his hair that had fallen forward as he struggled to move Julia, his expression was worried and his words ragged.

I pointed to the napkins. "But you'll have to let go of the napkins and that could start the bleeding again. I don't think you're supposed to move a person with a possible head injury."

"We'll be quick," Graham said, dropping the napkins and sliding his other hand under her shoulder.

The door inched open, and Rebekah's head appeared before I could reply.

"Hold that door," Graham said to her.

"I'll do no such thing." Rebekah's voice, crisp with authority, immobilized Graham. She stepped into the small space, and I shuffled up onto the stairs to make room for her. She picked up the bloody napkins and reapplied them to Julia's forehead. "Now, I need you to hold these napkins here to her forehead," she said, addressing Graham. "Yes, exactly like that. Don't remove them. The ambulance should be here in a few minutes." As soon as Graham started following her instructions, her tone became soothing. She continued to speak as she checked Julia's pulse, her eyes, and then gently ran her hands along each one of her limbs. "Mr. Markham, the resort manager, has been notified, and he will see that the EMTs are brought directly here."

Rebekah removed a small zippered pouch from one of her pockets, took out a pair of scissors, and snipped the strap of the camera. She gently untangled it from Julia's hair and bunched it together with the camera, which she held out toward Graham. But when Rebekah began her examination, he'd moved around to Julia's other side. While holding the napkins to her head with one hand, he had taken one of Julia's hands in his other hand, and I could tell he didn't intend to let go.

"Here, I'll hold it." I reached out for the camera as the faint wail of a siren sounded. Graham asked, "She's going to be okay, right? She will wake up in a few minutes, won't she?"

"You don't have to worry. The emergency techs here on the island are excellent, and if we need to, we'll call for an air evac to Brunswick."

I couldn't help but notice that Rebekah didn't actually answer his question.

Tips for an Organized Wedding

A bride needs lots of lists to keep track of everything:

- Contact list of vendors
- Contact list of wedding party members
- Guest list
- Contact list for the big day with information on other people to call (besides the bride/groom) if the unexpected happens
- Gifts received list to write thank-you notes

Chapter Eleven

After the EMTs disappeared out the heavy wooden door, I stood there a moment in the sudden quiet. The EMTs had assessed Julia's condition, carefully strapped her to a board, then moved her to a gurney. The last view I had of her, she was on the gurney, being rolled away through the doorway to the alcove, Rebekah on one side and Graham on the other.

After the EMTs arrived, I'd stayed up on the narrow staircase, out of everyone's way. I realized I felt a bit unsteady. I gripped the smooth wood of the banister and sat down on one of the steps, the camera still in my hands. The wooden stair treads felt hard and unforgiving, and I shivered. How badly hurt was Julia? The injury on her forehead looked bad, but did she have any internal injuries? She'd been so pale and motionless.

My gaze went to the pool of blood. The white walls and bare stair treads of the utilitarian staircase made the splash of the bright red at the foot of the stairs stand out. The low murmur of the waiters' conversation resumed in the dining room and filtered through the heavy door. I sent up a prayer for Julia and the medical people who would take care of her. I didn't know exactly what she'd done since she arrived on Camden Island—what she might have done to Summer—but I hoped she recovered from her fall.

I fished my phone out of my pocket and dialed Mitch's number. I could hear the kids' voices in the background when he answered. I told him about Julia's fall.

"Is she going to be okay?" Mitch asked quietly.

"I don't know. Rebekah said something about airlifting her to the mainland if they needed to."

"That doesn't sound good."

"I know. Maybe they won't need to do it."

"Are you okay?"

"Yeah. A little shaken up—you know how it is, you see something like that, and you can't help but think of how fragile life is." I blew out what the stroller brigade exercise leader called a cleansing breath. "But I'm all right. Just taking a few minutes to get my equilibrium back. I haven't seen Redding yet, and someone needs to tell Summer and Brian what has happened."

The line was silent for a moment, then Mitch said, "Let's wait and see what we hear about Julia's condition."

"I don't think we should wait. Graham went with her. Who knows how long he'll be gone? I hate to be insensitive and bring things back to the wedding, but the rehearsal and dinner are in"—I paused to check my watch—"three hours. Is this terribly crass to bring this up now? I hate to focus on wedding details at a time like this, but I don't know if Graham will be back by six. If Julia is transferred to the mainland . . . well, he may not make it back tonight or even tomorrow for the wedding. Brian and Summer need to know so that they can make plans." I ran my fingers along the grain of wood in the banister, keeping my gaze focused on it, not the blood on the floor. "I wish we didn't have to tell them," I added. "There's already been so much that has gone wrong."

"I know," Mitch said, and I could hear the concern in his voice. "But you're right. They need to know. Summer's pretty tough. She can handle it. I'll get the kids settled with the cousins who are babysitting tonight. Then I'll talk to Summer."

"Okay. I'll meet you in our room after I talk to Redding. Don't forget we have to change for the rehearsal."

"I know. Suit and tie," Mitch said grumpily. Despite all that had just happened, I smiled at his tone. Mitch didn't exactly enjoy dressing up.

"You'll look devastatingly attractive," I said. "And it won't be as bad as the tux you'll wear tomorrow."

"Don't remind me."

A woman in a resort uniform pushed through the door as I ended the call. She held a basket of cleaning supplies and started when she saw me. "Are you okay? Do you need help, ma'am?" she asked.

"No. No, I'm all right," I said as I put my phone away. "Just taking a break."

She nodded as she bent over the puddle of blood to clean it up, and I grasped the smooth wooden banister to lever myself up. It seemed that it was hours ago when I'd pushed through that door on my way to talk to Redding about Patricia. I turned to climb the stairs. I dropped Julia's camera off in our hotel room. I'd either return it to Graham or leave it with the front desk, if I didn't see Graham.

I went to the conference room. Redding was entering the room with Craig when I arrived. I held up a hand to draw his attention. "Sorry to interrupt. When you have a minute, I have some information for you."

"All right. I'll be with you in a moment." Redding

motioned me over to a set of club chairs positioned by a window.

My definition of "a moment" and Redding's definition were completely different. I sat in the chair, intermittently checking the time. At the half-hour mark, Craig emerged looking shaken. His scared expression reminded me of the kids when I caught them doing something they knew they shouldn't, which was at odds with his beefy physique. He nodded to me once, then headed out. Redding strode out of the room and stopped abruptly. He'd clearly forgotten I was waiting. "I'm sorry, Mrs. Avery, I can't speak to you right now. I have your cell phone number in the statement we took earlier." He took a few steps away from me and moved down the hall as he spoke. "I'll track you down as soon as I can."

Frustrated, I watched his back disappear around the corner, wondering if he'd just gotten the news about Julia. If that was what he was rushing off to check on, I could have given him the inside scoop. Well, that was that. I couldn't force Redding to listen to me. I headed back to our room and let myself inside. The first thing I saw was the thick binder of wedding details that I'd deposited on the bed after my lunch with Summer. The accident with Julia had pushed everything else out of my mind except how it would impact Brian and Julia, but there were still a ton of wedding details to follow up on. I had confirmed everyone's showtimes before lunch and tennis, but I only had a few hours to do final checks for the rehearsal and dinner.

I flipped to the section related to the rehearsal and set off in a quest to mark things off my list. First, I stopped by the gazebo where the wedding would take place. The chairs would be set up tomorrow. For the run-through tonight, chalk outlines had been placed on the grass, marking off the aisle and the areas where the wedding party would stand. Everything looked in order there, except for the clouds banking in the sky to the west. What had been a thin strip of wispy clouds now had grown thick and dark. I turned and hurried away from the ominous sight, reminding myself that there was a backup plan. The wedding could be moved indoors.

I hurried through the dining room, but paused for a second in the alcove. It was quiet there, and my thoughts went immediately to Julia, but I reminded myself I had things that must be done, so I pressed on to the kitchen and confirmed that the menu for the rehearsal dinner was already being prepped.

Corsages and boutonnieres made of white roses accented with lily of the valley and sweet pea had been delivered and had been placed in a special refrigerated storage area in the kitchen, which was reserved for floral arrangements. A quick peek into the banquet room at the end of the dining hall showed that the resort staff were laying out place settings while the florist moved from table to table, positioning centerpieces with the same flowers as the bridal bouquet. I checked off the last item on my list, thinking that the details related to the wedding itself were going exceptionally well. If only I could get everything else to run as well.

I was on my way back to my room to change when my phone rang. I assumed the unfamiliar number was Redding, but the male voice wasn't quite as deep as Redding's. "Ellie?"

"Yes. Who is speaking?"

"It's Graham. I need you to do something for me."

Graham was the last person I expected to hear from, but I had created a contact list for members of the wedding party with names of people they could call if something came up—names of people other than the bride and

groom—and since my name had been at the top of that list
I should have expected the call, but it still surprised me. I'd
assumed it might be hours before anyone heard from Graham. "Yes, of course. Where are you? How is Julia?"

"We're at—I don't even know the name of the city—
whatever city is closest to Camden Island on the mainland.
Julia is stable, but still unconscious." He let out a shaky
breath. "They want to keep her here for now, which is good.
I think. They're not talking about transferring her anywhere else, so that means she must be doing okay, right?"
He didn't wait for me to answer. He continued, his words
rushing together. "Anyway, now that things have calmed
down they need to admit her. Officially, that is. She's definitely in the hospital, but they need to do all the paperwork, and I don't have any of her information, her
insurance or anything like that. I don't have her parents'
phone number either, or I would have called them. I don't
even know where her phone is. Maybe it fell out of her
pocket?"

"I don't think so," I said. "I went up the stairs after
you . . . left, and I didn't see anything." The servants' stairs
were so barren that a cell phone would have been easy to
spot.

"This is terrible." Graham's voice sounded more and
more ragged as the conversation progressed. "I have to let
someone know she's in the hospital."

"It's okay. Just tell me what you need." I hadn't been
around Graham much, but the flustered, breathless tones
coming over the phone weren't like anything I'd heard
from him before.

"Sorry. Julia didn't have her purse with her. I'm sure she
left it in her room. If you could get the resort to open the
room, and look for her purse, that would be a start. Anything you find could help me out."

"Sure. Not a problem. Let me get the manager," I said

as I changed direction and headed for the desk, keeping Graham on the line. It took a few minutes to sort everything out, but soon I was following Mr. Markham up the stairs to the second floor. "Okay, we're on our way now. I'll call you back after they let me in her room."

"Thanks, Ellie." Graham sounded a little calmer now, but there was still an edge of worry in his voice. "I'm glad you gave out that contact list to us earlier. I really don't want to bother Brian or Summer with this."

"That's okay. That's what I'm here for. I'll check the room and call you right back." I'd told everyone that if they had any issues to call me and that I would help them sort out any problems that came up. I'd hoped to keep Summer out of any stressful situations, but I'd never imagined something like this.

Mr. Markham lingered on the threshold after opening Julia's door. It was similar to the other rooms I'd seen in the resort, but since the building had been a home at one point, all the rooms were a bit different. I figured some walls had been knocked down and some rooms combined to make space for bathrooms and storage closets for the resort. Julia's room was a bit smaller than mine or Summer's and it had a different layout with the bath tucked around a corner, but the bedding, curtains, and furniture all looked similar to the other rooms I'd seen. This room was very tidy. Not one piece of clothing was draped over a chair or the bed, and no stray pairs of shoes were scattered around the floor.

I'd expected her purse to be tossed on the bed or in a chair, but I didn't see it anywhere. I glanced in the bathroom. Her cosmetics bag and a flat iron sat beside the sink, its unplugged cord trailing over the tile floor. I moved to the large wooden armoire and opened it. Her clothes rested in neat stacks or hung on hangers on the rod. I saw an edge of leather half hidden behind a swimsuit cover-up. I pushed it aside and pulled the leather bag, a purse, out of the armoire. "I think this is it," I said over my shoulder to Mr. Markham.

Julia's purse, a satchel in a supple brown leather, would normally have made my mouth water—I love purses and handbags—but I was too focused on finding anything that would help Graham to indulge in a little purse envy.

I found her wallet and looked through it. I pulled out her driver's license and then flipped through a stack of credit cards until I found a laminated card with a policy number for health insurance. I called Graham back.

He answered on the first ring and I read both numbers off to him "Great. Thanks so much. That will help. Did you find her cell phone?"

"No, I haven't seen it. The resort manager and I will look around here some more and then maybe he can check the Lost and Found?" I looked toward Mr. Markham, raising my eyebrows. He nodded.

"What kind of phone is it?" I asked.

He named a brand, but I wasn't familiar with it and asked exactly what it looked like. "It's one of those huge ones with the oversize screen," he said. "You can't miss it. She has a cover on it with a picture of high heels and the screen saver is a picture of a palm tree on a beach."

"Okay. I'll call you back in a minute."

I handed off the wallet and the purse to Mr. Markham. "Perhaps these should go in the hotel safe?"

"Yes, of course." He slipped the wallet into an inside pocket of his suit jacket. "I will take care of it as soon as we leave here."

"Graham wants us to keep looking for her cell phone," I said, reaching past the hanging clothes to pat the back edges of the armoire storage area. "Nothing here."

Mr. Markham tucked the purse under his arm and moved to check the carpet around the nightstands. I scanned the pristine desk and opened a few drawers, but only found a resort notepad and a pen.

My phone buzzed. I didn't recognize the number so I answered as I moved across the room to Julia's suitcase, which was resting on a suitcase stand in the corner of the room.

"Mrs. Avery, Detective Redding, getting back to you. I'm available now, if you can come back to the conference room, I can see you."

I didn't have long before I needed to change for the rehearsal dinner, but after Redding's lecture to Patricia about how the investigation took priority over wedding activities, I wasn't about to mention it. "I can do that. It may take me a few minutes to get there, though."

Like the purse, the suitcase was a high-quality brand trimmed in leather. I wedged the phone onto my shoulder and unzipped the suitcase.

"I should be here for the next half hour or so," Redding said.

As I flipped the top of the suitcase open, Mr. Markham said, "Here it is." I could see him out of the corner of my eye, bracing a hand on the bed as he stood up, holding a large phone.

"I can come right now," I said as I reached to close the suitcase, but stopped when I glanced inside. I stepped back and shifted the phone off my shoulder into my hand. "On second thought, you're going to want to come to Julia Banning's room instead."

"The woman who was injured? Why?"

"She has a paintball gun and a socket wrench in her suitcase."

*   *   *

Redding arrived within minutes. Once we sorted out why Mr. Markham and I were in Julia's room, Redding's attention turned to the suitcase. He pulled on a pair of gloves. "What did you touch?"

"Quite a bit." I glanced around the room. "The armoire and the desk. And the suitcase. I unzipped it, then put my finger under the edge and flipped it back."

"I see." Redding leaned over the suitcase.

I hadn't touched it again, but Mr. Markham and I had spent the time waiting for Redding to arrive staring into the suitcase. A lightweight sweater, the one that Julia wore last night at the bonfire, had been placed so that it partially covered the paintball gun, which was on the very bottom of the suitcase, but the distinctive shape of the gun handle as well as the barrel were easy to distinguish as they stuck out beyond the fabric draping over it. A plastic tube of red paintball pellets was shoved down in one corner beside a socket wrench.

Redding took out a pen and used it to edge a Windbreaker up, which revealed a sandwich-sized zip-top plastic bag filled with brown leaves. I wasn't an expert on plants, but I was pretty sure the shriveled leaves were poison ivy. The warning rhyme *leaves of three, let them be* popped into my thoughts as I looked at the bag.

Before Redding removed his pen and the Windbreaker dropped back, I also saw the glint of several silver lug nuts in the groove at the bottom edge of the suitcase. I'd inched forward to look over his shoulder. I hurriedly shifted back a step as Redding turned, his gaze sweeping around the room. He went to the window, which looked out over the front of the resort, and examined the frame and glass.

It was like the window in our room, a paned single-hung window with two thumb latches and no screen on the outside. He didn't touch anything, just pulled his phone out of his pocket and made a call, requesting a crime scene technician. "Pay special attention to the window and the suitcase," he said before ending the call.

I glanced back at the suitcase and tried to rearrange my thoughts. Was I so wrong, so off base, about Patricia? I wished I hadn't contacted Redding so quickly. If I'd waited an hour or two, the paintball gun, lug nuts, and socket wrench would have been found, and I could keep my crazy theories to myself, but, like Mitch said, I'd opened the box. I was sure Redding wouldn't forget I'd wanted to talk to him, but at this point, what was the use of pointing out to him the possibility that Ned was blackmailing Patricia? It looked like I was completely wrong. The golf cart accident and the pranks all had been arranged by not two people as Mitch and I had thought, but a single person—Julia. And I had completely misread her, too. Despite the lovey-dovey atmosphere between her and Graham, she still must have been fixated on Brian.

Redding replaced his phone and moved to a door that connected to the next adjoining room. "Whose room?" Redding asked, looking toward Mr. Markham.

Since I'd flipped the suitcase open, Mr. Markham had been nervously wiping his forehead. He gave it another swipe as he said, "I believe that is Mr. Graham Murphy's room."

Redding used his gloved hand to try the doorknob. It turned, and he pushed the door partway open with his elbow, revealing clothes discarded on the floor and strewn across every surface, except the bed, which was neatly made. Obviously, the maids had been in earlier today and made the bed, but left everything else as it was. Redding let the door swing closed, then touched the dead bolt with a key slot instead of a lever. "I need this door to stay locked."

As Mr. Markham pulled a ring thick with keys out of a

pocket and locked the door, Redding pointed to the purse, phone, and wallet, which Mr. Markham had removed when I told him Redding was on his way to see the suitcase. Mr. Markham had lined the items up neatly on the foot of the bed. "And these belong to Julia Banning?"

"Yes. I found the purse in the armoire," I said.

"I handled it as well," Mr. Markham added. "I was going to put it in the hotel safe, but then . . ." His gaze shifted to the suitcase.

"Yes. All right. Thank you, Mr. Markham." Redding removed a plastic evidence bag from his inside pocket, shook it open, and prodded the items into the bag before sealing it. "If you'll see that the crime scene techs are admitted when they arrive?" Redding moved to the door to the hallway and opened it.

"Of course," Mr. Markham said as he and I filed through the door. "Let me know if we can be of any other assistance."

"Just make sure this door stays locked as well until the techs arrive."

Mr. Markham said, "I will have the access code changed and escort the technicians here myself as soon as they arrive." He nodded to Redding and moved down the hall, again running his hand along his brow line.

I gestured to the phone encased in the plastic bag that Redding held loosely in his hand as we followed a few paces behind Mr. Markham. "Graham wanted us to look for her phone so he could contact her family. He doesn't have the numbers."

"I see," Redding said. He maneuvered the phone around inside the plastic bag, then hit the button to wake it. An image of a palm tree filled the screen. "No pass code. I'll see that he gets the information. Now, what was it you wanted to speak to me about?"

"Oh, that. It's not important now."

We had been walking toward the main staircase, but Redding stopped, and I had to turn toward him. "If you have information related to the case, you're obligated to share it."

"I wouldn't exactly call it information," I hedged. "More like speculation. But everything in that room points to Julia. She was the one who did those things. . . ." Redding zeroed in on the uncertainty in my tone.

"You don't think she is responsible?"

"I don't know. A few days ago I would have said yes, she's the person most likely to be involved—because of her history with Brian. But after watching her with Graham the last few days . . . well, she *seems* to be in love with him." I looked down at the intricate vine pattern on the carpet. "The more I saw her and Graham together, the more convinced I was that she was over Brian. She seemed . . . well, she only had eyes for Graham. At least, that's what it seemed like to me."

"And yet Mr. Murphy doesn't have her family's phone numbers. Is their relationship a recent one?"

"I have no idea."

"So this speculation you have, it's not related to Julia?"

"No," I admitted.

"This case isn't closed yet, Mrs. Avery. It may be closed very shortly, but if you have any information . . ."

As Mitch said, I'd opened this box, and I couldn't put anything back in the box now. "I hope I'm completely wrong, and if I am, I would be so grateful if this . . . bit of information . . . didn't get out." I looked up and down the hallway. Mr. Markham had stepped into the elevator. Redding and I were alone in the hallway.

"I'll be as discreet as I can."

I nodded. I understood it was all he could promise. "Okay. As I said, it probably doesn't matter anymore, but it's about Patricia Abernathy and Ned Blackson. I think it's possible Ned was blackmailing her."

Redding's eyebrows moved up a fraction of an inch. "You'd better come with me to the conference room."

"Mom, where have you been?" Livvy asked as I practically skidded into the lobby.

It was a miracle I hadn't broken a leg sprinting down the stairs in my high heels. My shoes of choice were either tennis shoes or boat shoes. My usual activities of cleaning, sorting, and organizing, not to mention keeping up with two kids, required casual clothes. For client meetings I had a couple of business-casual outfits that I wore with medium heels, but I rarely wore a heel over an inch high, so I felt a bit tottery as I leaned down to reposition the barrette that was already slipping through Livvy's hair.

I drew in a breath to calm my racing heartbeat. "I had a meeting. I got here as fast as I could." I had spent the time in the conference room with Redding going through what I knew about Patricia and Ned while trying to avoid sneaking glances at my watch. I remembered Redding's sharp words to Patricia about the seriousness of a murder investigation and how it took priority over everything else. I didn't want to ask to cut things short so I could go change for a wedding rehearsal. Thankfully, he'd wrapped things up, and I'd been able to scoot back to the room to change into my silky wrap dress in a soft green. Then I'd twisted my hair up into what I hoped looked like an intentionally messy loose chignon and dashed for the lobby where we were all to meet.

"You look very nice," I said to Livvy as I smoothed her hair and snapped the barrette back into place. She had on a flower print dress and ballet flats with her cross-body purse, which hung heavily against her hip.

"Daddy fixed my hair," she replied, her tone indicating that he was to blame.

Mitch said, "You know hair bows are not my thing."

I shot him a quick smile. He was hopeless when it came to fixing Livvy's hair. I turned back to her. "You know you can't read tonight, right?" I said. She never went anywhere without at least two books, one to read and a spare, her "just in case" book, she called it.

Livvy frowned. "Mom, you know banning books is wrong. We have a whole week about that at school and how bad it is."

I managed to keep a straight face as I said, "This is only a temporary ban. I'm not saying you can't read the books ever, just not tonight. Or tomorrow at the wedding," I added, as I pictured Livvy sneaking a book out of her purse during one of the ceremony's songs as she stood in front of everyone.

Livvy looked like she wanted to argue, but I hugged her close and whispered in her ear, "It's okay. I'll let you stay up later tonight and read in bed."

That made her happy. I stood up and surveyed my guys. Mitch looked handsome in his suit and tie, but he was already shifting his head, moving his collar around. Nathan, a miniature version of Mitch, stood pulling at his tie, his pockets on his small suit coat bulging. I was sure they were filled with Legos and Hot Wheels. "You two clean up pretty good. Very handsome," I pronounced. Nathan's chest swelled, and Mitch settled his tie at his neck. "We may look good now, but I assure you, the last half hour wasn't pretty."

"I think you did a great job, considering you were on your own," I said. "Sorry I wasn't there to help." As we moved across the grass to the gazebo, the kids sprinted ahead, and, in a low tone, I told Mitch what had happened.

"Wow. So it was Julia after all," Mitch said, extending his arm.

I tucked my hand into the crook of his elbow. "Looks that way. Although, Redding seemed to take everything I said about Patricia and Ned seriously. Did you tell Summer and Brian?"

"About Patricia? No, I just found them a few minutes ago. I only had time to tell them about Julia. Brian has asked one of the ushers to stand in for Graham."

Summer saw me and moved across the grass. She reached out and gripped my hand. "It's awful about Julia, isn't it?"

I agreed, but kept all other news to myself. This wasn't the time to tell her about the suitcase in Julia's room. Brian called for everyone's attention and summarized what little information he had about Julia, simply saying she'd had an accident and was in the hospital. "I know we are all hoping and praying for her recovery." He looked Summer's way as he said, "Summer and I don't want to do anything unsuitable, but since you have all gathered here this weekend, we feel we should go ahead with the rehearsal and ceremony."

I heard several murmurs of agreement as Brian clasped his hands together and said, "In that case, we'll continue."

Someone had a question for Brian and he turned away to answer it as Summer looked toward me. She widened her eyes. "It's finally here, our wedding rehearsal."

She was smiling widely and shot a quick glance at Brian who, despite being in the middle of a conversation with one of his groomsmen, seemed to feel her gaze and looked toward her. They exchanged one of those wordless glances that only couples who know each other very well can indulge in.

"Well, let's get this show on the road," I said.

Brian heard me and said, "Yes, let's get going. We have filet mignon waiting." Several of the groomsmen murmured their approval.

Summer rolled her eyes and said to me, "It's always about the food with them." She pressed a hand across her midsection. "But come to think of it, I haven't had a thing to eat since lunch."

"Do you want me to get you something? I'm sure the kitchen could put together a little snack for you." I didn't want Summer to get light-headed or feel shaky during the rehearsal. The lunch we'd shared on the terrace had been several hours ago.

"Oh no. I'm fine. Feeling great, actually." She half turned so she faced the group surrounding us and raised her voice. "Okay, everyone, go to the places Ellie assigned you. When everyone's in position"—she turned and looked toward the members of the string quartet set up inside the gazebo—"the music will begin. Ushers, you're up first."

Summer moved around, deftly organizing everyone into the correct order for the procession. I'd offered to run this part of the rehearsal for her, but she'd waved me off, saying, "I do this sort of stuff all the time for the congressman. It will be a piece of cake." She worked the crowd like an expert, shifting people into position, including the mothers-in-law, who were carefully avoiding each other. When she came to Yvonne, Summer gave her a sunny smile, which Yvonne returned, but she only gave Summer a small polite upturn of the corners of her lips.

The music started up. "That's my cue," Mitch said, kissing me on the cheek before he strode off. I motioned for Nathan and Livvy to follow me. Earlier when I'd checked the setup, I'd pre-positioned the box with the ring pillow and basket for flower petals, placing it behind a lattice screen that divided the audience seats from the staging area where the attendants waited. I handed Nathan the silky pillow.

"Why do the rings have to have a pillow? And why do I have to carry it?" Nathan asked, and I could tell he was having serious second thoughts about toting around the frilly pillow.

"Tradition. Aunt Summer asked you especially to do this. It's a very important job. Out of all the cousins, she picked you," I said, hoping to cut off any protests. He looked for a long moment at the pillow, then said, "Okay, but I'm not doing it again. No more weddings."

"That's fine. Let's just get through this one."

I handed Livvy the empty basket. "Where are the flower petals?" she asked. "You said there would be petals."

"There will be tomorrow. Today, just pretend. Hurry, get in line over there in front of Aunt Summer."

The music started. The minister took his place under a wire arch positioned over the entrance to the gazebo. Tomorrow, the arch would be decorated with flowers and would frame Brian and Summer as they exchanged their vows on the steps leading to the gazebo. Mitch began the walk down the aisle with his mother on his arm.

A shout, loud enough to be heard over the music, caused heads to turn. "Wait! I'm here." The musicians faltered to a stop as we all turned in the direction of the voice.

Graham, dressed in a T-shirt, khaki shorts, and flip-flops, jogged across the grass.

Chapter Twelve

Graham's jog trailed off to a brisk walk. "Sorry." He sucked in a deep breath. "Sorry, man. I tried to get here before it started."

Brian, who had been waiting off to the side, trotted over to Graham. "What are you doing here? How is Julia?" he asked as they exchanged a brief guy hug, slapping each other on the back.

Everyone had all fallen silent at Graham's shout and the whole wedding party must have been curious about Julia's state because no one started talking.

"She's stable," Graham said, stepping back. "They have her sedated."

"Oh," Brian said. "Sorry. I thought since you were here that she might be . . ."

Graham looked down at the ground. "There's nothing I can do right now. The doctors told me to take a break, get out of their hair for a while. I'll go back later tonight."

"How did you get here? Hasn't the last ferry already run today?" Brian asked.

"I hired a private boat to get me over here. It's coming back for me at eleven tonight."

"You didn't have to do that."

Graham slapped him on the back. "I couldn't leave you hanging on the night of your rehearsal."

"Thanks, man. Glad you could make it, but if you need to leave, just head out."

Graham nodded and plucked at his T-shirt. "I'm not exactly dressed for this. Let me get changed."

"All right, I'm sure we'll have to run through it several times. I've got Lance standing in for you until you get back."

As the two men parted, I glanced at Meg. "Can you keep an eye on the kids for me? I'll just be a moment."

"Sure," she said, leaving the row of bridesmaids.

I hurried across the grass as fast as my heels allowed. "Graham, hold on."

I caught up with him at the top of the shallow steps where he'd paused when I called him. "Did Redding get in touch with you? Did you get the contact information for Julia's family?"

"Yes, her sister will be here tomorrow." Even though we were far away from the wedding party, Graham lowered his voice. "And he told me about what he'd found in Julia's suitcase. I can't believe it. I'm completely stunned that she would—" He looked away at the horizon. "I haven't known her that long, but I had no idea. I never would have suspected she'd do those things. I know Summer and Brian weren't happy that I brought her, but she kind of attached herself to me and wouldn't take no for an answer."

I thought of Redding's questions about their relationship. "So you have only been dating awhile?"

"About a month. The crazy thing is that I didn't even know she was the one who behaved so badly when Brian broke up with her. I met her online. Brian and I are both so busy that we don't see each other much, especially with him in Tallahassee and me in Macon. Our paths don't cross as much as they did when we were kids. I knew about his 'wacko ex,' as he called her, but I'd never met her. So I had no idea Julia was that girl until we arrived."

"But she had to have known if she brought all those things. She had to have planned it."

"I know. She never let on. When I got the official invite in the mail two weeks ago, Julia was with me. I didn't show her the invitation, only told her it was on Camden Island, but she must have seen the names on the invite or maybe she knew about the wedding some other way." He shook his head and blew out a sigh.

"It was in the newspapers here in Georgia and in Florida, anywhere Brian or Summer had family." I'd seen the copies of the newspaper announcements.

"She said she'd never been here, to Camden Island, and would love to see it, so I asked her if she wanted to be my plus one." He let out a little laugh. "I thought she liked me."

"For what it's worth, I thought so, too," I said, thinking of those adoring looks I'd seen her sending Graham's way. She must be quite an actress, but then again if she was motivated to hurt Summer she wouldn't want Brian to suspect she was involved, not if she wanted a chance with him later. And that had to be her goal, didn't it? Or else she was doing everything out of spite and revenge. I suppressed a little shiver, thinking how awful it would be if that was what motivated you. I wouldn't wish her condition on anyone, but if that was her mental state, then I was glad she was safely off Camden Island.

"So are you going back to the hospital?" I asked.

Graham lifted one shoulder in a small shrug. "I think I have to. I'm all she's got at the moment. I'll go back tonight and stay with her until her sister arrives."

"What do the doctors think?"

"They're not telling me much. I'm not official family or anything, but I overheard enough to know that they're worried about swelling of the brain. They've got her in a medically induced coma. Somehow, that may help the swelling go down."

"Oh, Graham," I said. "That's awful."

"I know, but they say they may be able to bring her out of it tomorrow or the next day." Graham looked over my shoulder as the strains of classical music floated through the air. "I didn't want to tell Brian how serious it was. He doesn't need that on top of everything else, you know?"

"Yes. Right. Well, I have to get back."

I returned and took charge of the kids from Meg, and sent them off down the aisle with instructions to walk super slow. "Pretend you're playing Mother May I, and you're only allowed to talk one medium step at a time." They did great, even when they had to do it over and over again. By the fourth run-through everyone had it down and even the minister's microphone was working. Graham had returned during the second round, dressed in a dark suit, threading his tie through his shirt collar as he walked across the grass. He blended in smoothly, handing over the ring from Nathan to Brian and escorting Meg down the aisle.

I could tell they were about to wrap up, so I whispered to the kids to go to Dad when they were dismissed, and I slipped away to check on the dinner in the banquet room. I wasn't the only one who'd had that idea. I entered the room and heard Patricia's nasal tones. "This is unacceptable. *Completely* unacceptable."

She was speaking to a waitress, a young woman with long, black hair tied back in a ponytail, who said, "I'll get another cloth and reset the table."

"There is no time for that now. Everyone is coming directly here," Patricia snapped. "No, I need to see the manager. I expect a discount for this sloppy presentation."

"What's wrong, Patricia?" I asked. The tables were arranged in a U-shape, with the head table forming the bottom of the U. Patricia was at the far side of the room at the end of one of the long rows that extended out forming the sides of the U.

"Look at this. This flower arrangement looks hideous, and there's water on the tablecloth."

The centerpieces on the tables held the same flowers Summer had picked for her bouquet: white roses, lily of the valley, and sweet pea. "That one does look a little beat up, but I think we need the florist, not the manager. I know she brought a few extra arrangements in case there was a problem."

The waitress arrived back with another tablecloth and several people following her. "The florist is in the kitchen, if you'd like to speak to her," the waitress said as she and her crew quickly stripped the table of the flatware, china, and glasses, changed the cloth, and began to reposition everything. Within a minute, the place settings were aligned and the tablecloth was pristine.

"Indeed, I do want to speak to the florist." Patricia stomped off, and I followed her, carrying the offending arrangement.

"That is not my work," the florist said when I set the centerpiece down on the counter in the little work area off the kitchen. Summer had told me that the resort catered so many events that they had a special area for floral preparations setup, but I hadn't really looked around it until now. I'd only taken a quick look earlier in the day to make sure the flowers had arrived.

A long counter filled one side of the narrow room and

the other held two large refrigerators, which were stuffed to overflowing with the flowers that would be used tomorrow for the arch, the centerpieces, the bouquets, the corsages, and the boutonnieres.

"You're saying that you didn't make this centerpiece?" Patricia asked, her lips pinched together in a way that made the fine lines radiating out from her lips stand out.

The florist, Denise, was a short, roly-poly woman in her forties. In the few interactions I'd had with her, she had been very easy to work with. She reached out one plump hand and spun the arrangement around so that she could see it from every side. She pushed it away with a look of distaste. "I did the initial arrangement, but I would never put something that looked like that on a table at an event."

She shifted the low vase around and pointed to the crumpled long green leaves of the lily of the valley and then gently cupped a crushed white rose that hung from a broken stem. "No, this is inexcusable. I will speak to the waitstaff. Someone must have bumped it or dropped something on it." She shook her head as she turned to slide open the door on the large refrigerator. "I have an assistant, but I check every arrangement myself." She pulled out a duplicate of the centerpiece and set it beside the beat-up arrangement. "I assure you I would not let that horrible-looking arrangement go out this door. Every arrangement on the table was in excellent condition earlier."

"I don't care whose fault it is, the fact remains that you tried to pawn off a subpar flower arrangement on us, and I will not have that," Patricia said. "I expect to see a discount on the final bill."

The florist ran her gaze over Patricia, then said, "I won't charge you for one of the centerpieces."

She'd obviously dealt with women like Patricia before

and had decided it was better to knock something off the final bill than argue.

"Thank you, Denise." I scooped up the new arrangement. "This will be perfect. Very smart of you to make an extra arrangement."

Patricia sniffed and seemed to want to linger, but I waved for her to precede me through the doorway. "We better get back out there before everyone arrives from the rehearsal," I said.

"Yes. I suppose so," she said reluctantly, then looked back to the florist. "There better not be any crushed or bruised flowers tomorrow. I'll check everything myself." She turned and stomped out the door, her words floating back, "You really have to watch these people. They will take advantage at every opportunity. . . ."

I paused at the door. "I'm sorry about that."

Denise waved her hand. "Typical monster-in-law. Don't worry about it. I've seen worse."

Glad I hadn't become a florist, I replaced the flower arrangement as the first of the wedding party came in the door. Mitch arrived with Livvy and Nathan, and I had them check the place cards until they found our four seats on one of the long sections. We settled into our chairs, Mitch and I in the middle, with a kid on each side of us. Summer and Brian took their seats at the center of the head table, and the food service began.

We had a delicious spring mix salad with feta cheese and dried cranberries, then filet mignon, baby red potatoes, and roasted mixed vegetables. The expensive steak would have been wasted on the kids, but Summer had thought of them. They were each served a bowl of gourmet macaroni and cheese, which they enjoyed, but their favorite part was that the menu for the dinner was impressed on large chocolate wafers, which had been centered on each dinner plate when we sat down to eat. I made the kids save the chocolate until most of their mac and cheese was gone. The kids finished eating long before all of the adults. I could tell Livvy was chafing under the "no-reading" ban, fidgeting, and looking longingly toward her purse, so I gave her my phone and told her she could take some pictures.

Eventually, Livvy asked if she and Nathan could go play board games in the library with their cousins. "Madison said she would be there." Madison was older than Livvy, and Livvy adored her. I'm sure we would hear "Madison this" and "Madison that" all the way home.

I glanced over at Nathan, who was licking the last of the chocolate from the fingers of one hand, while lining up his Hot Wheels cars around his plate. The servers were circulating through the room, topping off drinks. The toasts were about to begin.

"In a little while. After the toasts," I said.

Livvy sighed loudly and went back to taking pictures with my phone.

At the head table, Gus picked up a glass of champagne and cleared his throat. The murmur of conversation died away as everyone shifted their attention to him. "Everyone who knows me, knows I don't go in for this sort of thing." He circled his glass of champagne, indicating the room. "Fancy dinners, making speeches." Patricia, seated beside him, closed her eyes. I bet she wanted to stand up and rip that glass out of his hand and give the toast herself.

Gus cleared his throat again. He looked toward Brian and Summer, and his face relaxed into a smile. "But for you two, I'd do anything." He lifted his glass toward the couple. "Summer, welcome to the family." Brian and Summer clinked their glasses against Gus's. Beside me, I heard

the shutter click rapidly, and I wished I'd thought to silence all the sounds on the phone, but no one else seemed
to notice. Everyone was watching the front of the room.

Gus sat down and Brian stood to respond to the toast.
There was a moment during all the shifting and movement
that I thought Summer's face looked strained, but when
Brian glanced down at her, she smiled back as radiant and
beautiful as I'd ever seen her. I missed Brian's words because I was focused on Summer's face, but he must have
said the right things because a murmur of "aww" went
around the room when he finished. They touched their
glasses together, and we all sipped along with them. Summer put her glass down and that same look of strain came
over her again, but it vanished when Meg, who was sitting
on the other side of her, said something. Summer turned
her way, and I couldn't see her face anymore. Meg braced
her shoulders and stood, giving a beautiful, obviously
memorized toast, but it was sweet and Summer sent Meg a
special smile, then Summer raised her glass again toward
her maid of honor.

"How do you think Summer is doing?" I asked Mitch,
who had his arm along the back of my chair.

"She looks happy."

Graham toasted the couple, only saying a few words,
but everyone understood that he had other things on his
mind.

"Is that the last one?" Livvy whispered loudly. "Can I
go find Madison now?"

I glanced at Mitch. "They have been very good."

Mitch nodded. "Yeah, I think they can skip the rest of
the toasts." He tilted his head. "Come on, let's see if your
cousins are there."

Nathan pocketed his cars in seconds. "If only he'd clean

up his room so quickly," I murmured as Mitch edged behind my chair, the kids following him closely.

Mitch slipped back in during the pause after another toast. "They're playing Candy Land," he said. "Nathan's not too excited about it, but they promised Battleship was next."

After a few more toasts, there was a general shuffling as the event wound down. Chairs were pushed back, some people stood and moved to talk to different groups of people. Brian stood, buttoned his suit coat, and whispered something in Summer's ear before moving to a group on the far side of the room. Summer dipped her head and pressed her napkin to her lips, which was perfectly normal, but there was something about her posture, her slightly hunched shoulders, that didn't look right.

"I think I'll check on Summer," I said, standing. I slipped into Brian's vacated chair. Meg and the other of the bridesmaids had pulled their chairs closer and were looking at photos on someone's phone.

"Summer, are you okay?" Now that I was closer to her, I could see that her face was flushed.

She blew out an unsteady breath. "No. I feel like I'm going to be sick."

Tips for an Organized Wedding

A Wedding Budget

The first step to staying within your budget is to actually sit down and figure out a total amount you want to spend, which may involve discussions with various family members. Traditionally, the bride's family covers the wedding ceremony and reception while the groom's family takes care of the rehearsal dinner and the honeymoon, but there are plenty of variations on how expenses are covered, so make sure everyone is in agreement on who is paying for which portion. A shared electronic spreadsheet can help everyone keep track of expenses. Decide what portion of the day is most important to you and allocate the budget accordingly.

Chapter Thirteen

"**I** do not want to throw up at my rehearsal dinner," Summer said through clenched teeth.

"No, of course not. Let's get you out of here."

Summer stood, tottered for a second, then regained her equilibrium. I'd reached out to steady her, but she put up a warning hand.

She didn't want anyone to know she wasn't feeling good. I could understand that. I remembered the nearly hysterical reaction of one of the bridesmaids to the poison ivy. Summer shuffled along the edge of the room. Once I was sure she wasn't going to fall over, I managed to catch Mitch's eye and motioned my head toward the door. The banquet room was at the back of the restaurant's dining room. Mitch met us outside the banquet room doors.

"Summer, you look overheated," he said. "Do you need some air?"

"She's not feeling good," I said.

Summer ran a hand over her forehead. "It came on so quickly. It just hit all at once. Oh, I hope it wasn't something in the food. That would be terrible, to food-poison the wedding party."

"I'm sure you'll be fine in a little bit," I said, but I wasn't sure of anything.

Summer pressed a hand to her abdomen and grimaced.

"Let's get you up to your room," I said. "Do you think you can make it?"

She nodded and swallowed thickly. Mitch said, "I'll get Brian."

I shuffled off, one hand under Summer's arm and the other around her back as we moved through the tables of the dining room. I led her to the elevator. She wasn't in any shape for the stairs. Thankfully, the little alcove was empty and the elevator came almost immediately. She leaned against the wall as the elevator creaked into motion. Her cheeks were bright pink now. She rubbed her eyes. "Ellie, what's wrong with the lighting in here? You look odd."

"Nothing." The lighting looked normal to me, but then I looked more closely at her eyes. Her pupils were dilated, which I knew couldn't be good. A *ding* rang out as the doors opened. She had her room key card in her pocket, and I got her through the door and into the bathroom before she threw up.

I held her hair back for her, then handed her a wet washcloth as she collapsed back against the tile wall. "I'm calling Rebekah," I said.

She raised her hand a few inches, but she moved slowly as if the small movement took a great deal of effort. "Oh, don't do that. I think I feel a little better." She'd tipped her head back against the wall and spoke with her eyes closed.

"I'll get you some water," I said, and moved into the room. I didn't care what Summer said, my "mom senses" were tingling. Something was very wrong.

Rebekah arrived, took Summer's vital signs, and reached for the phone. "We need to get her to the hospital."

"The hospital?" Brian said. He was on the floor of the bathroom beside Summer, his arm around her shoulders. She hadn't wanted to move.

Rebekah didn't answer him. Instead, she spoke into the phone. I couldn't understand what she said, but her words were sharp and there was concern in her gaze as she turned back to us. "The ambulance will be here shortly."

Summer was lying against Brian, her face flushed and her limbs droopy. Her lethargic manner alarmed me more than her nausea and her flushed skin. Summer was not one to stand by and let others decide what was best for her. She wasn't speaking up—in fact, she didn't seem aware of the conversation at all—and that concerned me. Brian ran his hand across Summer's forehead, brushing back her hair. Her eyelids fluttered, but that was her only reaction.

Rebekah said to Brian, "Her pulse is slow and erratic, and her pupils are dilated. Those symptoms combined with the gastric distress indicate she may have ingested a toxin."

Brian blinked once, then said, "How long until the ambulance gets here?"

"It should only be a few minutes."

Brian looked toward Mitch. "Can you find Caroline? I want her to come with me."

"Of course." Mitch leaned over and touched Summer's cheek. "Hang in there, Summer." She didn't respond, and Mitch hurried out of the room, his face tight with worry. My heart went out to him, but I was glad Brian had asked him to find Caroline. He'd feel better doing something rather than just standing around, which was all I could do as Rebekah and Brian cared for Summer as she roused and her body tensed with another attack of nausea.

I slipped out of the crowded bathroom and waited in the hotel room until I heard the sirens. The EMTs came, and the whole awful scene that had played out earlier with Julia was repeated—the confusion and rush that accompanied the arrival of the EMTs, the calmness of their voices as they asked questions and moved Summer to a gurney, speaking to her in normal, everyday voices, informing her of their every move even though Summer barely acknowledged them.

I watched the gurney trundle away down the hallway, Caroline on one side and Brian on the other, feeling scared and worried. They took the gurney down through a service elevator, and I sprinted down the main staircase to the lobby and out through the main door. I flew down the shallow steps at the edge of the veranda and rounded the corner of the resort in time to see the ambulance lumber down the shell drive at a moderate pace. It had happened very quickly and since they had emerged from the service entrance where there were only a few spectators, I doubted most of the wedding party knew what had happened. I had hustled Summer out of the banquet room quickly, and apparently Mitch had managed to tell Brian and Caroline what had happened discreetly.

I crunched across the shell drive and joined Mitch and Rebekah. Mitch turned to me. "Rebekah says that they will probably call for a medical air evacuation and take her to the nearest hospital."

"It's that serious?" I asked, my heart sinking. Summer had looked awful, but I'd hoped that Rebekah would be more reassuring.

"Yes, I'm afraid so," she said, her gaze full of sympathy.

"What do you think happened?" I asked.

Rebekah glanced away, clearly not wanting to speculate.

Mitch said, "Please tell us what you're thinking. You already know that someone made sure Summer came in contact with poison ivy. There were other incidents as well. Someone may have . . ." He swallowed, overcome by emotion.

"Upped their game," I said, finishing the sentence for him. "That's what you're thinking, isn't it?" He gave a reluctant nod, and I added, "I don't want to think about it either, but with everything that's happened . . . it could be possible."

"But you know what that means, don't you?" Mitch asked.

"Yes." I didn't want to think about what else that meant. "We were wrong about Julia."

"I'm afraid I'm lost here," Rebekah said, breaking into our intense conversation. "There's obviously some huge undercurrents that I'm missing."

I looked at Mitch with raised eyebrows. He gave a small head nod, and I said, "After the incident with the poison ivy, we were pretty sure that Julia—the woman who fell down the stairs today—had planted the poison ivy. She had some . . . issues with Summer's fiancé, Brian, in the past. The police found evidence in Julia's room today. It looked like she was responsible for the pranks on Summer as well as the golf cart accident."

"Wait." Rebekah took a step back. "You're saying that the woman we sent off to the hospital earlier today—the one who fell down the stairs—was responsible for that photographer's death?"

"Well, it looked that way, but now . . ." I shrugged. "Julia's in the hospital off the island. There is no way she could have done anything to Summer, unless she was able to give Summer something that had a delayed reaction?"

Rebekah shook her head. "No, the onset of digitalis toxicity usually takes place fairly quickly."

"Digitalis?" I said, weakly. "Isn't that the poison that shows up in a lot of mystery novels? It affects the heart?"

"Yes, that's the one. But I'm not sure that digitalis was involved here," Rebekah cautioned. "It may be something completely different, but the dilated pupils, the flushed skin, the lethargy, all combined with nausea and vomiting . . ." She shrugged. "They will work it out at the hospital. They'll run toxicology reports and figure out exactly what it was."

I closed my eyes briefly. I didn't want to think about Summer and poisons, but the fact remained that she was on her way to the hospital. "But you think there's a strong possibility that she was poisoned?" I asked.

"Yes, I'm afraid so. I hope not, but that's what my gut tells me."

Mitch said, "You said it acts quickly. Are we talking hours or minutes?"

"It depends on the dose and the concentration. If it was digitalin—that's the medicine—there are certain time frames, but if she consumed it in the raw state—foxglove—then it would depend on how much was in the plant, which varies from plant to plant."

I frowned at Mitch. "I wonder if Summer was on any medicine?" I turned back to Rebekah quickly. "The medicine for poison ivy. Would she still be taking that?"

"Yes, she would need to take it over several days."

My thoughts were spinning through all sorts of horrible possibilities. "I don't like to even think about this, but is there any way someone could have switched out the medicine for the poison ivy with this digitalin? Do they look the same?"

Rebekah considered for a moment. "I'm not as familiar with digitalin but I believe it is dispensed in a small round tablet, similar to the medicine I prescribed for her poison ivy, but the prescription I wrote for her would have been in a blister pack. You know what those are? A flat, foil-backed sheet with each pill encased in a plastic bubble that you punch out."

"Yes, I know what you're talking about," I said. "So it would be harder to switch out a tablet in one of those blister packs."

"But not impossible," Mitch said darkly. "You called Redding today, right?" At my nod, he reached for my phone, transferring the number to his phone. "I'm going back to Summer's room. I have one of Brian's key cards," he said as he moved away, speaking over his shoulder. "I'll ask Redding to meet me there."

He strode away quickly, and Rebekah murmured, "That seems like a long shot. If someone wanted the bride to ingest digitalin there are easier ways to see that it gets in her system, like grinding it up and adding it to her food."

"The rehearsal dinner." I pressed a hand to my mouth for a second. "Summer and I had lunch together today. We split two appetizers, and I'm fine. I don't think it could have happened at lunch."

"Hmm . . . what did she have to drink?" Rebekah asked.

"A bottled water, and I watched her open it. No, if it was in something she ate, it had to have happened at the rehearsal dinner. I talked to her before the rehearsal, and she told me she hadn't eaten anything since lunch. I asked if she wanted some food, but she said no, that she felt great. I have to get back to the banquet room."

Rebekah said, "Yes. That's a good idea. Tell the detective I'm available to answer any questions he has."

"Thanks," I called, already half jogging across the shell drive. I reached the resort and hurried through the dining room, but I came to an abrupt halt at the threshold of the banquet room. Every table had been cleared, even the table-cloths had been removed. A crew of about four employees were shifting the bare tables around into a new arrangement, probably for another event on the following day.

I crossed the room to the door the servers had used during the evening and found it opened into the little alcove between the main dining room and the kitchen. The swinging wooden door that hid the servants' staircase was directly across from me. I turned and pushed into the heat and bustle of the kitchen. "Where are the dishes from the banquet room?" I asked the first person I saw, a young woman unloading champagne glasses from a plastic square tray with high edges.

She shook her head. "*No inglés.*"

I moved to another woman, who stood at the center of the kitchen with a tablet in hand, and repeated my question. She gave me a puzzled look as she waved her hand toward a stack of clean white plates on a set of industrial chrome shelves. "They're done."

"And the food? Where's the leftover food?"

The woman put her hand on her hip. "It's gone. If you forgot your doggie bag, I'm sorry, but the banquet food was cleared away. Now, I need to ask you to leave. Resort guests aren't allowed in this area."

"It's incredibly important. Surely, you don't run all the leftover food down a garbage disposal, do you? There's got to be trash or a compost pile or something left over." I spotted a man pushing a large trash can across the room and moved in his direction. "Could it be in there?"

She gripped my arm and pulled me back. "Why?"

I should have called Mr. Markham before charging in here, I realized belatedly. His word carried weight. This woman thought I was just some crazy guest who'd probably had one too many. There was only one way to get her to take me seriously. "Someone may have been poisoned."

She stared at me a moment, her gaze running over my face. I must have looked significantly shaken because her eyebrows lowered into a frown. "Does this have something to do with the commotion at the service entrance tonight?"

"Yes."

Her shoulders came down and her gaze went to the ceiling. "Of course it does." She turned on her heel and called out, "Mel! Get those trash bags from the banquet room and put them aside."

I pulled out my phone to call Mitch and realized I'd just missed a call from him. I'd turned the ringer off before the rehearsal and had forgotten to turn it back on. He'd followed up his missed call with a text.

Redding here with me in Summer's room. No sign of her medicine being tampered with.

I switched the ringer on, then called him. He answered right away.

"I got your text. Is Redding still with you?"

"Yes."

"Good. He needs to come to the kitchen. After you left, Rebekah said that an easier way to poison Summer would be to add something to her food. I'm in the kitchen now. They've already cleared the banquet room and washed the dishes, but the garbage is still here."

"I'm putting Redding on."

Mitch handed over the phone, and I repeated what I'd told Mitch.

"I'll be right down. Make sure those bags aren't thrown away."

Redding arrived in the kitchen within a few minutes with Mitch at his side. Redding huddled with the woman with the tablet along with Mr. Markham, who had arrived shortly before Redding. The woman must have called him. Redding asked about the food, and they pointed out the bags of trash.

Redding nodded. "And the drinks?"

"The glasses are already washed," the woman replied.

"What about the bottles you served it from?" Redding asked.

She pointed to rows of plastic crates stacked along one wall. "We recycle glass. The wine, beer, and champagne bottles are over there. Probably the top three or four were from that dinner, but there's no way to know exactly which ones came from the dinner. They'd just be added to the crates."

"No one touch those until my techs get here."

I'd shifted off to the side, trying to keep out of the way of the constant busyness of the kitchen staff, but as soon as Mitch entered the kitchen, he spotted me and came to stand beside me. "Mom just called me," he said. "They're keeping Summer at the local hospital on the mainland for now. Her blood pressure is low, and she's still feeling sick. They're doing tests."

"So they don't know for sure what's caused it?"

"No."

"How are your parents?"

"Pretty shaken up." Mitch would have said more, but he spotted Redding crossing the room toward us.

"Mr. and Mrs. Avery, I understand that this is a very stressful time for you. Thank you for the information you've provided, but I suggest you return to the wedding party events and let me take it from here."

Mitch glowered at him. "My sister is in the hospital. You can't expect us to go away and pretend nothing has happened—" I slipped my hand into Mitch's and squeezed.

It took quite a bit to get my normally laid-back husband riled, but once he was worked up, he wouldn't back down.

"No, I wouldn't expect you to," Redding said, his voice calm. He glanced around the room. Most of the kitchen staff were moving through their routines, but a few people were staring at us. "We don't know for certain that your sister was poisoned. Until I get word on that, I have to move cautiously. But if she was poisoned and the person who did it thinks it wasn't picked up on, then the chances of that person relaxing and making a mistake, giving themselves away, is greater. Do you see what I'm saying?"

"I see your point. I don't like it, but I see it," Mitch said.

"Good. Then can I count on you to put out the word that something disagreed with your sister, and she was hospitalized as a precaution?"

Mitch gave a reluctant nod. "But I expect you to keep us updated on the investigation. If she was poisoned—"

Redding interrupted Mitch. "We will make sure she's safe. I'll do everything I can. I promise you that. I've got a sister of my own, so I understand your reaction."

I could feel Mitch's arm, which had been pressed against mine, relax as he loosened his grip on our linked fingers. He gave a short nod, which Redding returned.

I let out the breath I was holding. "All right," I said. "Come on, Mitch. There's nothing else we can do here." I tugged on his hand.

"I suppose you're right." He slowly followed me out of the kitchen and through the dining room.

"Oh! The kids—how long has it been since they went to play board games?" I asked, a sudden attack of mom-guilt mixed with panic coming over me as I realized that I hadn't kept an eye on the time.

"Relax," Mitch said. "It's only been about an hour."

"Really? It seems like so much longer."

"I know."

In the lobby, we turned the corner to go down the hall-way that led to the library and almost collided with Yvonne. She jumped back, and I reached out automatically to steady her as she wobbled on her stiletto heels. She gripped my forearm. "Do you know about Summer? Have you heard that she's in the hospital? That can't be true, can it?"

Mitch and I exchanged a glance, and I said, "Yes, I'm afraid so."

Her face, which had been tense and worried, went pale. "Oh, no," she murmured, "I had a voice mail, but I hoped . . ." Her hand fell away from my arm, and her whole body sagged.

Mitch reached out, hooked his hand under her forearm to steady her, and led her to one of the padded benches that lined the hallway.

She collapsed onto the bench. I sat down beside her. "Can I get you something? A glass of water, maybe?"

Her gaze was focused on her hands, which had fallen into her lap. She clenched her cell phone in one hand and lifted it slightly.

"I had a message from Brian, that Summer was sick. I hoped that she was okay, but then someone said she'd been taken away in an ambulance . . . He'll be devastated and worried." She lifted her gaze to mine, and I was surprised to see tears glittering in her eyes. I recognized that motherly instinct to comfort your child, that desire to smooth away the hurt and worries of life—or if you couldn't do that, to at least share the burdens. She blinked rapidly and swallowed hard. "He said he'd call me later, but he's not going to, not after the way I behaved toward Summer." She dropped her head and sniffed.

I sent Mitch a *help me here* glance, and he shrugged, then gave a little head shake that I knew meant *I have no idea what to do.* "I, ah—I'll go find some tissues," Mitch said, then set off down the hallway.

Internally, I shook my head. A man would rather deal with a gun-toting mugger than a crying woman. I turned back to Yvonne. "I'm sure that's not true. He's probably just busy getting her to the hospital and everything sorted out. Once things calm down, I'm sure he'll call you."

She pressed her finger to her upper lip, but tears seeped from her eyes, tracking through her mascara and eyeliner. "Yes, but don't you see—that's why it's so bad." She sniffed, raised her head, and wiped her fingers under her eyes, smearing her makeup even more. "We've always been close, Brian and I. We didn't have those horrible tense, angst-filled teenage years that are so common. Brian was a good kid. He was so concerned about his GPA."

She rolled her eyes. "The GPA, the college admissions, the extracurricular activities, the college application essays. Sometimes I couldn't believe Brian was my child. Had I really given birth to this goal-oriented, focused boy who wanted to be a lawyer? I mean, my son, a *lawyer*?" She laughed and I could see that there was pride behind her consternation. "But I had. He did everything exactly right, followed the rules, and excelled while he did it. So we skipped a lot of those painful teenage things. Brian was so adultlike, even from the time he was about twelve. Always focused on the future, making the best choices. It was easy to depend on him." She heaved out a sigh that moved her shoulders. "I see that now. That perhaps I depended on him too much. Perhaps I was just a teeny bit selfish."

I bit my lip and let her continue.

"And now he's chosen a perfectly wonderful girl, and by pushing her away, I've pushed him away too."

Mitch returned and held out a box of tissues.

"Thanks," she said as she took one and wiped her face, but there wasn't much damage control she could do. She only smeared the black mascara and liner more.

"Well, I don't know Brian very well, but he doesn't seem the type of person to hold a grudge. I'm sure you can make amends."

She thought about it for a moment, then gave a little nod. "Yes. It's possible, I suppose."

"And Summer wants to patch things up. I know she does. You and Summer both want Brian to be happy. Surely it will work out."

"Yes, it might," she said slowly. "When you look at it like that . . ."

"We'll let you know, if we hear anything," I said.

"Alright." She dabbed her eyes again, then squared her shoulders. "Thank you, I would appreciate that." She stood and shook out her skirt. "Thank you for listening, too."

"Anytime," I said, shooting a reproachful glance at Mitch.

"I think I'll check with the front desk, see what time the first ferry leaves in the morning," Yvonne said.

As she walked away I said to Mitch, "Great job, getting the tissues."

"I think I detect a note of sarcasm in your tone," Mitch said.

"Yes. You practically sprinted away once the tears were imminent."

Mitch tossed the tissue box on the bench and wrapped my hand around the crook of his arm. "Smartest thing I could do. Leave the women to talk, fetch tissues. I have learned that when a woman is crying, it's best to not say too much. Usually, whatever I say is the wrong thing. Best to keep quiet and get the tissues. Besides, I wasn't sure if those were real tears or just great acting," Mitch said as we moved down the hall.

"I think they were real."

"She *is* an actress."

"Yes, but there was something raw and exposed. I think she was legitimately upset. And I doubt she'd ruin her makeup if she was just pretending to be worried."

"Well, time will tell," Mitch said.

"Yes. Speaking of time, it's been a while since we heard anything from your mom and dad. They didn't happen to call you while you were off getting tissues?"

"No, I called them," Mitch said, and the lightness vanished from his tone. "I just wanted to check in. No change."

Chapter Fourteen

The tap of rain against the window woke me. I rolled away from Mitch's shoulder, slipped out of bed, and peeked between the curtains. The clouds that had been on the horizon yesterday had rolled in, casting a grayish tinge over the view. Raindrops streaked the window, blurring the landscape, but I was still able to see that the chalk lines on the grass had been washed away. The framework of the arch, marking the entrance to the gazebo where Summer and Brian would have stood today to exchange their vows, looked barren without its layer of flowers.

I heard Mitch stirring, and I turned away from the gray view. The first thing he did was check his phone. "Anything?" I asked.

"No."

"Well, at this point, no news is good news, I think," I said, dropping down onto the foot of the bed. Mitch's parents had called at three in the morning to let us know that Summer's vital signs had stabilized.

Mitch fingered his phone. "Do you think it's too early to call?"

"No, I doubt anyone's gotten any sleep."

I reached out a hand. "I'm sure she's doing either the same or better."

He nodded, but dialed anyway. I went to shower. I knew it wouldn't be long before the kids were awake, and any tiny bit of jump on the day that I could get, I needed.

When I emerged from the bath, the kids were snuggled into the bed with Mitch.

Livvy looked at me, her face stricken. "Aunt Summer is in the *hospital*."

We hadn't told the kids last night, agreeing that it would be better to wait until they weren't tired—kids took everything harder when they were exhausted—and we hoped we would have better news today.

"Yes," Mitch said, "but she's doing fine."

"She is?" I asked, joining them.

"Her vital signs are back to normal and she's feeling better. They want to keep her until tomorrow morning, just for observation."

"Thank goodness." I squeezed Mitch's hand.

"I'm going over on the first ferry to give Mom and Dad a break."

"Oh, good. I'm sure they need some rest. I'll stay here and work all the wedding details."

"The wedding," he said, running a hand over his face. "I forgot for a second. This was supposed to be her wedding day."

"She can't get married now?" Livvy asked.

"No, she can still get married, but it may not be here. They may have to reschedule."

"But why can't she just get married tomorrow?"

I closed my eyes, and the list of vendors scrolled through my head: the food, the flowers, the tux rentals, the musicians, the photographer, the minister. They would all have to be cancelled and rescheduled.

"Mom, what's wrong?" Nathan asked. "You look all pale and sick, like Tanner did right before he threw up all over the carpet in reading circle."

I opened my eyes. "Thank you for that lovely image," I said, ruffling his hair. "Nothing is wrong. There's nothing that can't be rescheduled," I said, looking over Nathan's head to Mitch.

"Who knows," Mitch said. "Brian may get his wish. They may *have to* elope."

Three hours later, my phone rang as I left Mr. Markham's office. I didn't recognize the caller ID, but I always answered in case it was a new organizing client, but it wasn't a new client. I recognized Summer's voice before she said more than hello.

"Summer! How are you?"

"I'm fine now, but they won't let me leave yet. Never go in the hospital, Ellie They're determined to find something wrong with you."

"But you did have something wrong with you, and it was pretty serious," I said, feeling so relieved to hear Summer's bouncy tone.

"Yes, I know. And I know I sound totally ungrateful and selfish, but I want to get out of here and get married, but they won't let me leave. They say they need to observe me for at least twelve more hours. I told the nurses I'm leaving tomorrow morning, no matter what."

I heard the muffled sound of Caroline's voice in the background. Summer must have tilted the phone away because her voice faded. "Yes, Mom, I am calm . . . No, let me finish talking to Ellie . . . Right, only a few more minutes."

Summer's voice came in louder as she pulled the phone back to her mouth. "So yeah, since Mom's not helping me break out, I need you to come over here so we can talk wedding stuff."

"Wedding stuff?"

"Strategy," Summer said shortly. "What we're going to do."

"Oh, I'm already on it. I just met with Mr. Markham and discussed shifting the ceremony to tomorrow. I've contacted all the vendors, too."

"Wonderful. Oh, Ellie, I knew you were just the person to help with my wedding. You really should do this full-time. You could probably make a mint."

"We'll see. Let's get through this wedding first," I said.

"Right. Okay, so can you come over on the ferry with Mitch? There's still time. It doesn't leave for another thirty minutes. I'd really appreciate it."

"Let me see if I can find someone to watch the kids. It's still pouring rain. They've cancelled all the outdoor activities today, so all the kids are going bonkers." The novelty of old-fashioned board games had worn off. Earlier this morning, I had left Mitch to explain why they couldn't go swimming in the rain.

"Ask Madison to watch them," Summer said. "Tell her I'll pay her double her usual babysitting rate."

"Okay, I'll see what I can do."

Madison couldn't turn down Summer's offer. She said she was saving up for a prom dress, so Mitch and I were able to take the ferry together. It was quite a different ride than our trip over, which had been filled with sunshine and happy expectations. The rain had tapered off for the moment, but the overcast sky turned the sea a gunmetal gray, and the air was chilly. We spent the trip in the interior cabin where I flipped through the wedding binder,

double-checking to make sure I'd contacted everyone involved in the wedding and told them of the delay.

Yvonne was on the ferry too. After a brief greeting and
a quick smile, she retreated to the other side of the cabin. I
wondered if she was embarrassed about sharing so much
with me yesterday.

I lost track of Yvonne when we arrived at the dock. The
rental car company was there to meet us, as Mitch had
arranged, and it wasn't long before we were at the hospital. When I pushed through the door of Summer's room,
she was sipping juice from a straw. She had an IV in her arm
and a bad case of bedhead, but she looked alert and happy.
Her color was good, and when she saw Mitch and me, she
extended her arms. Mitch hugged her close and murmured,
"You gave us quite a scare. Glad you're doing okay now."

"Me too."

Brian had been seated on the end of the bed, but he
stood when we arrived. Mitch's parents, who had been in
chairs on the far side of the room, stood as well. Dark circles shadowed their eyes, and they had that worn-out look
the kids get when I let them stay up too late. We all exchanged greetings, and then Mitch pulled his parents aside
to coordinate. He planned to take them back to the ferry
so they could get a few hours of sleep at the resort, then return later in the day.

They gave Summer hugs and promised to be back before dinner, then they left with Mitch. Yvonne slipped
through the door as it closed after them.

Brian, who had just settled back onto the foot of the
bed, stood and said, "Mom." His voice was weary, as if he
didn't want to deal with her right then. "I don't really have
time right now . . ."

Yvonne flinched a little at his tone, but she put a big
smile on her face. "No, don't get up. No need to worry. I'm

not here to stay. I just wanted to bring you this." She handed the to-go cup of coffee to Brian. "It's a hazelnut latte."

"Um, thanks," Brian said.

She turned to Summer. "And I didn't know if you could have anything to drink, so I brought you these instead." She held out a stack of glossy magazines to Summer. "I'm glad you're feeling better."

Summer took the magazines. "Thank you."

The two women looked at each other for a moment, then Yvonne said suddenly, "Well, I'll let you rest." She hurried from the room.

Summer and Brian exchanged a considering look. Then Brian said, "I think she means it."

Summer sighed. "You better go after her."

Brian kissed Summer on the forehead and headed for the door.

"But tell her she better not try to boss me around after we're married," Summer called after him. "She can't forget that I'm your wife."

"I won't let her forget," Brian said before he left.

"Going to be your wife," Summer amended as she folded her arms over the magazines. "Well, that's quite an about-face."

"Yes. I talked to her last night. She was so upset. She seemed very different than I'd seen her—contrite almost."

"We'll see if it lasts. She didn't quote any Shakespeare, so maybe it will. How about Patricia? How's she taking it?"

"I spoke to her this morning after breakfast. She was . . . concerned."

"About the fuss, I imagine."

"Well, yes." I didn't say anything else. Summer had enough to worry about and didn't need to know that her future mother-in-law thought that possibly being poisoned was a selfish and unreasonable thing to do on the eve of your wedding.

I took Brian's place at the foot of the bed. "So how are you?"

"Oh, I'm better now." She shivered. "You don't want to know what they did to me." She hit a button and raised the bed so that she was in more of a sitting position. "Let's talk wedding stuff. I need something to get my mind off all this." She raised her arm with the IV attached and indicated the hospital bed.

"Okay," I said. "The good news is that all the vendors feel awful for you, and since you had arranged for everyone to stay overnight tonight, almost all the guests and most of the vendors, like the florist and musicians, will be able to stay on until tomorrow. Even the minister can stay. He's taken the whole weekend off. But after tomorrow . . ."

"They can't hang around any longer waiting for the bride to get released from the hospital. I understand. Don't worry. I'll be out of here and back on Camden Island by noon tomorrow. Now, what's the bad news?"

"There's no problem with the reception. Mr. Markham said the resort will be happy to slide the reception to Sunday. The ballroom isn't booked, but . . ." There was no way to soften the news, so I just came out with it. "The gazebo area is rented for tomorrow."

"What?" Summer sat forward, and the magazines slid toward the side of the bed.

I caught them before they hit the floor. "I'm afraid so. Mr. Markham says it's a huge event and has been on the books longer than your wedding. Some political fund-raiser thing."

Summer fell back against the pillows. "But that means that we don't have a wedding venue. The contract we signed with the resort was very specific about cancellation.

It doesn't matter if we have all the other stuff—the minister, the flowers, the musicians, the food. We have to have somewhere to put it all."

"Mr. Markham went over your options with me. He said they would be happy to apply the deposit you've paid toward a new date."

"No," Summer said adamantly. "We are not rescheduling. Brian and I are getting married this weekend. Even if we have to do it in the hospital chapel, we are getting married."

I stacked the magazines on a rolling tray beside the bed. "I thought you'd say that, so I asked about other options for this weekend. I think Mr. Markham is slightly worried that you and Brian may sue the resort, so he's very open to working with you to find a solution."

Summer's forehead wrinkled. "Sue Camden Island? Why would we do that? None of this is Mr. Markham's fault."

"I know that, but you know how sue-happy people are now. Something goes wrong and they bring a suit just to see what they can get from a big company or corporation. And Brian *is* a lawyer."

"But he's not that kind of lawyer," Summer said.

"Right. You and I know that, but Mr. Markham is motivated to make sure you and Brian are happy. As happy as you can be, anyway, after all that's happened."

Summer sighed. "I'd be happy to forget all the fancy stuff with the ceremony and just get married. You know, something basic." She'd been plucking at the blanket that covered her lap, but as she said the last sentence, her hand stilled. She gazed across the room toward the window. We were on a high floor and it was raining again. Beyond the rain trickling down the glass we could see the thick layer of gray clouds. "What's the weather forecast for tomorrow, do you know?"

I checked my phone. "Clear. High around seventy-five."

"I have an idea." She pulled the rolling tray closer and picked up her phone. "Let me call Mr. Markham." She was scrolling through her contacts when the door opened and a young Asian man in scrubs and a white jacket entered the room.

Summer lowered her phone. "Hi, Dr. Mori." As she put her phone back on the tray, she said to me, "I'll get in touch with Mr. Markham as soon as I can."

Two other people also in scrubs trailed into the room behind Dr. Mori. One of them maneuvered a rolling cart with a computer monitor and keyboard through the door while the other held a tablet. The doctor moved to Summer's bed, and I backed up. "I'll wait outside."

"No, I'd rather you stayed," Summer said to me.

"How are you feeling?" Dr. Mori asked Summer.

"Great. One hundred percent ready to get out of here."

"You do look much better. Your color is more normal, if a little pale."

"I'm always pale," Summer countered quickly, and picked up a strand of hair. "Redhead, you know."

Dr. Mori checked Summer's pulse, listened to her heart, and examined her eyes while the people behind him scurried around Summer as they scanned her wrist bracelet, then tapped and typed away on their computer equipment.

Dr. Mori tossed his stethoscope around his neck and said some medical jargon that I didn't understand to people with him, then turned back to Summer. "You've improved. Your heart rate and blood pressure have normalized. Any more nausea?"

"No, none."

"Okay. Then I want you to stay overnight, and if things stay the way they are now, I'll discharge you in the morning."

Summer sighed. "I can't talk you into letting me out today?"

"No, I don't think that would be wise."

"Well, then *early* in the morning, right?"

A smile turned up the corners of Dr. Mori's mouth. "Because you're a bride, yes, early in the morning." He reached for the tablet, which his assistant handed over. "Now, about these test results." His face went serious. "Your blood contained a glycoside."

Summer shook her head. "I can tell from your tone that's not good, but you're going to have to spell it out for me."

"It means that you ingested a toxin."

Summer glanced at me, her face falling. "I hoped that it was just food poisoning or something . . . else. Silly of me, I know."

I glanced at the doctor and saw that he wasn't puzzled. "You know the background? What's happened to Summer during the last few days?"

"Yes, Detective Redding spoke to me last night. I've already sent him a copy of the test results."

"Was it digitalis?" I asked. "I spoke to the nurse practitioner on the island. She said it might be digitalis."

"It could be. The signs Summer was exhibiting when she arrived certainly were consistent with a digitalis overdose, but there are other poisons that function the same way. It could also be convallatoxin, another toxic glycoside. I've requested another test to narrow down the results. Try not to worry about it. You are recovering, and that's the important thing." He said he would return to check on her in the morning and left the room, his entourage trailing along behind him.

Summer dropped her head back onto her pillow when the door closed behind him. "I don't understand this at all. It couldn't have been Julia who did this to me. She's still in the hospital. In fact, she's on another floor of this hospital. I asked about her as soon as I began to feel like my normal self again. Who hates me so much that they want to poison me? I mean, if I really stretch my imagination I can see that someone like Julia, someone who's a little"—she circled her finger at her temple—"crazy, might shoot paintballs at me or try to smear me with poison ivy, but those things were small compared to actually poisoning me."

"I don't understand it either," I said, and went on to tell her Mitch and Redding had checked her room for signs that someone had tampered with her medicine, but had come up empty.

"So that means it probably happened at the rehearsal dinner," Summer said, a frown on her face. "But I didn't eat much. With all the talking and chatting, and making sure everyone was having a good time, I wasn't focused on food. I didn't have any of the salad and only had a few bites of the steak and vegetables."

"That may have been a good thing," I said. "Did anything taste different or funny?"

"No, everything was wonderful. I was happy that it had turned out so well, that we weren't having one of those horrible rubber-chicken dinners."

"And no one gave you anything else? A breath mint? A stick of gum?"

"No. I only had whatever everyone else had."

The door swished open and Brian entered. Summer reached out her hand to him. "Oh good, you're back. The doctor was just here." She went on to relate what he'd told us, and I slipped from the room, figuring they needed some time alone. I was sure with the hospital workers and the other visitors, Summer and Brian probably hadn't had a minute alone.

I pulled my phone out and called Redding. He surprised me by answering. "This is Ellie Avery," I said. "I'm at the hospital with Summer. Her doctor just gave her the news that the test results showed that she was poisoned. The doctor said he had sent the results to you?"

"Yes, I have them. I've dispatched a deputy to the hospital. He should arrive within the next ten minutes. I'm actually on my way there as well. I'm going to recommend that your sister-in-law reduce the number of visitors and postpone her wedding."

"I don't think you'll have much luck with that last one. She's determined to get married tomorrow."

Redding's gusty sigh came over the line. "Yeah, well, I have to float the idea."

"Any results on the food from the rehearsal?"

"Using the place cards, we've been able to narrow it down to two bags of trash. Our techs are working on it. I've asked for a rush, but this isn't like those TV crime shows. We probably won't get results for a while."

"Days?"

"At least."

Now it was my turn to sigh. "Well, I can tell you that Summer said she didn't eat much at dinner, so her food was probably barely touched. She didn't have any of the salad, only a few bites of the steak and vegetable side dish."

"Okay, that's helpful. I'll pass that along."

I hung up, peeked into the room, and saw that Brian and Summer were deep in conversation. So, I took the elevator down to the cafeteria and bought a bottled water and a chocolate muffin. I figured I'd burned off enough calories worrying about Summer to justify the splurge.

I was moving through the tables to a seat near a window when I saw Graham. I moved across the room to his table. He was seated across from a woman. Her back was to me, and all I could see was brown hair cut in a pixie style.

Graham saw me approaching and stood. "Ellie! You must be here to see Summer. How is she?"

"Doing better."

"Oh, that's good." He turned to the woman still seated at the table. "This is Julia's sister, Audrey."

At her name, she looked up quickly and seemed to notice me for the first time. "Sorry," she said, standing and extending her hand. "This has all been such a shock. I'm not all here." Now that she was looking at me, I could see a resemblance between the two sisters. They both had heart-shaped faces, but Audrey's chin was more pointed. Her short hair, no makeup, and casual T-shirt and jeans made me think that she wasn't a fashion plate like Julia, but then again, maybe she just threw some clothes on and hit the road so she could get to her sister's side as soon as possible.

"It's okay. I'm sorry about Julia. How is she?"

"The same," Graham said. "No change, which the doctors assure us is good."

Audrey glanced down at the muffin I held and said, "Why don't you join us? Graham was on his way to get some food for us. I haven't had anything since this morning, but everyone assures me I should eat even if I don't feel like it."

"Oh, I wouldn't want to intrude."

"No, please do," Audrey added, and pulled out the chair beside her.

I reluctantly slipped into the seat because I didn't see how I could turn it down without being rude, and Graham went off to the food area.

As soon as I was seated, Audrey turned toward me. "You must be part of the wedding party."

"Yes. The bride is my sister-in-law."

"So you were around Julia these last few days?"

"Yes."

Audrey flicked a glance toward the food line where Graham was pushing a tray and selecting food. "So how did she seem?" There was a tension in her voice and an intensity in her gaze as she watched me.

I unwrapped the plastic around the muffin, buying myself a little time to figure out how to word my response. "She seemed a little nervous at first, but mostly happy," I said, thinking back to all the times I'd seen her and Graham cuddled together and the loving looks they'd exchanged. "She really seems to like Graham."

Audrey seemed to relax a little. "Good. That makes me feel better."

I broke off a bite of the muffin for myself, then offered her a section, but she shook her head. "Why do you ask?" I wondered if Graham had told her about the incriminating things found in Julia's room.

Audrey licked her lips. "I suppose you've heard about what happened after Brian and Julia's breakup?"

"Yes. I heard a few things."

"Yeah, well, she went overboard there for a little while. She's the first to admit it, now. So when I found out that she was at Brian's wedding ... well, I was shocked. I thought she'd put all that behind her. She certainly sounded like she had." Audrey gazed across the room and her expression softened. "I was so happy for her. She said she'd finally found a guy she really loved. And he loved her, too."

"Graham," I said, thinking that Graham hadn't seemed quite so smitten with Julia when I talked to him earlier. Had Julia been indulging in wishful thinking when she described her relationship to Audrey? Or had Graham's feelings cooled?

"Yes."

"But you were worried about her this weekend?" I asked. "Is that why you asked about how she acted?"

Audrey nodded. "She called me on Wednesday. She was so upset about the wedding. Especially after she'd switched everything around at the last minute. She was supposed to come see me this weekend. We were—" Audrey broke off as Graham set down a tray with two sandwiches and packages of chips.

"I wasn't sure what you'd want," he said. "I got ham and turkey. Your choice."

Audrey reached for the sandwich closest to her. "It doesn't matter. Anything is fine."

I finished off my muffin and dusted the crumbs from my fingers. "It was nice to meet you, Audrey. I better get back to Summer's room. My husband should be back by now."

Graham asked, "So what's the plan with the wedding?"

"We're not sure yet. The tentative plan is to go ahead with the wedding tomorrow if Summer is released in the morning. I'm not sure where, though. I'll call you when things are settled."

Graham nodded. "Just let me know."

Audrey looked up from her uneaten sandwich. "Yes, now that I'm here, you don't need to be with Julia every minute. Although I know she would want you nearby. She'd say that, if she could . . ." She looked away as she tried to control a surge of tears. She swallowed. "Sorry." She picked up a napkin and pressed it to her eyes.

Graham shifted in his seat uncomfortably and gave me what I thought was a warning look. So he hadn't told her about the paintball gun and the poison ivy. Well, I couldn't blame him. There was only so much you could unload on a person at one time. Seeing her sister in a drug-induced coma was probably all that Audrey could handle at that moment.

I pushed my chair back. "Let us know if anything changes, okay?"

Graham nodded, and I slipped away, feeling awful for Audrey and for Julia. Even if Julia couldn't have poisoned Summer, she could still be responsible for the paintball and the poison ivy. How horrible to know that once she woke up—if she woke up—she'd have to face the consequences of those actions. If she really did those things. I sighed and called Mitch. He was already back and in Summer's room. I said I'd be up in a minute and detoured to the gift shop where I browsed the selection of plants.

I skipped over the pink and blue arrangements for new moms and was contemplating an ivy when a woman with an apron over her striped shirt asked if I wanted some help.

"Yes, I need something cheerful. Two arrangements, in fact."

"We have a medium-size arrangement with daisies. Nice and bright and happy." She took one out of the refrigerator and set it on the counter, then picked up a different vase. "Or if you want a completely different arrangement in blue with some purple and pink accents, we have this nice one with poppies, snapdragons, and foxglove. Bit unusual, this one, but really nice."

Something about her words bothered me, but I couldn't pin it down.

"Or we have roses," the woman said, drawing my attention back to the counter.

"No, the daisies and the blue arrangement will be fine. I'll take them both."

She moved to the cash register and rang the sale up. I told her to send the daisies to Julia and the poppies to Summer.

The woman paused as she wrote out the instructions. "Now, this one isn't going to someone who has pets, is it?" She pointed the pen at the poppy arrangement.

"No. No pets at all."

"Oh, good. I always like to make sure because some folks will take the arrangements home, and they have no idea that the foxglove is poisonous."

"What?" I looked up from signing the credit card receipt.

"The foxglove." She touched the bell-like flowers hanging in from the tall central stem. "They're quite poisonous to animals and even people."

I scribbled the rest of my signature and called Mitch. When he picked up, I said, "We have to get back to Camden Island. I think I may know what made Summer sick."

Tips for an Organized Wedding

Once your budget is set, there are several ways you can keep costs under control.

- Keep the wedding party small
- Limit the guest list
- Check prices for days other than Saturday. You might save a significant percentage on your venue by picking a Friday or Sunday as your wedding day
- Off-season weddings, like winter weddings, can also cut costs

- Pick in-season flowers
- Use more greenery and fewer flowers for arrangements
- Consider other options for centerpieces and decorations besides flowers such as candles with greenery, floating candles, or even accents that echo the setting or time of year, such as shells for a beach wedding or pine boughs and pinecones for a holiday wedding
- Serving brunch or only cocktails will be less expensive than dinner for the reception
- For the reception and the rehearsal dinner, a buffet-style meal will usually be cheaper than a sit-down dinner
- Barbecues and picnics are additional options to cut food costs
- To keep costs down for an open bar, either limit the selection of drinks available, go with house beers and wines, or limit the time the bar is open
- Hire a deejay instead of band or create your own playlist
- Pick a smaller layered cake for photos and the cake cutting, then add a sheet cake to serve guests
- Keeping the "wedding" word out of the conversation with vendors—use "party" or "event"—until the price is agreed on as there are often price bumps when the "w" word is mentioned

Chapter Fifteen

"No, I didn't use any foxglove at all." Denise shook her head.

"None? Are you sure?" I asked.

"Yes, come look for yourself." Denise, who had been seated on a rocking chair on the back terrace, closed the book she had been reading and stood up. Mitch and I followed her through the resort to the flower preparation area. She waved her hand at the glass coolers. "See, no foxglove."

She was right. In my excitement to return to the island and ask her about foxglove, I'd completely forgotten that Summer had chosen white and cream flowers with only bright green leaves for accent colors. On the ferry back to the island, I'd done a quick Internet search on my phone for foxglove, and in all the pictures of the poisonous plant, the flowers were purple. I swiveled toward Mitch. "Could it be somewhere on the grounds? In the landscaping?"

"I'll find out," Mitch said, already turning away as he pulled up a picture of the plant on his phone.

I turned back to Denise. I had probably offended her by insinuating that one of her plants was used to hurt Summer. "I'm sorry . . . I was just so sure . . ."

But Denise didn't look upset. She stood staring at the flowers behind the glass, tapping her chin with a finger. "But there is lily of the valley."

"Lily of the valley?"

"Yes. It's poisonous, too, like foxglove. My cat got out of my yard a few years ago and ate some lily of the valley that was growing in my neighbor's garden. It was just a little bit, and she recovered, but the vet told me every part of the plant is poisonous—leaves, stems, flowers, everything."

"And there was that arrangement yesterday that was messed up." We stared at each other a moment, then I said, "Do you still have it? The arrangement?"

"Yes. I never throw out anything until the actual event is over. Just in case, you know." Denise went to the farthest end of the refrigerator and reached inside.

"No, wait. Don't touch it," I said.

"What?"

"Fingerprints." I pulled out my phone and typed the words *lily of the valley* and *poison* into the browser's tiny search bar.

"Oh." She let the glass door slide closed. While I waited for the results to load, we both stared at it. She had placed it in the very back, and we couldn't see it very well. "Can you tell if any flowers are missing?"

Denise squinted. "This side looks fine, but I'd be able to tell you for sure if I could turn it around. I used five sprigs of lily of the valley in each arrangement."

"Here we go," I said as I clicked on one of the results and scanned the text. "Highly poisonous, like you said. It's a convallatoxin," I said, stumbling over the word, but remembering the doctor today had mentioned it when he spoke to Summer. "Symptoms include nausea, vomiting, flushed skin, disorientation, dilated pupils, decreased heart rate, and coma." I closed the browser and switched to the phone with shaking fingers and dialed Redding's number.

As I listened to the buzz of the phone ring on the line, Denise asked, "Summer, did she have those symptoms?"

"Almost every one."

Redding picked up. "Detective Redding. Ellie Avery again. Sorry to call you again, but I've found another possibility for the poison."

Redding was on his way back to Camden Island when I talked to him, and I stayed with Denise until he arrived. Wearing gloves, he removed the plant from the cooler and put it on the counter. "You said you could tell if something was missing?" he asked Denise.

She leaned over the arrangement, but didn't touch it. "Yes." She nodded decisively. "This plant is missing two of the lily of the valley stems."

Redding made a note. "And you said it was Patricia Abernathy who pointed out that this plant had been tampered with?"

I nodded, then Redding said, "Tell me again what happened."

"As the rehearsal ended, I went to the banquet room to check on everything for the dinner. I'd been in before the rehearsal and everything looked great, but when I got there the second time, Patricia was already there. She was upset about that flower arrangement," I said, nodding at the one with the broken stems. It looked worse now than it did yesterday. "Patricia wanted to speak to the manager, but I said we should find Denise. I was sure she could actually fix it."

Redding looked toward Denise. She settled her back against the counter. "I was in here—cleaning and straightening up when Mrs. Abernathy came in." Denise tilted her chin toward her chest and said in a tone that indicated that Patricia's reputation was something to be aware of, "You know who she is? One of the mothers-in-law?"

"Yes. I know her," Redding said.

Denise gave a quick nod. Redding's voice conveyed that he was aware of how difficult Patricia could be. "When I saw her I knew something was wrong," Denise continued. "She's one of those people who is never happy. She pointed out the damage to the arrangement and was very upset."

"Was the lily of the valley missing yesterday?" Redding asked.

Denise's forehead wrinkled as she contemplated the arrangement. "Possibly. I'm afraid I was only focused on the damage. I didn't count the stems."

Redding nodded, then asked, "So Mrs. Abernathy carried the vase in here and put it down?"

"No, that was me," I said.

"Did you handle this as well?" Redding asked, pointing to the flower arrangement.

"Yes," Denise said.

"The waitress touched it too," I added. "She moved it to replace the tablecloth. Water had spilled out of the vase."

Denise said, "But I did touch the vase when I checked the arrangement."

"Yes, I'd expect that." Redding bagged the whole thing, vase and all, in an evidence bag, then placed it in an empty cardboard box that had been stashed under one of the tables. "Is this room open all the time? Anyone could come in?" he asked.

"Yes," Denise said. "I don't have a key. I usually don't worry about locking up the floral arrangements."

"Of course not," Redding said as he stripped off the gloves. "I'll have one of my deputies contact you. We'll need to get your prints for elimination purposes." He tucked the box under his arm as he turned to me. "We'll begin re-interviewing everyone who was at the dinner, see if anyone saw anything suspicious. Now, can you point me in the di-rection of the waitress you spoke with yesterday, Mrs. Avery?"

"Yes, I'll try." I moved into the kitchen area with him and pointed out a thin woman in her early twenties. "That's her there. The one with her hair in a ponytail."

As Redding headed in her direction, Mitch came into the kitchen. He shook his head at my expectant look. "Nothing," he said. "No foxglove in the landscaping, but the groundskeeper said he couldn't be sure it wasn't grow-ing wild somewhere around the island. What's this about the lily of the valley?" Mitch asked as we left the kitchen and went back through the dining room. By the time we were in the lobby, I'd caught him up on what had hap-pened. I glanced around, looking for Patricia, but I didn't see her on the front veranda. "I think Redding will be in-terested in talking to her, and I don't think it will be a pretty sight."

"Yes, but he's got to explore that possibility."

"I know," I said with a sigh. "With Julia out of the pic-ture, it pushes the questions about Patricia and Ned back to the front of the investigation."

"And don't forget about Yvonne," Mitch said.

"After what I saw today in Summer's hospital room . . ."

"But that's today. She was all for making up with Sum-mer today, but how did she feel earlier?" Mitch asked. "Maybe she thought another scare would cause them to call off the wedding or postpone it."

"She did seem cool toward Summer at the rehearsal," I said, thinking of the brief small smile I'd seen her give Summer. "And it was only after Summer went to the hospital that she changed." I shook my head. "But I still think that Yvonne was legitimately grief-stricken about Summer's condition."

"Maybe it was guilt."

I blew out a sigh. "Okay, so she's a possibility, along with Patricia." I looked away. "I can't believe we're back to this, thinking that one of Summer's mothers-in-law would deliberately endanger her. What are we going to do tomorrow? If Summer is released and the wedding goes on, will she be safe? We can't keep an eye on her every second. She'll be eating and moving through the crowd. If anyone truly wants to hurt her, tomorrow would be another opportunity."

"I'm sure Redding is doing everything he can to find the person who did it." Mitch indicated with a tilt of his head that I should look over my shoulder. I turned and saw a deputy escorting Patricia through the resort. Her nasal tones were audible. ". . . incredibly inconvenient. I really don't see why he needs to speak to me again."

The deputy murmured something about follow-up questions, but Patricia noticed I had turned to watch her. Her angry gaze focused on me, and I turned quickly away to look out the window and saw two resort employees in raincoats carrying the metal arch around the side of the resort. I hurried outside, but stopped at the edge of the steps under the shelter of the roof overhang. The rain, which had beat down on us as we took the ferry back to the island, showed no sign of letting up. It continued to cascade down and puddles had formed on the shell drive and walkways. "Where are you taking the arch?" I called, raising my voice so that they could hear me over the steady rush of water through the gutters and drain spouts. One of the men shouted, "It will be around the back."

A man in a raincoat holding an umbrella stood at the base of the steps. At the sound of my voice, he turned, and I saw it was Mr. Markham. He pulled a walkie-talkie away from his mouth and said, "Don't worry, Mrs. Avery, your sister-in-law called me and gave me very specific instructions. I will see that everything is arranged, just as she asked. It will be no problem at all."

"You're talking about the ceremony?"

"Yes. A brilliant idea." The walkie-talkie crackled. "Now, you must excuse me, the rain is supposed to clear within the next hour, and we have to make up for lost time in setting up for the next event. Don't worry about the wedding. It is all under control." He turned away and spoke into the walkie-talkie as he moved through the rain toward the gazebo.

"What brilliant idea?" I asked Mitch who had come to stand beside me. "What's the plan?"

"Don't know, but apparently you don't need to worry about it. Mr. Markham has it all under control."

"But I like to know what the plan is." I watched Mr. Markham's figure as he joined a group of several other raincoated people in the gazebo.

"I'm sure Summer will let you know either tonight or tomorrow. Come on, we have enough to do as it is."

Mitch and I returned to the resort, crossed the lobby, and headed for the library. "You're right. I need to shift gears. It's definitely time to relieve Madison." I knew I was a bit of a micromanager, but I was an organizer, after all. Organizing was all about the details, and I didn't like being out of the loop.

We entered the library and Nathan's squeaky voice shouted, "Duck, Mom!"

I lowered my head and a barrage of white paper airplanes hit the door frame near me while one sailed over my head and into the hallway near the grand staircase.

"I win," Nathan shouted. "Mine went through the door."

I looked up and saw that Nathan, along with several of his cousins, draped over the second-story gallery that ran around the library. They all turned and pounded down the circular staircase, which was located in the corner of the library, then they dashed across the room and retrieved the paper airplanes.

I glanced around the large room, wondering how many irate people I was going to have to apologize to, but the room was empty except for the kids and Uncle Bud and Aunt Nanette, who sat on one of the sofas arranged on one side of the room. Queen was sprawled along the rug in a deep sleep. A long, modular desktop stretched across the other side of the room. It was topped with a row of computers as well as a couple of printers and formed the resort's business center. The contemporary lines of the setup were at odds with the rest of the room's sumptuous decor of ornate wood molding, embossed wallpaper, heavily brocaded drapes, an oriental rug covering the hardwood floor, and the leather-bound volumes that lined the walls on the lower level as well as the gallery.

Madison smoothed out the tip of one of the planes that had been crushed on landing and handed it back to one of the kids. "We kind of ran out of things to do after they got tired of playing Old Maid and coloring. Uncle Bud said this would be fine."

"As long as no one else is in here, it's fine," I said, eyeing the railing that ran around the gallery. It would be about waist high on an adult, so it was plenty tall enough to keep the kids safe when they were up there.

Mitch reached for his wallet. He handed Madison several twenties.

"Oh, I couldn't take this much," Madison said. "I charge the Drakes ten dollars an hour to babysit for them, but that's because their kids are terrors. Your kids are a piece of cake compared to them."

The kids raced back up the stairs and lined up along the gallery railing again, their planes at the ready. "Let's aim for the recycling bin," Livvy said, pointing across the room to the green-lidded container that sat at the end of the business center desk. "Ready, set, go."

"That's great to hear," I said to Madison, "but we were gone longer than we thought, and we didn't intend for you to watch all the younger cousins." And we'd also discovered there were two secrets to keeping good babysitters: return on time and overpay. We'd already blown the first one, but we could take care of the second.

"Well, okay," she said.

"Consider yourself off duty," Mitch said. "We've got it from here."

"All right. Thanks." She turned to the kids, who were barreling down the stairs again to get their planes. "Bye, guys."

They waved distractedly, and Madison left the room, tucking the money into her jeans pocket. The kids trooped up the stairs again and picked a new target. The planes sailed through the air over our heads as Mitch and I moved to sit down across from Uncle Bud on another couch.

"It was either paper airplanes or teach them to play poker," Uncle Bud said.

Mitch grinned at him. "Good choice."

"So how is Summer?" Uncle Bud asked.

"She's doing better," I answered as I gathered up the paper that the kids had left scattered over the coffee table, which was an accumulation of folded airplanes and crayon drawings.

"It looks like she'll be out of the hospital tomorrow," Mitch said.

"That's wonderful," Aunt Nanette said. "I'm so glad. I hate that all this has happened this weekend. It's just terrible. Will they go ahead with the wedding or reschedule it?"

I said, "Summer is determined to get married tomorrow, and at this point, I don't think she cares if the ceremony takes place here or at the hospital. Tomorrow is *the* day, rain or shine." I glanced toward the gray windows. "And I mean that literally." I reached down to pick up several paper airplanes that the kids had left under the coffee table.

"Glad to hear it," Aunt Nanette said. "And how are your parents?" she asked Mitch. "Do they need a break from the hospital?"

"No, I brought them back here today so they could get some rest," Mitch said.

His voice continued, and the conversation went on, but I had stopped listening. Most of the paper airplanes were made out of the resort's thick stationery, but a few of them were made from thin printer paper and several of the sections were covered in closely spaced print. I pried the folds apart. It was some sort of real estate sale contract for a property in Sarasota. Scrawled in a large messy handwriting across the top margin were the words *Attn: Graham Murphy. Ready to move on this. Need a response ASAP.*

Mitch clapped his hands together and called the kids down from the gallery. "Okay, kids, time for dinner."

Nathan pounded down the stairs and slid to a stop, his sweaty face only inches from mine as he gripped my hand. "Don't throw those away."

"What? The drawings?"

"No, the paper airplanes. We have to save them. And this one, too." Nathan carefully flattened an airplane so aerodynamically sleek that it looked like some sort of exotic origami. "Uncle Bud folded these especially for me. See this one? It's a fighter jet. And this one is a jumbo jet. We can keep them, right?" Several of the planes Nathan held were also made from the printer paper with small print on one side. I touched one of them. "Where did you get the paper to make these?"

"After we ran out of the scratchy paper Madison brought from her room, I got some paper out of the recycling bin." Nathan pointed toward the green bin. "I didn't use any of the printer paper," Nathan said, his voice serious.

Recently, he and Livvy had gotten in trouble for using a huge pile of the paper out of our printer tray for their art projects. I'd told them it was okay to use old paper out of our recycling bin, but not the new paper.

I stood and moved across the room to the recycling bin, which had a lid with a slot to deposit papers. The lid had a snap that locked into place, but it wasn't engaged. SECURE SHRED: PAPER DEPOSITED HERE WILL BE SHREDDED was printed on the outside of the bin. "Not so secure," I murmured. Nathan had followed me across the room and was repeating his question. "I can keep them, can't I?"

"Yes, as long as you put them in your suitcase," I said. "Then you can put them in your room when you get home." Since Nathan had zero interest in identity theft, I thought the papers would be safe enough.

"Okay," he agreed happily.

We rounded up the rest of the kids and deposited them with their respective families, then headed for the dining room to order dinner. Mitch and I split a massive order of spaghetti with meatballs the size of Wiffle balls while the kids had chicken strips. Mitch nudged the last meatball toward me. "What's that sad expression for?"

"No, no more for me." I put my fork down with a sigh. "I just can't help thinking that we would be at Summer and Brian's wedding reception right now."

Before Mitch could reply, Livvy, who had been twisted around backward looking out the window, swiveled back toward us. "Can we go swimming? It's stopped raining." The clouds still hung overhead, but I realized it wasn't quite as dark and gray outside as it had been only a little while ago.

"Maybe Mr. Markham's weather forecast is right. Maybe the storm has cleared," I said. The only water falling now was dripping off the trees when the wind shifted their branches. A small strip of bright sky glowed beyond the tree canopy. Mitch and I exchanged a glance, and I said, "It is early, and we don't have anything else planned for tonight. I mean, now we don't."

"I don't see why not," Mitch agreed. He checked the weather app on his phone and declared that the severe weather was out of the area. "So yes, we can go to the pool, but if it starts to rain again, out you come."

The kids let out whoops and that was pretty much the end of dinner. By the time we returned to the room, got everyone suited up, and found our way down to the pool, the requisite one hour since dinner had elapsed, and I waved the kids in. Broken clouds now covered the sky, but the patches showing through were pale blue.

Mitch jumped in the pool, spraying both kids. I wasn't ready to swim yet, so I settled into a poolside chair, but I'd barely got my swimsuit cover-up off before Livvy surged out of the water and ran-walked toward me, showering me with drops of water as she neared me. "Mom, I think I left my book in the dining room."

I wasn't surprised she'd brought a book to dinner. Her reasoning was that there might be a few spare minutes, and she was all about working in a chapter or two whenever she could.

I glanced at Mitch, who had swum over to the side of the pool near me and was listening with his arms propped up on the edge of the pool. "Rock, paper, scissors?" he asked.

I couldn't help but smile. "No, I'll go. You stay here on pool duty," I said as I pulled on my cover-up and flip-flops.

In the dining room, I found the book under the chair where Livvy had sat during dinner. The table was empty, and I was able to get the book, then slip back out of the dining room without disturbing anyone's meal, but I ran right into Patricia as I left.

"You!" she said, pointing a finger at my nose. "I know it was you. Don't bother to deny it."

Chapter Sixteen

I took a half step back from Patricia's pointing finger. "I'm sorry?"

"You told that interfering detective that I was in the banquet room and handled the flower arrangements. Who else could it have been? I doubt the florist or that waitress even knows my name."

I knew that statement was wrong—Denise certainly knew Patricia's name—but I didn't say that. It would only agitate her more to know she had a reputation with the vendors.

"He all but accused me of poisoning Summer, my future daughter-in-law. And"—her voice rose—"he wanted to know what my relationship was with Ned Blackson. Ned! The photographer. You're so nosy. I'm sure you are to blame for that, too. Well, I won't have it. It's harassment, that's what it is. I want it stopped now." She pointed her finger at me again, bobbing it up and down to emphasize her point. "Do you understand me? As if I'd have anything other than a professional relationship with a *photographer*."

I don't take being lectured well. Especially when the person doing the lecturing was as insufferable as Patricia. My resolve to keep my mouth shut evaporated. "Then why was he blackmailing you?"

Patricia reared back as if she'd had an electric shock, and her expression immediately shut down. "That is not true," she said, but her assuredness was gone.

"I don't think so," I said. "I think it's true. And Detective Redding must think it's a possible lead if he's asked you about it."

She pinched her lips together, then sighed. All the tension and righteous indignation that had been stiffening her manner seeped right out of her. She glanced around the lobby. "So I suppose everyone knows . . . or will shortly?" She didn't wait for a reply, but went on in a much more subdued voice than she'd used just moments earlier. "Well, it doesn't matter now. All the plans I had for this weekend . . . they're all ruined now."

"I haven't told anyone but Detective Redding," I said. "I felt I had to, after Ned died."

She stared at me a long moment, then rubbed her temple. I noticed that her fingers were trembling. "I need a drink. Come on, I'll buy." She turned and marched quickly into the bar that connected to the restaurant. I wasn't really in the mood to grab a drink with her, but she looked a bit—and I couldn't believe I was actually thinking this—fragile. I blew out a sigh and followed her into the bar. The last thing I wanted was for her to show up with a hangover in the morning.

My swimsuit cover-up, a loose cotton dress, wasn't what I'd pick to wear to the resort bar, but unless someone noticed the straps of my swimsuit at the neckline, no one would realize I was dressed for the pool. No one raised an eyebrow at my attire, but I was glad when Patricia sat down at a booth rather than on one of the bar stools. I slid onto a leather bench across from her. She'd already motioned the waiter over. "Scotch. Neat." She looked at me with eyebrows raised.

"Just soda water with a twist of lime for me," I said as I placed Livvy's book on the table. I wanted a clear head in the morning, too.

The waiter was back in moments, depositing the drinks on the small table between us. Patricia took a large slug of hers, checked that the booth behind her was vacant, then settled back in her seat. "I may have overreacted. Just a tad. When I think about it now, with everything that's happened this weekend, well, what Ned threatened to broadcast . . . it's not that important in the big scope of things, but several months ago . . . well, I didn't want it getting out."

"Didn't want what getting out?"

Patricia sighed again, then leaned forward and lowered her voice a notch. "That Gus had joined one of those far right, extremist groups."

"You mean like a new Nazi party?" I hadn't heard about anything like that going on, but I wasn't exactly up on all the news. Being a mom and running a business—even a part-time business—took up most of my time and attention. I didn't follow politics or the news as closely as I probably should. I sipped my bubbly drink and waited.

"No. Worse. It was one of those conservative groups," she said, lowering her voice so much that the last two words were barely audible.

I shifted in my seat. "I'm not sure I understand," I said, but I was afraid I did. I just wanted to be perfectly clear on what Patricia thought.

"Well, you can imagine what a disaster that would be, if it got out. I mean, those people, they're for guns and taking the country back—whatever that means—but it doesn't sound peaceful, does it? And . . . well, I don't know what else they're for, but it's not good. I know that."

She scanned the room again and must have been satisfied that everyone was out of range and continued in a low, confidential tone. "I mean, all the important influential people, all the people who *matter*, are on the other end of the political spectrum, if you know what I mean." She raised her eyebrows at me and gave me a knowing look. "If word got out that Gus was participating in those . . . circles, well, Brian wouldn't have even a ghost of a chance of making a political career."

I clamped my lips together. I'm not an apolitical person, but I make it a policy to never talk politics with clients or strangers. "I see," was all I said, and I was quite proud of myself for my restraint.

"Of course you do," Patricia said comfortably.

The thought that I might not agree with her had never crossed her mind, I realized. But, in fairness, that was how she operated one hundred percent of the time on all subjects—her opinion was right and best and everyone should agree with her.

Patricia picked up her glass for another drink and gulped some more scotch. "You know the ironic part? I invited him to our house. I thought it would save time." She looked away and shook her head. "If only we'd gone to his studio it never would have happened. Ned never would have known. But no, I had to go and ask him to come to our house." She twisted her glass around as she said, "Gus hates having his picture taken, but we needed a professional shot for the ballet program. We're gold medallion sponsors, you know, and they always have their pictures in the program. I thought Gus would throw less of a fit if he didn't have to go somewhere. Ned agreed to come to our house and took the pictures very quickly."

She signaled the waiter for another drink. "Another for you?" she asked me, but I declined. Patricia continued, "I had an appointment and had to leave immediately after the photos were taken. I left Ned and Gus chatting about football." She widened her eyes. "You would think that would be a safe subject. Men can talk about that for hours. I never thought . . ." She trailed off for a moment, then said, "Apparently, Ned saw a flyer Gus had brought home, and asked Gus about it. Well, that was all it took. Gus is very passionate about politics. He told Ned about their group and Ned must have hinted he wanted to be involved because Gus invited him to the next meeting." She reached across the table and placed her hand on my arm. "I found out all of this through Ned, who was only too happy to tell me as he showed me photos from those meetings. Ned had offered to 'document' the meeting for Gus—free of charge." She laughed, a sharp braying sound. "Turns out, he planned on me reimbursing him."

"The art show," I said as the waiter arrived with a tray and fresh drink.

She took the new drink from the waiter but waited until he'd left before she spoke again. "Yes. That's what he asked for, but I talked him into taking on Summer's wedding. It's a significant job. He agreed, but as soon as Summer signed off on Ned as the vendor, he came back to me about the art show again. Of course, I couldn't have everyone know what Gus was involved in. It just wouldn't look good, so I agreed to sponsor the show. I do lots of work in the arts community. It wouldn't raise any eyebrows."

"But how could you expect to keep Gus's politics a secret?" Surely, if Gus was attending rallies or meetings, his participation was public knowledge. How could you blackmail someone whose secret was already out?

"Oh, didn't I explain that? These meetings were to *set up* a group. Planning meetings. Gus is a founding member." She shook her head and sipped her drink.

"Once I realized how deep Gus was into it, I convinced him that they should wait until the summer to go public. You know, concentrate on the fall campaign season. I figured that after a few months had gone by he'd take up some new interest, and his political dabbling would melt away. I was wrong, though. He's still interested in it. I've tried bridge, fishing, and that fantasy football thing, but nothing has grabbed his attention." She rubbed her temple again. "I wasn't sure where it would end. I could tell Ned was very pleased with the situation and wasn't going to leave me alone."

"So Ned wasn't satisfied with the job of photographing Summer's wedding and an art show?"

"It was foolish of me to assume that he'd be happy and go away. No, he wanted more."

"That's why you looked relieved when he died."

"You noticed that?" She shifted her gaze away across the bar and looked truly embarrassed for the first time. "It's true. I'll admit it. His death made my life a lot easier, but now . . . with all the other things that have happened this weekend, no one is going to want to link themselves with Brian. It's such a shame. Such a waste. Like I told that detective, I didn't kill Ned or try to hurt Summer."

"But you were still worried after he died, too. That's why you went to his room, to look through his things."

"How did you know about that?" she asked.

"My room is a few doors down from Ned's. After the accident, I saw you slip out of his room and sneak off down the stairs. Why else would you be in his room?"

She didn't reply, just looked into her glass.

"How did you get in there?"

She swished the scotch around and gave a tiny shake of her head. "I told a maid I'd forgotten my key card. Of course she let me in."

Of course she would, I thought. Patricia could be very intimidating.

"Did you find anything?"

"No. It was a long shot. I realized that the police probably had already been there to search and had probably taken his camera. But I had to check . . . on the off chance that he had brought photos. The guest list contains quite a few powerful people. . . ."

She didn't need to finish. With her handpicked selection of guests, Ned would have had a great opportunity to show the photos to any number of people who Patricia wouldn't want to see them.

"But as I said before," Patricia went on, "Ned's death might have made it easier to make sure Gus's political dabblings didn't get out, but overall his death cast a pall over the weekend and left a bad taste in the mouth of a lot of important people. Too many things have gone wrong. No one will want to link themselves with Brian after this."

"Something that Brian is completely unconcerned with." The voice came from the other side of a decorative half wall that divided the bar. The booth on the opposite side of ours creaked and Gus's head appeared as he stood.

Patricia paled and reached for her glass, but it was empty again. "Darling, I had no idea you were here."

"Obviously." Gus walked around the dividing wall and sat down in the booth next to Patricia.

She fingered her glass nervously and raised her hand to signal the waiter, but Gus stopped her before she could get her hand more than a few inches in the air. "Don't you think you've had enough? Wedding tomorrow morning, and all."

"Yes, I suppose you're right."

I watched their interaction, fascinated. I hadn't seen them together very often and my impressions of the time I had watched them had been that Gus was definitely in the henpecked husband category, but Patricia, despite her tough words earlier about nipping his political aspirations in the bud, seemed downright conciliatory at the moment.

Gus took a last sip of his drink that he'd carried with him and set it down. "I don't make any apology for my political opinions." He shifted, turning his shoulders sideways so that he was looking directly at Patricia. "Everyone has a right to express their opinion—that's what I'm interested in preserving, by the way. Your advice on waiting until the summer to kick off the group was sound. Volunteers burn out if you work them constantly, and we do need to focus our energy on our main priorities. I decided to follow your suggestion because it was good advice, not because I was bored with the group. So you're going to have to give up on the idea of me dropping it. It's too important. Just like you're going to have to butt out of Brian's career."

"But I'm helping him."

"He doesn't want your help."

"But he's young. In time—"

"Patricia, you need to let it go. Brian will make his own way," he said in a tone that indicated the subject was closed.

Patricia got a mulish look on her face, and I expected her to protest, but Gus pulled several pages of lined paper from his pocket and put them on the table. They had been torn from a spiral notebook and little bits of paper from the ragged edge dappled the table. "Now, I think we need to agree to disagree on political things. I'm not changing my mind any more than you're willing to change yours, so we should just leave it. I think we need to find something we can agree on, something we can work together on." He tapped the papers. "I think we need to start our own foundation."

Patricia had been on the verge of protesting, but she paused, clearly surprised. "A foundation?" she asked, and I could see she was turning the idea over in her mind.

Gus pushed the papers so they were in front of Patricia. "All my thoughts are right there. You put so much time and energy into all these causes of yours. Let's concentrate on something we can both agree on. Focus all that drive and energy into something we both care about."

Patricia reached for the papers and unfolded them as Gus continued. "There are lots of people out of work now and lots of people have lost their houses. I know those are two of your pet charity concentrations."

Patricia's gaze had been skimming over the paper, but she looked up. "I didn't think you cared about any of my charity things."

"Oh, I always pay attention to what you're doing." He smiled at her, and she grinned back. I'd been feeling like a third wheel for several minutes, so I reached for Livvy's book. As I scooted to the end of the booth, Gus continued, "I think we could do something like Habitat for Humanity—they do a lot of good work—but add in a training element. Instead of using volunteers to do the work, we could use the construction itself as an on-the-job training program. Plumbing and electricity, building trades, those aren't glamorous, but if someone has those skills it could put food on the table."

"I think I'll leave you two alone to discuss this. . . ." I murmured.

"Oh, Gus, this is an interesting proposal." Patricia flipped to another page. "This really could work." She had a look of happy fascination on her face that I'd frequently seen on both of the kids' faces—Livvy when she first held a new release from a favorite author and Nathan when he got a new set of Legos.

"With you in charge, I think it could," Gus said.

I slipped out of the booth and said good-bye to them. They murmured replies, but Patricia was already flipping back and forth through the pages. As I left, Gus stretched his arm along the back of the booth and pointed to something on the paper. "Let me explain this part . . ."

I signed the slip at the bar to bill my drink to our room and slowly headed back to the pool, thinking that as crazy as Patricia's story was, I believed her. I also had a hard time picturing Yvonne swinging so far from one end of the emotional spectrum to the other—hating Summer enough to actually harm her then shifting to repentance and becoming the welcoming mother-in-law? No, I just didn't think she could make that big of a change. I thought her remorse was genuine, but I didn't really think that she'd intended to physically harm either Ned or Summer. Sure, she wanted to break up the wedding, but I didn't think she'd resort to murder to do it.

And that left exactly zero suspects.

I opened the door to our room, and Mitch put a finger to his lips. "Kids are in bed."

"Already?" I'd returned to the pool and found the chaise longue chairs we had been using were empty. I had checked the time and realized how late it was. I had spent quite a while talking with Patricia. I'd headed to our room, figuring I'd find Mitch in the middle of getting the kids ready for their bedtime routine.

"Yep," Mitch said. "We did the whole bit—bath, pajamas, teeth, bedtime story, prayers. The whole checklist."

"Wow. You are awesome. Remind me to do something nice for you later."

Mitch waggled his eyebrows and moved toward me.

"Not that nice. They're your kids, too."

Mitch laughed and pulled me into his arms. "Where were you?" he asked between kisses.

"Patricia waylaid me as I left the dining room. Accused me of siccing Redding on her about Summer and Ned."

"Well, you did," Mitch said.

"I know. And I pointed out that Ned was blackmailing her."

Mitch lifted his head from my neck.

"Yes. It was rather juvenile and impulsive, but I did get the whole story on Ned. He was blackmailing her—"

"Mooommm, are you coming to tuck me in?" Livvy called from the adjoining room.

"So big she needs a cell phone, but still wants to be tucked in," I said to Mitch, then called out that yes, I'd come tuck her in.

"We better enjoy it while we can," Mitch said. "It won't be long before she'll be putting up Do Not Enter signs on her door. You can fill me in on all the details about Ned in a little while."

Swimming had done in Nathan. He was already sleeping hard. He sprawled across the bed, his limbs limp, breathing heavily. I kissed his forehead, then moved to Livvy's bed.

She was propped up on the pillows, the light of my phone glowing on her face.

"What are you looking at?"

"The pictures I took at the rehearsal dinner."

"Ah," I said as I snuggled in next to her and wrapped my arm around her shoulder. "That's a good one," I said. "You got everyone." She'd zoomed out and had Brian and Summer at the center of the table with Meg beside Summer and Graham beside Brian. The rest of the bridesmaids and groomsmen filled out the table. Everyone was smiling and happy. "It's a video." Livvy touched the screen and the scene jumped to life as a jumble of conversation and laughter came out of the speakers. One of the waiters moved through, topping off the champagne glasses, and then Gus stood to make his toast. The video ended and Livvy switched to another picture.

"I like this one better."

The photo was a close-up of Summer and Brian as they clinked their glasses together. Their gazes were locked on each other, and they were both smiling widely. It was hard to believe that only a short time later Summer would be at the hospital.

"Is Aunt Summer going to be okay?" Livvy asked in a small voice.

"Yes. Didn't you hear us talking about it in the library tonight? She's doing much better and will be back tomorrow morning."

"Yeah. I heard." Livvy snuggled deeper into the curve of my arm. "But sometimes grown-ups are wrong. They think one thing, but then something else happens."

"Well, that is true. We're certainly not always right."

"Yeah, I know."

I had to bite back a smile at her confident tone. Oh, boy. The teenage years weren't far off. I could feel them getting closer by the minute. "But, Aunt Summer is much better. Her doctor told her she could leave in the morning if she was feeling good. And she is determined to get married tomorrow, so I'm pretty sure she'll be here tomorrow.

There's not much that can stop Aunt Summer when she sets her mind to something." I squeezed her close in a hug. "Now, let me say a good-night prayer for you, and you can get some sleep. Tomorrow's going to be a big day."

"Okay." Livvy's skinny arms went around my neck, and I inhaled the scent of soap and shampoo, then she handed me my phone and slid lower in the bed. Her eyelids were droopy, and I could tell that the time in the pool had worn her out, too. I said a quick prayer for her and for Summer, then kissed Livvy's forehead and tiptoed from the room.

At breakfast the next morning, I checked my phone. No messages or missed calls. I sighed, then switched to look through my photos.

I hadn't slept well. My thoughts were on an endless confusing loop, alternating between trying to figure out who would want to hurt Summer and thinking about details related to the wedding ceremony. I still didn't know what Summer had coordinated with Mr. Markham for the ceremony. I'd stopped by the front desk to ask him this morning, but was told he was in a meeting and that he'd call me. I'd also called Summer twice this morning. It was early, but from what I remembered of my time in the hospital after the births of Livvy and Nathan, the nurses would have already been in and out of her room several times by now. But she hadn't answered or texted back, which wasn't like her.

I swished my finger across the screen, dragging each picture into view, then sending them off again. Someone had poisoned Summer at that dinner. If only I could find something in the photos . . . but there was no one caught suspiciously reaching toward Summer's plate or lingering in the background behind her chair.

"Ellie. Your food," Mitch said.

I looked up to find the waitress hovering behind my shoulder with my omelet. I pulled away my arms, which had been propped on the edge of the table, and slipped my phone into my tote bag beside the wedding binder. A huge stack of pancakes was deposited in front of Mitch and smaller versions went to the kids.

"Nathan, your food is here, too. Put that away—" I said as he sent one of the paper airplanes he'd made yesterday zooming through the air. He was aiming for his cousin's table next to us, but the plane went farther, sailing over the table and bouncing off Graham's shoulder blade. He turned around to see what had tapped him on the shoulder and spotted the plane on the floor behind his chair.

"Nathan, go get your plane and apologize to Mr. Murphy," I said.

Nathan prepared to slide off his chair, but Graham had already swiped up the plane from the carpet and was at our table. He smoothed out the tip of the plane, which was a little bent, as he handed it back. "No need to apologize. Here you go, buddy. That's quite an impressive plane."

"Thanks, my uncle made it for me. He says it's an F-15."

"Nice," Graham said before he returned to his table.

I heard my phone ringing in the depths of my tote bag. As soon as I pulled it free, I recognized the number. It was Redding.

"Mrs. Avery. I have an update for you. You are the point of contact for the Avery family?"

"Yes, I suppose so."

"Good. I tried to contact your sister-in-law but got her voice mail. I understand she's leaving the hospital today?" he asked.

"Yes, that is the plan."

"Glad to hear she's better." His voice became more seri-

ous. "I have results from the tests on the food from the rehearsal dinner."

"That was fast."

"Well, apparently the police commissioner got some
feedback from someone involved in the case, and he was
able to expedite things."

I sensed Patricia's hand at work. I bet she called . . . someone, someone with influence, who could make things move
faster.

Redding let out a frustrated sigh. "There were no traces
of any poison."

"No trace?" I asked. "Nothing at all?"

Mitch looked toward me. I tilted the phone away and
said in a low voice, "It's Redding. He says there was no
poison in the food from the dinner."

Mitch's eyebrows drew together. I'm sure my expression
mirrored his.

"None," Redding confirmed. "All the tests for the food
and the drink came back negative."

"But that doesn't make sense," I said. "Could she have
been poisoned some other way? Through touching something? Or breathing . . . I don't know, fumes or vapor?"

"I've got a call in to our consultant, asking those very
questions. Make sure your family keeps a close eye on her
today."

A commotion at the entrance to the restaurant drew my
attention. I turned and saw Summer and Brian enter the
room, holding hands and smiling. "We will. Thanks for
the update," I said to Redding.

Summer and Brian paused at a table where Summer exchanged hugs and exclamations with her bridesmaids, then
they came over to our table. Summer moved around the
circular table, depositing hugs all around, but giving Livvy
and Nathan an especially tight squeeze. Brian went to Gra-

ham and they shook hands. "Good to see you, man," Graham said.

"We're glad to be back."

Summer embraced Mitch then turned to me, a huge grin on her face. "I can't tell you how glad I am to be here. Nothing gives you an appreciation for good health like being in the hospital."

"I thought we might not see you until later," I said.

"Are you kidding? Those people were in and out of my room at five a.m. If they could take my blood that early, they could certainly start the paperwork to get me out of there."

Brian said, "Yes, she was quite unstoppable. And once the nurses heard it was our wedding day, they moved even faster."

"So the wedding is *really* going to be today?" Livvy asked.

"Yes, really. Are you ready to dress up?" Summer asked.

Livvy nodded. Nathan shrugged.

"Oh! Graham, we have more good news." Summer swiveled toward him. "The doctors are bringing Julia out of the coma today."

He looked surprised. "Oh, ah—good. I didn't realize. No one said anything to me."

"Don't worry. I talked to her sister—Audrey, isn't it?— who said the doctors say Julia is doing better. They expect her to come out of the coma just fine. You should be there."

"That's wonderful. But what about the wedding? The ceremony and everything. I don't want to bail on you," he said as he looked toward Mitch.

"Don't even worry about that," Brian said. "You need to be with Julia. Go on. Nothing is as important as someone's health," Brian said as his glance strayed to Summer.

"That's right. Go on," Summer said, patting his arm. "With everything that's happened, it really brings into perspective what's important. Who cares if we have an uneven number of bridesmaids to groomsmen?"

"Don't let Patricia hear you say that," I said in a low voice.

"You know what?" Summer said. "She can be upset if she wants to, but things like that aren't worth wasting any worry on."

"I'm sure one of the ushers can stand in for you," Brian said, his glance going to Mitch. "That will even up the numbers and keep everyone happy. You wouldn't mind, would you?" Brian asked Mitch.

"Not at all. I'd be happy to do it," Mitch said.

"Let me make a call." Graham returned to his table where he'd left his cell phone. He stood there a moment, the phone pressed to his ear.

I motioned for Summer to pull up a seat from a nearby table. "So tell me about the new ceremony. What do you need from me?"

"Nothing," Summer said, a grin on her face. "It's all taken care of."

"Everything? Are you sure?"

"Yes. It's only a few little tweaks. Everyone can still meet at the same places, just the location of the ceremony has shifted. The reception is still the same."

"Summer, I really think we should go over the changes."

"No time. Here comes the rest of the Avery clan," she said, eyeing the group of aunts and uncles who had just entered the dining room. "I know every one of them will want to hug me and make sure I'm okay. Then I have to get to the spa for my hair and makeup."

"Well, okay," I said. "It's your wedding." If she wanted

to go with the flow that was fine. I'd try to handle things as they popped up. I studied her face closely. She looked awfully relaxed for a woman who had endured multiple pranks and a bout with poison. I waved her closer and asked in a low voice, "Did they give you something at the hospital before you left?"

"What do you mean?"

"Maybe something to relax you?"

"No, why?"

"I don't know. You seem to be handling the stress of your wedding day really well, considering, you know, what's happened over the last few days."

"I'm determined to not worry about it," she replied, also speaking softly. "Brian is on hyper-vigilant alert." Her glance shifted to Mitch. "As well as Mitch, Dad, and you. Not to mention all the other assorted relatives who are here. This is probably the safest I'll ever be."

Graham returned to our table as he ended his call. "It's all good. I spoke to Audrey. I'm going to check in with Julia this morning, but I'll be able to make it back here in time for the wedding."

Livvy tugged on Summer's hand. "Aunt Summer, I thought he"—she pointed to Brian—"wasn't supposed to see you before the wedding."

"That's an old wives' tale."

"A tale?" Livvy said with interest. "That's like a story, right?"

"No, an old wives' tale is an idiom."

Nathan snickered, and I leaned forward to clarify. "That's a grammar term. Idiom, not idiot." I'd learned a lot about how little boys' brains worked during the last few years.

"Oh," he said, clearly disappointed.

Summer said, "The old wives' tale is that if the groom sees the bride before the wedding on their wedding day, it's bad luck, but that's just a superstition. You know, something that people believe, but it's not based on fact. We're having no more bad luck around here." Summer said the last sentence almost as a declaration.

Brian nodded and reached for her hand. "I think there's some people who want to talk to you."

They walked away hand in hand and were engulfed in the group of relatives near the doorway. I watched them and saw that Brian was keeping an eye on Summer. Mitch was as well. Summer was probably right. She probably was safer now than she had been all week. I turned back to finish my breakfast. Despite Summer's relaxed attitude there was a lot to do before the ceremony today.

"Mom, that's Dad's glass," Livvy said.

I looked down at the glass of orange juice and realized she was right. This glass was almost empty and I'd only had a few sips from my nearly full glass. I replaced Mitch's glass, setting it down. "They were so close together. I picked up the wrong one and didn't notice." A thought jolted into my mind. "Oh," I said suddenly.

Mitch looked up from his plate. "Ellie, are you okay?"

"The champagne," I murmured, reaching for my phone and bringing up the pictures of the rehearsal. I flicked through them again, then looked at Mitch. "I was wrong. So wrong. This changes everything."

Tips for an Organized Wedding

Delegation is the key to making sure the big day runs smoothly. Even if you plan everything yourself, you can still hire a wedding day coordinator. Or, a cost-cutting option would be to draft a trusted family member or friend for this role, but it can be a stressful job. Make sure that if you recruit a friend or family member, he or she is okay with essentially "working" on the wedding day. A detail-oriented person who doesn't mind handling any crisis that pops up is an ideal choice.

Chapter Seventeen

"Changes what?" Mitch asked as he cut into his stack of pancakes.

I shifted my chair closer to Mitch and showed him the pictures of the rehearsal. "It was the champagne. The poison was *in* the champagne."

"But Redding said there were no traces of poison in anything they tested," Mitch said.

"Yes, but they weren't able to test the individual glasses. They'd already been washed by the time Redding got there. They tested the residue in the bottles and there wouldn't have been anything in the bottles that were served to everyone because the poison was only added to one glass, the one Summer drank from. Look at her champagne glass," I said, tapping the phone's screen. It was the photo of Summer and Brian that Livvy took seconds before they drank their first toast. Their narrow champagne flutes were pressed together and while the rims of the glasses were at the same level, the difference in the amount of liquid was easy to see now. Before, when I'd looked at the pictures, I'd been so focused on looking at people, searching for someone furtively slipping something into Summer's food that I'd overlooked the disproportionately large amount of champagne in Summer's glass.

"See? Hers is filled almost to the top, while Brian's is only about two-thirds full."

"Yes, it is, but that's not proof—"

"Of course not. We can't be one hundred percent sure, but you know how they are, these event dinners." We'd attended many formal dinners, called Dining-outs, as part of Mitch's military career, as well as various Hail and Farewell events that were usually much more casual. "They don't top off everyone's glass to the brim at events like this one," I said. "When the servers make their rounds they give everyone roughly the same portion, but they certainly don't fill your glass completely. I'm sure it's a money-saving thing for the resort."

"So you think someone added some sort of liquid that contained the poison to Summer's glass?"

"Yes. Think about it. Of all the food and drink served that night, it would be the one thing the poisoner could be sure she'd consume. Maybe not a lot, but she would have to at least take a few sips following the toasts. If the poison was highly concentrated . . . it might be enough."

"Enough to make her sick and send her to the hospital," Mitch said, his voice tight.

I lowered my voice even more as I flicked back to pictures that Livvy had taken. She was quite the shutterbug and had taken thirty or forty, so the moments before the toast were well documented. I found the video, made sure the sound was off on my phone, then hit play. The image came to life, and there was only a slight wobble in the picture as Livvy panned across the head table, capturing a waiter as he moved along filling each person's champagne glass. He finished serving everyone at the head table and I knew the video would end in a few seconds. I paused it. "Look at the glasses," I said, handing the phone to Mitch.

He zoomed in and slid the picture back and forth, studying each glass. "But they're all the same. No one has more than anyone else."

"Right." I took the phone back, skipped over the section where Livvy panned away from the hand table, then moved to the last frame of the video Livvy had taken. "Now look at this."

"Yes, I see it. It's fuzzy, but I can tell there's more in this glass, but . . ." Mitch looked up at me. "But it's in front of Brian, not Summer."

"I know," I whispered. I flicked my finger over the screen, sliding the next picture into place, which was of Summer and Brian clicking their glasses together with Summer holding the fuller glass.

"But that means . . ." Mitch looked away from me, his gaze scanning the room as he worked through it.

"That Summer picked up the wrong glass, like I did just now. It's easy to do at formal dinners with all the silverware and glasses. I know I have to check and see which glass is mine sometimes."

Mitch clicked the screen, making it go black. He turned more toward me. "So the poison was meant for Brian?"

"Yes, I think so. Which changes everything. Maybe it's *Brian* who is in danger, not Summer. If Ned hadn't taken the golf cart, Brian would have been driving. He would have had the accident."

Mitch glanced swiftly around the room, then ran his arm along the back of my chair so he could lean in and whisper in my ear. "But what about the poison ivy and the paintball?"

"Distractions, I think," I said, voicing one of the thoughts that had been buzzing through my brain for the last few minutes. "Setting the stage so that the incident with the golf cart would look like an accident. It would be considered another prank, but one that had gone horribly wrong. There's only one person who could have coordinated it all. . . ."

I waited, to see if Mitch would come to the same conclusion I had. His gaze scanned the room and came to rest on a table not far from us. Mitch looked back at me, his eyebrows raised.

"Graham. I think so too. He could have planted the paintball gun, the poison ivy, and the socket wrench in Julia's room very easily, using the connecting door. And he was sitting right beside Brian at the dinner. Who would have a better opportunity to add something to his drink than the person seated beside him? He could have taken some of the lily of the valley from the flower arrangement that was damaged. He went in the resort to change while all of us were at the rehearsal. I spoke to him on the steps, but I didn't go inside with him. He could have slipped into the banquet room, taken some of the lily of the valley, and then gone upstairs, or he could have taken some on the way down, but I'd assume he'd have to cut it up, or pulverize it or something before he added it to Brian's glass. No one would drink something with bits of leaves or flowers floating in it. So it would make sense he would take it on his way upstairs so he could"—I swallowed, not wanting to think about how cold and calculating he'd been—"prepare it."

I looked across the room at him. He sat half turned away from us, his face in profile. The waitress reached to move his empty plate. He nodded at her and smiled. "How can he look so normal, so friendly? And the way he's been treating Brian . . . how can he act like his best friend and then try to poison him? I don't understand."

"Neither do I," Mitch said. "Who knows why? But you better tell Redding."

"Yes, and send him these pictures, too," I said.

Graham stood and pushed his chair in. He headed for our table. I immediately dropped my phone to my lap like a kid caught trying to pass a note in class. He gave us a polite nod. "See you in a few hours."

Mitch said, "Okay. Give Julia our best wishes for a speedy recovery."

"Thank you, I will." For just a second his gaze slipped from Mitch's face toward Nathan, then he smiled. "See you later this morning."

Curiously, I looked over at Nathan. There was nothing to see except his plate swimming in syrup. He'd taken advantage of our preoccupation with the photos to drench his pancakes. He lifted a soggy bite to his mouth and chewed in satisfaction. Why that extra moment of attention from Graham? There was nothing to look at but a sticky little boy . . . and his paper airplane, which was balanced on the top of an unused coffee cup from his place setting.

"Ellie, did you hear what I said?"

"Hmm, what? I'm sorry." I turned back to Mitch.

He looked toward Graham's back as he walked through the tables to the restaurant's entrance. "Julia. He's going to visit Julia this morning."

I felt my eyes widen. "And they're bringing her out of the coma today," I said, a sick feeling coming over me. If we were right, and Julia wasn't guilty of all the pranks, if she was just a scapegoat whom Graham had set up to take the fall for him, she'd be able to deny everything if she was awake. I reached for my phone, as Mitch said, "Approaching monster-in-law at two o'clock."

"I can't get sucked into wedding details . . . or even arguing with her right now."

"You go," Mitch said. "I'll run interference for you."

I slipped away from the table, automatically shoulder-
ing my tote bag, which had been on the back of my chair.
I'd only gone a few steps when I darted back and scooped
up the paper airplane. "Just borrowing this for a minute,"
I said to Nathan.

He would have protested, but his mouth was too full. I
turned and escaped as Patricia picked up her pace, her
gaze fixed on me. As I hurried away, out of the corner of
my eye I saw Mitch stand and move into her path as he
said, "Ellie will be back in a moment. Minor emergency
that requires her attention. Why don't you wait here with
us for her?"

Mitch really was great. Not many husbands would sac-
rifice themselves to casual chitchat with the likes of Patricia, I thought as I scurried through the tables. When I
reached the lobby, I slipped into a chair that was nearly
hidden under the huge leaves of a potted banana plant and
dialed Redding's number. It went immediately to his voice
mail. My shoulders dropped. I didn't want to leave this as
a voice-mail message. I hung up. I'd try again in a second.

While I waited, I pried the folds of the paper airplane
apart and skimmed the text. It wasn't the same page I'd
looked at yesterday, but it was definitely part of a real estate contract. Mentions of escrow and title company details filled the tiny text.

I looked consideringly toward the library, debated for a
second, then stood and quickly paced down the hall. Except for one person at the far end of the table, the business
center area of the library was deserted. I went to the recycling bin. It was still unlocked so I flipped it open and dug
around inside.

"Um . . . I don't think you're supposed to do that." The
woman at the table frowned at me.

"Just looking for some papers that were thrown in here by mistake." I shifted the papers around, but there weren't any documents like the one I held in my hand.

I let the lid fall back into place and redialed Redding's number as I strode out the door of the library. The phone rang again. If he didn't pick up this time, I would have to leave a message.

I went back to the lobby, intending to leave my message then return to the dining room, but then I had another thought. There were more airplanes upstairs in Nathan's suitcase. Just as I turned toward the stairs, Graham stepped inside the lobby from the veranda. My steps checked slightly as I twisted my head around so I could see where he was going. He paused, caught sight of me, and his gaze dropped to the paper airplane in my hand.

A slight change came over his features as his gaze connected with mine. He looked determined and . . . not angry exactly . . . but cross. Probably exactly the way I looked when Livvy forgot her lunch and I had to turn the van around and rush back home to get it before the late bell rang at school.

For a second, I considered sprinting across the lobby back to the dining room, but that would take me right into Graham's path, and I didn't want to get anywhere near him at this moment. Maybe I was wrong. Maybe I'd misread him. Perhaps he had simply forgotten something and returned to the resort to get it before he left the island, but I didn't want to find out. I turned and headed up the stairs at a quick pace, but nothing that would look unusual or draw Graham's attention back to me if I'd been mistaken about the way he looked at me.

Redding's voice in my ear startled me. I'd been so focused on Graham, I'd stopped listening to the ringing line on the phone. I pressed the phone to my ear and realized it was Redding's message, not his voice that was coming through the phone. I took a deep breath, preparing to launch into my message as I reached the landing. The grand staircase folded back on itself and I switched direction, turning back to face the lobby as I climbed the next set of stairs. I gripped the handrail and looked over the banister to the set of stairs I'd just climbed. Graham was already halfway up, taking them two at a time, his long strides eating up the distance between him and the landing. He looked up quickly, his gaze going right to me. He was clearly checking my progress.

All thoughts of playing it cool and strolling down the hall to my room evaporated when his gaze settled on me. He was coming after me. I was his goal, his target.

A long beep sounded from my phone. I jerked the phone back to my mouth. I'd completely stopped listening to Redding's voice-mail greeting. "Redding. This is Ellie. Ellie Avery."

I sprinted up the steps toward the second floor, putting on a burst of speed that would have impressed my fellow neighborhood walking companions, the Stroller Brigade. "It was Graham," I said, then sucked in a breath. Adrenaline and sprinting up the stairs had robbed me of my breath. "Graham—" As I cleared the last step and came out on the landing, I put my hand in the little interior pocket of my tote bag where I usually placed my room key card, but the pocket was empty. "I don't have it," I muttered under my breath, remembering that when we'd left the room this morning, I didn't have my key, but Mitch had his, so I hadn't worried about it.

I didn't want to turn around and go back down the stairs and encounter Graham. It was irrational, but thoughts of Julia and her accident on the stairs flashed through my mind. *No, avoid Graham.* A quick glance over my shoulder showed that he hadn't reached the landing yet. Instead of turning to the right to the hallway that contained our very securely locked room, I darted to the left to a smaller door marked with an exit sign.

It was the only place I could go. There were no maids or carts or open doors anywhere in sight on the long hallway that stretched out to the right. The knob turned easily in my hand and I slipped inside the shadowy hallway as my phone emitted a long beep, the signal that the voice-mail recording had run out.

I ended the call then redialed, scanning the small, dim room. It wasn't a hallway. A narrow window high above my head let in a stream of light, illuminating a thin metal handrailing. My fingers traced along its upward curve. A circular staircase.

I leaned over the railing, peering downward. The staircase seemed to twist on for a long way, but when I thought of the high ceilings in the lobby and the airy grand staircase, it would be quite a long distance between the second floor and the ground-floor lobby. A muted noise from the hallway had me scooting up steps, climbing toward the thin stream of light. The third-floor landing should be closer. I could get out of the stairway faster by going up.

I moved up as quickly and quietly as I could, assuming it was another servant staircase. There hadn't been a lock on the door below, and I didn't want to give away my whereabouts by making any noise. If I could get to the next floor, presumably the servants' quarters that I'd toured a few days ago, I should be able to find the other set of stairs that we'd taken during the tour and follow them back down to the main floor where there were lots of people.

The phone rang in my ear as I continued up the steps. After a few turns, I expected to come to a small landing that jutted out from the twist of the stairs, like the one below, but the stairs continued to spiral upward, giving off an occasional creak as I carefully moved up the treads. Redding's outgoing voice-mail message finally came on as I came even with the narrow window that was letting in the light. My thighs were beginning to burn. Surely I should have reached the next floor by now? I'd covered more than enough distance vertically to be at the third floor.

I leaned toward the center support and glanced up for a quick check. The stairs continued to corkscrew upward for several more twists. That's when it hit me: I wasn't on a servants' staircase. I was in the old bell tower that soared over the resort. The bell tower we had peered up into after the bachelorette party that the guide, Emma, had guarded so that we wouldn't go up. I was in the bell tower that was closed for safety reasons. Suddenly those creaks that I'd mentally written off as part of an old building sounded a lot more ominous.

I turned around to make my way back down. Hopefully, Graham would have come out on the second floor, not seen me, and assumed I went into my room. I doubted he knew which rooms were ours. If he hadn't decided to wait in the hallway for me, I could slip back into the hallway and return to the main floor.

Far below me, the door that I'd entered through from the hallway opened. I froze, one foot poised in the air. Because I was so high I couldn't see who had opened the door. The metal of the staircase blocked my view of the doorway and its tiny landing, and there was no way I was going to lean over the railing and reveal myself. If I didn't move . . . perhaps the person would close the door and go away. Winded from the climb, I tried not to breathe.

I'd completely tuned out Redding's voice-mail greeting, which had been droning away in my ear, but his words stopped and the high-pitched tone, the signal to leave a message sounded. It wasn't extremely loud, but the small, silent, enclosed space of the bell tower seemed to magnify the faint sound.

The door below opened wider, throwing more light onto the staircase, but it was briefly blocked as a figure moved through the door and hit the metal treads at a running pace.

I whirled and ran toward the top of the steps as fast as I could, my tote bag banging against my side. The sound of our feet hitting the stairs reverberated up and down the tower.

"Ellie again. I got cut off," I said into the phone as I flew around the last twists of the staircase and stopped at a flat wooden panel placed at an angle above my head. I traced my fingers along the edge, and they brushed over a chain draped loosely across the panel. At my touch, the chain rattled, then slipped clear of whatever had been holding it in place with a noisy cavalcade of metal striking metal as the chain hit the stairs and slithered through the treads.

I felt the outline of a doorknob. I twisted and pressed forward up the rest of the steps. The little door was like an old-fashioned cellar entrance. I pushed it back and continued up the rest of the steps out onto the square viewing platform where a fresh, cool breeze whipped over me, feeling wonderful after the stuffy, closed tower. A narrow metal handrail ran around three sides of the staircase opening. Dead-ending into the door and getting it open had only taken seconds, but it felt like much longer with each thump of the footsteps echoing up through the tower.

"Like I said before, it was Graham," I said into the phone as I glanced around the tower. "He poisoned Summer. I have pictures that show her glass had something extra in it."

Four arched windows, one on each side of the tower, gave an amazing 360-degree view of the whole island, from the water sweeping up the beaches to the crumbled stones of the ruin in the distance. A glance down to the roof of the resort below did funny things to my stomach, and I quickly transferred my gaze back to the bell tower. There was no bell in the eaves overhead, but the sturdy beams that had once supported the bell stretched across the top of the tower.

The wind whipped my hair into my face, and I tilted my head to get it out of my eyes as I flipped the door closed, but there was no latch on the outside of it, no way to secure it in place. Rough wooden flooring planks covered a foot or two of space between the handrail and the window openings. I swept my gaze over the tiny walkway area around the door, but there was nothing, nothing I could use to brace it to keep it closed.

I moved around to the side opposite the opening for the stairs, getting as far away from them as I could, which wasn't very far in the tight confines of the tower. I said into the phone, "But the poison was actually meant for Brian. Summer picked up his glass by mistake."

The doorknob rattled, a hand shoved the door, throwing it open with a crash, and Graham moved up the last steps to the platform. He was winded and breathing hard. I flashed back to the morning we'd seen him on his run. With the beginnings of a potbelly, his heavy breathing, and bright red face, it had been obvious that working out was not high on his list of activities. He looked worse now. He gulped in air, his gaze flashing from my face to the phone.

I backed into a corner. The rough surface of the stucco dragged at the fabric of my shirt. At least it was a solid wall at my back and not one of the open windows. I knew time left on the message must have been close to running out. "As to why he did it," I said with my gaze locked on his, "I have no idea, but I think it has something to do with a real estate deal in Sarasota. I'm sure you'll figure it out. He's just chased me up the bell tower at the resort."

"Give me the phone," Graham said between gasps.

"Stupid of me to go up into the tower, I know," I said into the phone. "I didn't realize at the time it was the bell tower when I started up the stairs. But he's here with me now. Graham. Graham Murphy. So if anything happens to me, you'll know who did it." The beep signaling the end of the message cut off my last words.

I hit the end button and said, "Even though it cut me off, I'm sure he'll get the gist of it. The best thing to do would be for us to go back down the stairs."

He didn't reply, just stood there, his hands on his hips, working air in and out of his lungs as he watched me. The wind stilled for a moment, and I thought I heard a creaky metal sound. Was someone else on the staircase? I wasn't sure. A gust of wind whistled through the window openings, blocking out all other sounds.

I shifted my shoulder, letting my tote bag slide down my arm to my hand. "No need to be upset," I said, trying to use the same soothing tone as I did when Livvy or Nathan were upset. "I'm sure once you explain everything, it will be fine." I tightened my sweaty hand around the handles of the tote bag. With the wedding notebook inside it, it was actually quite heavy.

"The phone"—he paused for breath—"hand it to me," he repeated, his chin down.

"Sure." I tossed it toward him, intentionally throwing it wide, so he'd have to step away from the staircase opening. He took a half step so he could catch the phone, and I darted around the metal handrail for the stairwell. If I could get just a few seconds' start on him, I thought I could make it back down the stairs. I wasn't in spectacular shape, but I was in better shape than he was. I had been winded when I reached the viewing platform, but I was already breathing slower than he was.

I was on the first step down when he lunged for me. He caught my shoulder and threw me backward. Instinctively, I let go of the tote bag and reached out to break my fall as I hit the worn floorboards. Pain shot through me as I scrambled away, but he was on top of me, his hands closing around my throat before I could get any distance between us.

His red, sweaty face was bent over mine, too close. What scared me was that he wasn't infused with rage or anger. He applied pressure with a workmanlike concentration, his face almost impassive. I punched at his shoulder, clawed at his eyes, twisted, and kicked out, but he only turned his head away so that I couldn't reach his face. The pressure on my throat didn't lessen.

My vision went cloudy, then weird, pulsing black blobs appeared.

I reached out, my hand tracing along the floor as my vision distorted and darkness crept in at the edges. My fingers connected with something cool and round. Through the haziness, a thought connected somewhere in my fuzzy brain, and I realized I was touching a metal ring of the wedding binder. It must have fallen out of the tote bag when Graham knocked me down. I curled three fingers of my left hand through the ring and heaved it at Graham's head.

I must have connected with a sensitive spot because the pressure on my throat went away immediately, and he reeled back. I blinked and worked to suck in air. It burned and felt terrible, yet wonderful at the same time. As I blinked and cleared my vision, I saw papers from the binder flickering around the tower as the wind drove them into corners or swept them out the windows. But the fluttering papers were only a background to Graham, who had a hand pressed to his face over his eye. Blood seeped through his fingers as he gasped in pain, but he moved back toward me, his visible single eye fixed on me. I crawled backward.

Mitch emerged through the staircase opening. He took one swift glance around the tower and landed a right hook squarely on Graham's jaw that sent him sprawling onto the rough planks of the floor.

Chapter Eighteen

A couple of hours later, I sat on one of the library sofas. Mitch was beside me, his arm stretched along the back of the sofa lightly brushing against my shoulder. After knocking Graham out, Mitch had stayed at the viewing platform with me, calling first Redding then Mr. Markham, who called for an ambulance. When the paramedics arrived, they attended to Graham first, then carted him away and informed me that the corner of the binder that I'd thrown at him had hit him in the eye. "He may not see again out of that eye," the paramedic said.

Since Graham had been trying to choke the life out of me at the time I'd hit him, I wasn't able to muster up much sympathy for him. Redding had informed me that once the hospital finished patching up Graham, he had been placed under arrest.

Nathan's paper airplanes had been collected from his suitcase and were now flattened and stacked on the coffee table between Detective Redding and me. Uncle Bud was on the veranda with Livvy and Nathan teaching them how to fold new airplanes to replace the ones that the police had confiscated.

"I'm thoroughly confused." Summer sat in one of the leather club chairs near me. Brian perched on the arm beside her. "I know the hospital pumped me full of drugs and stuff yesterday, so maybe I'm still loopy on the aftereffects of those, but did you say it was *Graham* who did all those things?" She looked at me with concern, as if maybe I'd mixed up my words.

"I'm afraid so," I said as I glanced at Brian, who looked stunned.

Summer looked at him, too, out of the corner of her eye. "You're sure?"

"Oh, yes, I'm absolutely sure." Brian looked doubtful, so I added, "I'm positive it was Graham who choked me." I rubbed my throat where the skin was tender. Mitch assured me that my throat only looked a little bit pink, but I knew I'd have huge black bruises in a few days. Explaining that to Livvy and Nathan would be fun.

The paramedics had looked me over after they'd attended to Graham and said they couldn't detect any permanent damage. They had recommended that I go to the hospital for a more thorough exam. I'd refused. I would go see my regular doctor when we returned to North Dawkins, but I wanted to stay close to Mitch and as far away from Graham as I could. I thought it was rather ironic that Graham would be going to the same hospital where Julia and Summer had been taken.

Brian shook his head and looked toward Detective Redding. "I'm having a hard time taking it all in as well. If you could give us some more details?"

"Yes, that's why I asked you all here," Redding said. "I figured it would save time. In case you want to, um, continue with the events you had planned for the day."

Summer looked militant, and I thought she was about to launch into an adamant affirmation, but then she caught herself and glanced over her shoulder to Brian. "I suppose it depends on how everyone feels," she amended, glancing back to me.

"Oh, I'll be fine. I'm a little shaken up, but now that I've got my feet back on solid ground, I'm doing much better. Certainly better than Graham." I hadn't seen Graham since our encounter at the tower. Redding had already interviewed me alone. After Graham left for the hospital, I'd given Redding a blow-by-blow description of everything that had happened since breakfast.

Redding cleared his throat. "So Mrs. Avery, let's start with the photos you mentioned in your phone message, if you're able to talk . . ."

"Oh, yes. I can explain. Sorry about the incoherent messages. Talking while running isn't my strong suit." I glared at Mitch, who I knew might want to throw in a quip about running not *ever* being my strong suit to lighten the somber atmosphere, but he only raised his eyebrows, silently communicating a look to me that said, *I wouldn't dare bring that up here*. He removed my phone from his pocket and handed it to me. "I picked this up off the floor of the tower."

"Thanks," I said as I brought up the photos, then handed the phone to Brian. He had already forwarded the photos to Redding. I explained about the photos on my phone and the volume in Summer's champagne flute and how the poison had actually been in Brian's glass. "Summer picked up the wrong glass," I said. "Once we sorted that out . . . well, the rest fell into place."

"But why poison me?" Brian asked. "Graham is my cousin. Why would he do that to me?"

I glanced at the crinkled and folded papers on the coffee table. "I'm not exactly sure, but I think it has something to do with a real estate deal." I described how Nathan had taken the papers from the recycling bin. "I didn't think anything about it until breakfast this morning. Nathan flew his plane across the room and tagged Graham with it. When Graham returned the plane, he definitely noticed the paper. There was such a large amount of money involved . . . I don't know. It just seemed it might be possible that it had something to do with everything that had happened. I took the paper airplane with me when I left the restaurant, and when Graham saw me in the lobby with it . . . well, it sounds weird, but his gaze locked onto it, then his face changed, and I knew I wanted to get away from him. Somehow it's linked."

Brian reached for the papers and scanned the print.

Redding said, "I made a couple of calls during the last few hours and can fill in the gaps. I spoke to one of Murphy's coworkers at his law firm in Macon, a Ryan Philmore. I believe you have a recently deceased aunt on your mother's side, Gloria Dupree?"

Brian nodded. "Yes, she died last month."

"Were you aware that Murphy's firm handled her legal matters, including her will?"

"Yes, he mentioned he had put her in contact with someone in their office."

"Did he say why he didn't do it himself?" Redding asked.

"I don't know. He works mostly in corporate."

Redding made a *hmming* noise then said, "Well, that's not the way Murphy's colleague Ryan Philmore felt. He said Murphy could have easily handled the will—it was very simple—but he hadn't wanted to take the time." Redding consulted his notebook. " 'The lazy dog pawned it off on me,' according to Mr. Philmore."

Brian blew out a sigh. "Yes, well, Graham isn't extremely altruistic."

Summer rolled her eyes. "Graham has never done pro bono work—ever. I'm not surprised he couldn't find time to do a will for Aunt Gloria."

Redding said, "Apparently, he came to regret it. Besides the house your aunt lived in, she owned another piece of property, a small beach house in Sarasota. She received it as an inheritance from her deceased husband's brother two years ago. She left both properties jointly to you and Murphy. Mr. Philmore sent me a copy of the will."

"What?" Brian said.

Redding took out his phone, tapped on it until a document appeared, then handed it over to Brian. "Your aunt appointed Murphy as the executor. Did he mention your aunt's will to you? That you were a beneficiary?"

Brian had been scrolling through the document. He looked up, his face puzzled. "No. Nothing. He never said anything about it."

"I thought so." Redding flipped to another page in his notebook. "Mr. Philmore said that Murphy told him he would personally inform you of the terms of the will. I gathered from Mr. Philmore that it's not usually done that way, but since Murphy was a friend and work colleague, Mr. Philmore agreed. Murphy's phone has been entered into evidence. His e-mail was on his phone and even though I've only had a quick look through it, I've already found that Murphy contacted a Realtor in Sarasota last week. Their exchange of e-mails indicates that Murphy floated the idea of putting the property on the market and asked for a ballpark valuation. The Realtor sent comps from one to three point five million dollars."

There was a stunned silence in the room for a moment.

Brian cleared his throat. "What? Are you sure? What kind of property is it?"

"I'll read you the Realtor's summary to Murphy," Redding said. "*A two-bedroom bungalow, constructed in 1952. Needs a lot of work—roof, exterior paint, new windows, etc. Located on a busy section of prime beachfront, and surrounded on three sides by high-rise condos, which makes it a prime location. I personally know of at least two investors who would be very interested purchasing it.*" Redding gestured to his phone that Brian still held. "There are photos of it on there. I pulled up the address on a mapping app."

Brian tapped the phone, and Summer and I both craned our necks to get a look at the photos.

"It's cute. Tiny, but cute," Summer said.

I was close enough to Brian to get a glimpse of a tan Craftsman-style bungalow with white trim dwarfed on either side by two high-rise condos.

"So he agreed to sell it?" Summer asked, lifting the real estate papers that Brian had handed off to her when he took Redding's phone to read the will. "This is an offer to purchase the property. How could he do that? Didn't the will have to go through probate? He couldn't even put it on the market."

"He couldn't," Brian said, his voice stunned. "Not legitimately."

"Oh," Summer said, her shoulders dropping. "But Graham has never been one to color inside the lines."

Redding said, "The e-mails indicate that the Realtor floated the possibility of the property going on the market to a few potential buyers. One of them made an offer, despite it not being officially on the market." Redding pointed to the paperwork Summer held.

"But that still doesn't explain why he'd try to kill me,"

Brian said. "He could have bought me out. I would have sold it to him."

"No you wouldn't," Summer said as she took the phone from him. "Look at this photo when you zoom out. It's literally right on the beach. See that? Salt grass and sea oats and sea grape. Dunes right up almost to the front door. With all the work you've done to preserve beach ecosystems, I know that once you saw this, there would be no way you'd sell this slice of beach. And Graham would know that too," Summer said, her voice sad.

"Ah, I see," Redding said. "That fits. He knew you wouldn't sell, so he set in motion his plan to make your death look like an accident. If you die before the wedding, then he is the sole beneficiary."

The room suddenly felt colder, and I snuggled into Mitch's side. The thought of Graham carefully planning the timing of his cousin's death . . . no wonder he'd looked so removed and almost analytical up in the tower. He'd planned to kill Brian from the beginning, and I was only a bump in the road, something in the way of his goal.

Summer touched the papers. "And he went off and left this in a bin to be shredded?"

Redding nodded. "Very careless. He slipped up there, but it's difficult to plan the perfect murder. Normally, the hotel employees would have collected the paper and shredded it. No one would have known about the property deal if the bin hadn't been unlocked."

"And it looked like it was locked," I said. "It was only when Nathan told me where he got the paper that I realized it wasn't fastened."

Redding's phone rang, and Summer handed it back to him.

"Excuse me. I have to take this," Redding said. "Mrs.

Avery, if you wouldn't mind explaining Murphy's plan involving the pranks."

"Sure," I said as Redding moved off to talk on the phone.

"Pranks?" Summer looked toward me. "What is he talking about?"

"The paintball and the poison ivy. Graham must have been behind them. Anyone could have brought those things to the island hidden in their luggage, but Graham specifically invited Julia, someone who had a history with Brian. Graham knew that the first incidents would be blamed on Julia. Once those had taken place, he only had to loosen the lug nuts in the golf cart wheel. Brian should have been driving. Ned taking the golf cart was a coincidence. If he had been, Brian would have taken the turn that Ned did, and his death would have been written off as a horrible, tragic accident, one of a series of revengeful pranks gone wrong."

Summer leaned forward. "So you're saying that Graham set up Julia? She wasn't involved at all?"

"I don't think so. You and I both noticed how smitten she was with Graham. She wasn't acting like she felt any attraction to you, Brian. All her attention was focused on Graham. And she also seemed to be . . . I don't know . . . embarrassed when she arrived and saw you both. I had the distinct impression that she wasn't comfortable. At the time—after Summer explained the relationship history—I thought it was because she didn't like seeing you two together, but now I think it was because she didn't know this weekend was your wedding."

"What? Why would you think that?" Summer asked, clearly not sold on the idea of Julia not being the villain.

"Because I talked to her sister at the hospital. She said Julia had other plans. She was supposed to visit her sister this weekend, but that she'd switched everything around at the last minute, but that didn't go with the careful planning that would have had to have gone into the pranks and the golf cart 'accident.' Each of those things would have to be arranged and calculated out beforehand, especially the golf cart accident. The stretch of cart path that the wreck happened on was coordinated so that the wheel would come off, pitching the cart over, and throwing Brian onto the asphalt. Everything Julia would need to know—the use of the golf carts, the cart paths, the plan to picnic at the ruin, even the tidbit about the resort providing a special 'bride and groom' golf cart—was there on the resort's website. But she would need time to figure it out and plan each step of the pranks and the golf cart wreck so that it would be accepted as an accident. That's a lot to do at the last minute."

Redding had stepped to a corner of the room to take his call. He ended the call and returned to the group, catching the last few words. "Speaking of Julia Banning, I was interviewing her when your calls came in, Mrs. Avery."

"So she's out of the coma?" I asked.

"Yes. Her prognosis is good, but the first thing she told her sister was that she didn't want Graham in the room. He'd pushed her down the stairs."

Summer shook her head, a look of amazement on her face. "So it's true. Graham really did use her. He set her up to be the scapegoat. Do you think she suspected Graham was behind the incidents? Why else would he push her down the stairs?"

"Yes," Redding said. "You said she appeared to be very involved with Murphy, and she told me herself that she thought she was in love with him, but she noticed something that bothered her. Julia said she went into his room through the connecting door after he returned from his run. She startled him, and he dropped the fanny pack. It clinked when it hit the floor, and she caught a glimpse of something silver-colored inside. She stated that she asked him what it was. He told her it was a metal water bottle. She said she didn't think anything about it until the next day when they were leaving to go for a walk on the beach. Graham suggested they stop at the resort's shop to pick up some bottled waters. Julia said that when she suggested filling up his water bottle, he looked like he didn't know what she was talking about. She said it felt odd to her. Apparently, it wasn't the first thing he'd said to her that didn't seem quite right, so later she slipped into his room and took a look in the fanny pack. She found a socket wrench and lug nuts."

"We saw him that morning on his jog," I said. "He stopped to talk to us, Mitch and me." I explained about our detour to show the ruin to the kids. "I did think it was a little weird that he had brought a fanny pack on a jog. You know, it would be bumping against your hip the whole way."

Brian said, "Just the fact that Graham was jogging is weird. He doesn't like physical activity at all. I was always trying to get him to play golf or racquetball or tennis, but he never wanted to."

I looked toward Redding. "If he brought the fanny pack with him on his run, and he was at the ruin, was he retrieving the socket wrench and lug nuts?"

"Yes, I believe so. He probably decided he didn't want to have those things on his person immediately after the accident—that would be instantly incriminating—so he hid them to be retrieved later."

"And it wouldn't be easy to hide a socket wrench in your clothes anyway," Mitch added.

"Unless he was wearing something like cargo pants or shorts, but I think he was wearing a pair of khaki shorts with a T-shirt."

"That's right," Summer confirmed. "Patricia was a little

put out with him that he hadn't dressed appropriately for the garden party theme."

"So his jog was just cover for him when he returned for the socket wrench and lug nuts that he had hidden," I said.

Redding looked unhappy. "Yes, we searched the ruin, but the area is so large that we must have overlooked it."

Mitch said, "They could have been anywhere—buried or hidden in a tree or shrub or even in the ruin itself. I noticed several loose flagstones as well as crumbling masonry. Any small gap could have been a hiding place."

"So what did Julia do when she found the socket wrench and lug nuts?" I asked. "Did she confront him?"

"No. She called the front desk and asked for my contact information. Unfortunately, it appears that Murphy overheard enough of the conversation that he became worried."

"And so he pushed her down the stairs," Brian said, his face a mixture of horror and disgust.

"Yes," Redding said. "It did happen only a few minutes after her call to the front desk. She said she made an excuse about running down to the gift shop alone—said she needed more batteries—but he must have followed her."

"And the main elevators were slow," I remembered. "So she must have headed for the back servants' stairs like I did, thinking it would help her get downstairs quicker."

"But it only made it easier for Murphy to attack her," Redding said.

I shivered, thinking of those moments on the stairs when Graham had tried to get me to leave and when he'd wanted to move Julia. I was so glad Rebekah had arrived as quickly as she did. With both of us there, he couldn't do anything but watch as Julia got medical care and was taken away to the hospital.

Brian, his face pale, said, "I still can't believe it. Graham did all that and then tried again at the rehearsal dinner."

"Unluckiest murderer I've ever seen," Redding said.

"But determined," I added. "I wonder how he knew about the lily of the valley—about it being poisonous?"

Redding shrugged. "Don't know. There's nothing about it on his phone, so he didn't search for information on it there. Maybe it was just general knowledge he picked up somewhere along the way. I do know that we can nail him on that. The other things—the paintball and plastic bag with the poison ivy, even the tire lug nuts are iffy. None of those things have any prints on them, which is suspicious in and of itself. But the lily of the valley, we've got him on that. I've searched his room. The coffeepot that the resort provides in each room was broken. He'd dumped the pieces in the trash, but there is definite residue on the broken glass and in the trash. My crime scene tech says his fingerprints are all over the coffeepot. Preliminary tests on the fragments show traces of the toxin administered to you." Redding looked toward Summer. "It seems he chopped up the plant and boiled it, concentrating the liquid before adding it to the champagne. We also found a small bottle of shampoo that the resort provides in his jacket pocket. The bottle had been emptied of shampoo, but there was a residue in the bottom. It's been sent to the lab for testing."

Redding flipped his notebook closed. "I think that about covers everything. Did you have any questions?" he asked, looking toward Brian and Summer.

Brian just shook his head, and Summer said, "I'm so stunned, I don't know what to think. I mean, I knew Graham liked to skate close to the edge, but . . . murder? Of his own cousin? And trying to hurt Julia and Ellie, too? I'm just . . . astonished."

Redding slipped his pen into his jacket pocket and stood.

"One to three point five million dollars is a lot of motive. I've seen people kill for less. A lot less."

"I have a question," I said, figuring that if I didn't ask now, I probably wouldn't get another opportunity. "One thing that bothered me was that golf cart we saw leaving the ruin right before Ned's wreck. Did it have anything to do with all this?" I asked, waving my hand at the real estate papers.

"No. I was able to run that down this morning. Completely unrelated to this case. The cart was used by a couple returning from the golf course. They decided to take a detour on the way back to the resort to see the ruin. They have no connection to anyone in the wedding party."

"I see," I said. "Thanks, I don't like to have leftover bits and pieces that don't fit into the pattern, so to say."

"In this case, they weren't even part of the pattern. Just a stray complication." Redding put his hands in his pockets and relaxed a bit. "All right. I'll need formal statements from you all, but that can wait until later." He checked his watch. "I believe you have a wedding on the schedule."

Summer looked to Brian. "I know I was very adamant this morning about the wedding having to be today, but after all that's happened with Graham, well, if you want to put it off until later, I understand."

"Do you want to put it off? Having second thoughts about marrying into the Murphy family?" Brian asked.

"No," Summer said quietly, her gaze fixed on his face. "No second thoughts. I'm marrying you. Whether that's today or next year, doesn't matter to me."

"Then today it is."

Tips for an Organized Wedding

The day after a wedding can be almost as busy as the big day itself. Don't forget to arrange for rental items to be returned as well as transportation to the airport for out-of-town guests as needed. Designate someone to collect all gifts at the reception and either transport them to the new couple's home or arrange for them to be shipped, if the wedding is not in the bride and groom's home city.

Chapter Nineteen

The soft strains of the string quartet flowed through the air, and I straightened Nathan's tie then gave him and Livvy a quick hug. "All ready?" I asked. Out of the corner of my eye, I saw the ushers escorting guests to their seats.

Nathan nodded. Now that the actual moment had arrived, he didn't look a bit mutinous, as I'd been afraid he might. He looked a little scared. "Don't worry," I whispered. "You'll do great. Just walk slowly down the aisle and wait until Uncle Brian motions for you to come over to him. Easy-peasy."

He nodded, his gaze fixed on the end of the aisle where Brian and the minister stood under the flower arch. Behind them the endless horizon of beach and water stretched out as far as you could see. The sea breeze buffeted the flowers and ribbons decorating the end of each aisle and pulled at the women's dresses and ruffled the men's hair.

Livvy tugged on my hand. "Mom, some of the kids said I'm too old to be a flower girl." She looked over my shoulder at a row of cousins giggling in the back row of white chairs.

Why were kids so mean? I squatted down so that I could be on level with her. "Did you ever think that they might be just a teensy bit jealous?"

Livvy wrinkled her nose. "They would say that because they're jealous? Why would they do that?"

"Sometimes people don't like their situation, where they are in life, and they do and say mean things."

"Like Graham," Nathan popped into our conversation. News of Graham's actions and his arrest had spread quickly through the resort. I'd have rather sheltered the kids from it, but there wasn't a way to keep the news from them.

"Yes, unfortunately Graham is a grown-up example of that. But let's not talk about Graham right now. Let's focus on the wedding. Your cousins might wish they were in the wedding. After all, you get to dress up and be in the pictures. It's an honor to be picked," I said. Livvy looked thoughtful. "Just remember, you're doing it for Aunt Summer. She wants you here."

"Ellie, are you ready?" Mitch asked as he reached out a hand to lift me up. "It's time."

"Yes." I dusted a speck of sand from the lapel of his tux. He extended his arm, and I linked my hand through his elbow.

We moved to the main aisle around Patricia who was inching into position, her heels sinking into the sand. "Really, this is most disappointing," she said through gritted teeth. "Not at all what we expected."

Mr. Markham hovered near her. "Yes, I know it's not the original plan, but the bride and groom seem quite happy with it."

Gus gave a final tug to his collar and stuck out his arm. "Come on, Pat, let's get with the program. Only a few minutes, and we'll be in that grand ballroom."

"Yes, thank goodness. I don't think I'll ever get the sand out of my shoes."

We reached the red carpet that had been laid out on the sand, creating an aisle between the two sections of chairs. "Did I tell you how amazing you look?" Mitch asked as we walked. Moving at the slow pace down the center aisle with the music playing brought back memories of our wedding. Mitch had looked dashing in his dress blues with his ornamental saber. We'd had a small church wedding, nothing like this extravaganza, but it had been just perfect for us. We arrived at an empty row, and as I slipped into the seat on the end, Mitch brushed a kiss on my cheek as he murmured, "You're more beautiful today than the day we married."

Mitch escorted the rest of the guests to their seats, then joined me. Yvonne surprised me by turning up in a blush-colored dress with a lace overlay. She was so subdued that I wouldn't have known she was there except she was the first close family member escorted down the aisle to the re-served seats at the front. She sent Brian a genuine smile and turned back to wait for Summer's entrance. Patricia somehow managed to smile and grit her teeth at the same time during her walk down the aisle. Mitch's mom, Caro-line, already looked misty-eyed when she came in, and his dad waiting at the back to come in with Summer had that set, stoic look men get when they know something emo-tional is coming.

The bridesmaids and groomsmen took their places and Livvy and Nathan made it down the aisle without a mis-hap. I breathed a sigh of relief. The music changed to the wedding march, and we all stood. Summer appeared at the end of the aisle, looking radiant. Brian beamed back at her.

Mitch leaned in and whispered, "Despite the rocky start, I think they're going to be just fine."

Acknowledgments

I was in middle of this book when I got the news that my mammogram had a suspicious area, which is never news you want to hear. I had to put the book on hold while I worked doctor appointments and tests into my schedule, but I'm happy to report that all is well on the health front for me today. Thanks to Michaela for waiting for the book so patiently while I sorted everything out and for being supportive. Thanks to Faith for her encouragement and help with rescheduling everything. A big thank-you to the readers who look forward to the Ellie books. I promise the wait for the next book won't be so long. And, as always, I'm so grateful to my family, who brainstorm plot twists and listen to me while I ramble on about title ideas. You're the best.

"I do too."

I'm afraid I missed most of the ceremony because I was concentrating on sending mental vibes to the kids to stand still, which they did. Livvy's book didn't make an appearance—I knew she had one stashed somewhere, probably tucked away on one of the front rows—but she and Nathan stood statuelike during the vows and the ring ceremony, then they swept out along with the rest of the wedding party, and we all trooped off to the reception.

After I hugged each of the kids and told them they did a great job, they disappeared to join the other kids, and Mitch and I were left to enjoy our food completely alone. When the dancing started Mitch swept me onto the dance floor.

He swung me into a quick turn, then leaned back to look at my whole face. "So, wedding organization? What do you think?"

"Not for me. I'm leaving the bridezillas and the monsters-in-law to someone else. I'll stick to closets. No more weddings."

"Good plan, I think."

"Until Livvy's, of course," I amended.

Mitch groaned. "Elopement. Let's start talking it up now."